Text Classics

ELIZABETH HARROWER was born in Sydney in 1928 but her family soon relocated to Newcastle, where she lived until she was eleven.

In 1951 Harrower moved to London. She travelled extensively and began to write fiction. Her first novel, *Down in the City*, was published in 1957 and was followed by *The Long Prospect* a year later. In 1959 she returned to Sydney, where she began working for the ABC and as a book reviewer for the *Sydney Morning Herald*. In 1960 she published *The Catherine Wheel*, the story of an Australian law student in London, her only novel not set in Sydney. *The Watch Tower* appeared in 1966. Between 1961 and 1967 she worked in publishing, for Macmillan.

Harrower published no more novels, though she continued to write short fiction. Her work is austere, intelligent, ruthless in its perceptions about men and women. She was admired by many of her contemporaries, including Patrick White and Christina Stead, and is without doubt among the most important writers of the postwar period in Australia.

Elizabeth Harrower lives in Sydney.

RAMONA KOVAL is a writer, journalist and broadcaster. She is the author of *By the Book: A Reader's Guide to Life* and was the presenter of ABC Radio National's 'The Book Show' for many years. She now interviews writers for the *Monthly*'s book club. ramonakoval.com

ALSO BY ELIZABETH HARROWER

Down in the City
The Long Prospect
The Watch Tower
In Certain Circles

The Catherine Wheel
Elizabeth Harrower

Text Publishing Melbourne Australia

textclassics.com.au
textpublishing.com.au

The Text Publishing Company
Swann House
22 William Street
Melbourne Victoria 3000
Australia

First published in the United Kingdom by Cassell 1960
This edition published by The Text Publishing Company 2014

Cover design by WH Chong
Page design by Text
Typeset by Midland Typesetters

Printed in Australia by Griffin Press, an Accredited ISO AS/NZS 14001:2004
Environmental Management System printer

Primary print ISBN: 9781922147950
Ebook ISBN: 9781922148957
Author: Harrower, Elizabeth, 1928-
Title: The catherine wheel / by Elizabeth Harrower; introduced by Ramona Koval.
Series: Text classics.
Dewey Number: A823.3

CONTENTS

Playing with Fire
by Ramona Koval

ONE of the great pleasures of my reading life has been the relatively recent discovery of the work of Elizabeth Harrower. I was a child when she was first published, and by the time I was a serious reader she had stopped submitting her work for publication, aside from the occasional short story. Her books were not widely discussed, although Christina Stead and Patrick White had been admirers of them.

I wish now that I had read her acute insights into the human condition before embarking on my own messy life. In an interview I told Elizabeth this, and we both wondered if anybody ever listens to the lessons and advice proffered by others, especially in the pages of a book.

At the beginning of *The Catherine Wheel* (1960), Harrower's third novel and the only one not set in

Australia, we feel the icy winds of winter coming directly from Siberia, or at least from the direction Siberia 'was taken to be. Who knows where the wind was really coming from?'

Told in the first person, the novel puts us in the mind and body and small London bedsit of Clemency James, a twenty-five-year-old Australian law student living alone, studying for the bar by correspondence and giving French lessons in the evenings to pay the rent for her modest digs.

By the second paragraph we feel the cold in our own bones, our ears are throbbing along with Clem's and we are privy to her cheeky view of the grim realities of London: a city supposedly at the centre of the universe and a far cry from provincial Sydney, where Clem grew up. Here even the places across the road have 'enigmatic façades', as Clem herself does, noting her own appearance in the glass-panelled door as she seeks the relative warmth of her boarding house.

She has been disguised all her life as 'a nice quiet girl', but there is 'something unintentionally deceitful' about her overcoat. In postwar London, clothes send messages—'this uniform reserved for genuine socialists, this for hereditary shoppers in Harrods'—and Clem risks being accused of false pretences.

Again we are in Harrower's psychological territory, where things are not what they appear to be on the surface. She is acutely observant of the mores of

London in the late 1950s, of tearooms and restaurants and trips to the theatre; and, as ever, of the intersection of class and power.

Clem has a range of sensible and kind companions, like Lewis, a friend of a friend, an older man who dines with her on Friday nights.

> We'd finished a doubtful chicken vol-au-vent and were eating fruit salad. I listened in an amiable stupor brought on by food and heat. Once I looked up and saw our reflections in the misty mirror covering the wall behind the counter. Cheese boards and mustard pots stood on a shelf in front of it. My spoon was halfway to my mouth. Lewis talked, eating with an attention that somehow belied his faintly forbidding air of austerity. After all these years it still surprised me in a way to know that Lewis ate. He suspected that it even disappointed me a little, and was amused when I admitted it.

It is a world of social disguises, in which Clem has careful conversations while holding back what she really thinks. And it is her mind that is the focus of our interest and concern—in particular, the possibility of derangement when she takes up with the man who has been employed to wash the windows and to supervise the boarding house when its owner, Mrs Evans, takes off in the evenings to attend spiritualist meetings.

The man is Christian Roland, and his only jumper is yellow. In nature, yellow is the colour sometimes reserved for organisms with deadly poisonous intent, or for those trying to emulate them. Harrower offers such clues to her intentions throughout the novel; most seem to arrive subconsciously, penetrating our minds as we become further enmeshed with the lives of her characters and their relationships.

Christian is a strikingly handsome young man who has taken up with Olive, a drab and ingratiating older woman in whose house he has boarded. She left her husband and two daughters to strike out with him. Christian is all enthusiasm one moment and despair the next, delusion and world-weariness, aggression and alcoholic self-pity. He might as well have a neon sign flashing above his head: Danger! Keep Away!

And while Clem is knowing and clever and alive to his theatrics, she is also ready for an adventure. Little by little, she is lured into his fantasy world. She agrees to teach him French free of charge, using all her spare time; against her better judgement she does not resist the gravitational pull of planet Christian.

And judgement she has—we know it because she knows it herself—but sometimes people like to follow a story to see how it will end. When Clem gets closer to the flame of instability, she's no longer the 'nice quiet girl' that she first appeared to be. She's playing with fire.

Clemency, as befits her name, is lenient with Christian, even as she sees that he won't return the money he borrows from her, and doubts his story of a marvellous job in Paris coming up and a future life together, if only he can escape the clutches of Olive, who cares for him and controls him—at least, that is how he paints it.

Lewis and his sister Helen gently try to save Clem from herself. They see that the young woman they knew is going under. She resists them, pride and curiosity preventing her from pulling back from the brink. Can madness be infectious? Is this what's meant by *folie à deux*? Two impulses balance each other in Clem; she is both at the centre of the whirlwind and observing it—she 'listened like a scientist, listened like a lover'. The head and the heart.

We hope she is resilient. She reminds herself that she was 'immunised' long ago. We don't know by what. But in some immunisations it's the subsequent exposure which generates the population of active cells that maintain the defences against another assault. Once bitten, twice bitten. Perhaps the third time you bite first? Or not: 'And yes, not to worry, a kind insidious voice insisted in my ear, you can always die when it's too much.'

In conversation with Elizabeth Harrower I asked about Clem. It's as if she can sense Christian's turmoil, his madness—and yet he is engaging, firm in his opinions, somehow fascinating. Clem is keen to find out what might happen.

'There's a friend I have,' Elizabeth said, 'who talks about the charisma that is sometimes part of mental disturbance: that it has a sort of exceptional charm, exceptional attraction, magic, something quite special...People live dangerously to discover things. Sometimes it's a high price to pay.'

I marvelled at her uncanny understanding of relationships.

'I don't study people,' she replied. 'But I do somehow or other feel that I know something interesting about human nature that I have a deep wish to tell everybody. I haven't searched for it...These are just interesting things I know. I think I'll keep on like this to the end. Although I'm not writing, I'll still keep thinking.'

I love Harrower's *The Watch Tower* (1966), which is considered her masterpiece. But I love *The Catherine Wheel* more, perhaps because I'm a bit more like Clem than like *The Watch Tower*'s Laura. As do all the Harrower books, with their psychological mysteries and droll humour, their brilliant language and ear for voices, this novel takes your hand from the first page and draws you in.

So do follow. I promise that rich rewards await you.

The Catherine Wheel

The wind from Siberia as announced by the BBC came down Bayswater Road from the direction of Marble Arch somewhere in a straight line beyond which, half a world away, Siberia was taken to be.

Searing skin, and petrifying metal and wood, it took possession of London and this early day of the new year.

Gently, somehow sympathetically, with a secret sort of throb, my ears ached against it, but rather more drearily and with a sense of injustice my eyes watered as I narrowed them at the steely dark sky and swirling smoke. The centre of the universe! The brilliance of the winter season!

It was some time after three o'clock, and I was returning home from the shops of Notting Hill Gate. Beside me traffic trundled endlessly into town—saloons and commercial vans competing under swaying sodium lights, soon to be switched on. The air was fumy.

Ahead, the footpaths stretched empty but for the two or three muffled shapes that hurried past, bent bleakly, as I was, on some quick warm haven.

Across the road the enigmatic façades of a row of semi-public buildings ended where the railings of Kensington Gardens began. Just opposite this corner of the gardens Miss Evans had her service-house, and it was here I had a room with a diagonal view of bare black avenues and paths and empty seats and grass.

Reluctantly I had left my work for a few minutes to get food for the week, but as I jangled the loose change in my purse and fumbled amongst it with gloved and bloodless fingers for the key, I was aware of a profound unwillingness either to go back through these tall glass-panelled doors, or to remain outside.

My reflection looked glassily back at me through the elegant lines and curves of black wrought-iron. I glanced for a second, dispassionately, at the pale face and dark hair, at the amber eyes and almost childish mouth that had disguised me all my life as a nice quiet girl.

Even about my overcoat, I noticed, there was something unintentionally deceitful. The look of discreet simplicity advertised to knowing eyes its considerable cost. True, it was now three years since I had bought it in Sydney, but it had a boring monumental resistance to time and still contrived to seem subtly out of place in the local shops, as my other clothes did in Miss Evans's.

At home the single aim was to present a front of expensive elegance, whereas in London it was obligatory to show what one was and did: *this* uniform reserved for genuine socialists, *this* for hereditary shoppers in Harrods, and so on...Any other course, on discovery, left one open to a charge of false pretences.

I turned the key in the lock wondering what it could be like to fit so precisely into a mould. What *were* the legitimate trappings for an Australian, aged twenty-five, living alone in a bed-sitting-room, and studying for the bar by correspondence?

Shadows and the smell of cold stone and water in buckets engulfed me as the door closed on frivolous soliloquy. Upstairs books lay open on the table, and the routine waited to swallow me up.

I pushed at the swing-doors that led to a main hall, lofty and dim as a cathedral—with luck it would be as empty: no one would lay hands on me. I would snatch my milk bottle from the ticketed row by the wall and fly upstairs to those books over which it seemed I was already bent.

Oh, it wasn't exactly that I hurried with pleasure to send my mind on another assault course—I felt edgy and grated—but after two years of self-conditioning I had no way of overcoming the pattern imposed by my will. If I conformed absolutely, restlessness was smothered and there was peace—otherwise not.

Let there be no one!

Miss Evans stood at the bottom of the stairs, arms folded, talking to a man in a yellow sweater.

Well, anyway, private conversation. I could assume invisibility, collect milk, glide past...

'Here she is!' cried Miss Evans, obviously referring to me.

I was surprised, though not at all interested. Nevertheless I paused, and the three of us stood almost theatrically still, staring, separated by yards and yards of shadowy light and high walls and carpet-runner.

'Good afternoon, Miss James!' she called in that brisk forthright way of hers.

'Good afternoon, Miss Evans!' I stooped for the milk bottle.

The man unfroze, murmured something to her, and leapt upstairs carrying a variety of objects I couldn't distinguish through the afternoon gloom. Nor had I discerned his face. Only the message of the yellow sweater and its aspirations reached me, automatically.

'Well!' Miss Evans remained like a toll-collector at the end of the stairs, looking pleasant, challenging me to question her: 'Why did you say...?'

Her expectation that I should care was pathetic, ludicrous. I wasn't interested enough to wonder at her exclamation, much less to ask for reasons which, I knew, would light no response in me but exasperation at this delay.

'That young man,' she said, capitulating suddenly, as I raked up a smile to get past her. 'I was telling him you give French lessons.'

'Oh?' Now I stood slightly above her, on the first step.

Fifty-four they said she was. I was obliged to think once again, even through my reluctance, how pleasing her self-sufficiency was, her capability and ramrod back. Her arms and hands emerged from the three-quarter sleeves of her grey dress, round and clean, freed from the morning's chores for the afternoon's accounts. Or perhaps she would read a magazine in her room now, so nicely dressed, and eat a cucumber sandwich.

While I hovered, Miss Evans awaited some more positive query than that solitary 'Oh?' I faced this, and glancing upstairs added, 'Why? Is he...? Who is he?'

Delightedly she gave a chuckle, bearing me no grudge. 'His name is Christian Roland. He's a new young man to clean our windows. He just appeared at the door and offered to do the whole house, half-price, if I let him compete with my old firm, so...'

I smiled at her enthusiasm, narrowing my eyes in a friendly way, though in fact so hollow and detached that it was vaguely surprising not to rise slowly into the air. But I questioned her now, and her hands clasped, and her blue eyes lively, Miss Evans told me, 'Oh, we're great friends already, Christian and I. After he finished the downstairs windows I just made him a cup of tea and a bite—I was having one, anyway. So we had a good old gossip.'

'And he's learning French?'

'Yes. I thought we'd found you another pupil, but he probably wouldn't have enough money to pay, so that wouldn't do, would it?'

'No, I don't suppose it would.' And smiling what felt like a kind benevolent smile I went backwards up another two steps.

'Not that you need more work!' Gradually her hands fell to her side from the forceful cluster they had been at her waist.

Was it insulting to creep off surreptitiously, backwards, and still talking, up the stairs...? No. Hardly, I reminded

7

myself of the old formula: If they have nothing to do, you have. Remember—self-defence, bayonets fixed, barricades firm...

Now that I was definitely on my way, retreating step by step, I called down in a low voice of extreme cordiality, 'And did you decide to give him the job? With the windows?'

'Oh, yes! He's a nice boy to have about the place.' The bright satisfaction faded. 'Well, I must...' she murmured, and disappeared towards her room at the front of the house.

Released, I hurried up flight after flight, my throat and chest flaming with breathlessness, hampered by the basket and the icy milk bottle, trying to leave behind a small uncomfortable sensation of shame at my ungraciousness.

But, after all, that was hypocritical. For I was relieved, relieved, to brush the encounter off. And where was the obligation to be heart and soul with everyone who importuned attention? And, really, was graciousness my aim in life?

At the very top of Miss Evans's ancient sky-scraper, at the summit of all this decomposing matting, I let myself into one of the three single attic-rooms that shared a bathroom and kitchen. It was mine. I had the key. They were my square yards of freedom, and symbolized for me the greater, boundless freedom of my mind and person. And far below the flat recognition of its shabby walls and furnishings I never ceased to be aware of the gentle crooning assuagement that its existence caused about my heart.

The gas-fire popped alight. The flexible neck of the lamp bent over and spot-lighted the array of books and papers on the round table. Out of my coat, and with the food disposed in the cupboard, I shuddered for a moment or two in front of the fire, pressing the white frozen fingers of my hands together, shaking them, shivering through my teeth and smiling slightly with the pleasure of being free and me and alone and about to return to work.

The sweet ferocious calm that moved between my heart and lungs assured me now as it had done for years that examinations would be passed, and I would travel and work, absorbed and happy...

I sat down at the table and set out to capture concentration by a routine of self-hypnosis: eyes on print, eyes on print, EYES ON PRINT. Without thought I assumed as always that my mind would submit to the gymnastics required of it. I would remain at the table, or curled in an armchair, working over the week's new paper till I was overcome by that sensation of mental nausea and numbness that signalled: Enough! and then: Bed-time! Then, peculiarly sated by that feeling of blankness verging on sickness, I would sleep deeply and not dream.

It was somewhere after six o'clock and the house was alive with music and voices and slamming doors and jetting gas. On the stairs and in the corridors was a raw dank sooty smell of fog, but by the kitchen doorway where I stood talking to Mrs Parry, the warm and fragrant odour of fresh coffee circulated.

Mrs Parry, a widow, had recently returned to London from South Africa after an absence of twenty years. At first she had been nervous of Jan and me, but now she seemed to enjoy the nightly gathering at the kitchen door, where one of us cooked an omelette, while the other two stood by with eggs at the ready.

Two weeks ago she would never have asked a question, but now she said, 'And have you got to give any lessons tonight, Clem?'

'Oh no! Four nights for lessons, two for the reference library and one off. This is the library night.'

Her head, with its tight old-fashioned set, leaned over the frying-pan. 'And how do you come to be so good at languages?'

'Well, not languages. But my step-mother was French.' I could hear Mimi: 'When you go to Paris...' From Sydney it had seemed an extremely far-fetched emergency to invoke as a spur to learning. But how fortunate for me that she'd insisted! Not that I much enjoyed the hours spent tutoring Australian girls and backward children— I resented the draining off of that much energy—but I needed the money. It supplemented what was left of the legacy from my father and provided the smallest of buffers against sudden fear.

'You'll be glad to finish with your studies one of these days, I suppose. What made you think of that kind of work? The law...' Mrs Parry turned two pieces of toast on the griller.

'I worked for a solicitor in Sydney. That was it, probably.'

'Well, it's just as important for a girl to be qualified, I think. If I had my time over again I'd see I had something more than shorthand and typing to turn to at fifty.'

She poured black coffee into an earthenware pot.

Qualified. How conspicuous in conversation that word had seemed for those first months in London. At home, in Australia, relatively no one was qualified and everyone made money, whereas in Europe the exact reverse was true. How noble it had seemed! How almost disappointing that they minded at all about money!

'My father left me a small legacy,' I said. 'It'll just keep me till I get through the Finals.'

'You're a sensible girl not just to fritter it—especially when you've got no one to fall back on.'

'Mmm.' Taking credit where none was due. Of course some qualifications would help me to eat in my old age, but curiosity, not sense, had led to this. I had wanted to know *why*, would want to know not *how* but *why* about everything, always: this was only the beginning. So with my father's legacy I'd travelled a little, and now studied.

Yes, that was what I'd wanted, but...I sighed, and attended to Mrs Parry's conversation with such solicitude that she ate her omelette on the landing while I cooked mine.

'Jan's late tonight,' we remarked, going to our rooms.

Half an hour later Jan was sunk in one of the dark blue armchairs by the gas-fire, heavily trousered and sweatered, nursing a pair of velvet mules she'd brought in to display.

Now she was chirruping in a gay voice, 'And you didn't know Miss Evans was a spiritualist?'

'No.' I frowned. 'I knew she went to meetings with Mrs Slater—not that she was a medium.'

'But that's what I'm saying—she *is*. I went along to pay my rent before I came up this evening and I thought I'd never get out again. Apparently some Indian's got in touch with her, you know, from way out there. He's sending messages.'

'Oh dear. To Miss Evans?'

Jan bowed deeply. 'She wants me to go one evening.'

'Will you?'

'I don't think so.' She gave a nervous laugh. 'But then again it might be amusing. I'd love to see Miss Evans in a trance.'

Jan laughed very easily, at almost anything. In a sturdy mood this made her agreeable company, if disconcerting. Now she leaned forward, racked with mirth, her face hidden.

I smiled and looked at the fire, secretly appalled, priggishly feeling for Miss Evans, with whom Jan was friendly.

She came up from the laughing huddle over the bearded mules. 'But that's not all! You know how the Commander takes over as porter and doorman sometimes when she's out at night? Well, now she's roped the poor man in to escort her and Mrs Slater to the meetings—because of these race riots at Notting Hill. And five nights a week some window-cleaner character's going to be night-watchman. Christian someone.'

This much eccentricity in Miss Evans of all people was dismaying. I raised my brows in silent exclamation. 'I think I probably saw him yesterday. Is he the one who's learning French?'

'Is he? I don't know. Anyway he's here tonight. So's his wife.'

I shrugged. Soon I was due to go to the library.

Jan said, 'He'll probably make off with the rents. You're always hearing about things like that. We're going downhill fast! You can scarcely ask anyone home to dinner for the squadrons of females hanging about on the corner for customers, and that stair carpet, and the landlady seeing visions or whatever she does...'

Again Jan shook with laughter and again I watched with faint astonishment and admiration. What easy high spirits!

I studied her narrow face with its long grey-green eyes, the close-cut curly blonde hair. Jan was thirty, and worked in a bank in the City. London wasn't her town. With neither parents nor friendly circle, she had only acquaintances like me. And we had nothing in common but the bathroom and kitchen, and the distinction of being the youngest tenants in this old and middle-aged house. Yet for all this Jan was gay and had the light unclouded look of a girl whose emotions had never been touched.

'Well!' she uncoiled herself from the chair. 'I'd better let you go. Picture me relaxing in a scented bath while you trudge through the snow and ice to the library. It was just starting when I came in.'

Dear Jan! I gave her a look. As I started to speak someone knocked at the door and I hauled myself up.

'A pupil?' A touch of grey-green malice here from her eyes; she considered the French language an affectation.

'Shouldn't be.' I went to the door and Jan cast a curious eye over the woman waiting there, as she slipped past to her own room.

'Miss James? Your phone extension's out of order. Miss Carlton rang to say she can't come for her lesson tomorrow night but her friend will be.'

13

The breathless cockney voice came from a large round-shouldered woman of between forty and fifty. Oh, yes. The wife of the man...She was very sallow and her straight brown hair hung in a lank debutante bob to the collar of her black crêpe dress. While she spoke she gazed at me nervously, even deferentially.

I took the message and its unimportance in. A bitter draught spiralled up the stairs, stirring the woman's hair and skirt, moving coldly over my face. I smiled vaguely and thanked her. My hand moved the door to shut it, then halted, as I reluctantly acknowledged the obligation imposed by her humility to say something friendly—or at any rate, civil.

'What do you think of our stairs? I hope you don't have to climb to the top every time the phone rings!'

Shyly, like a child in front of her headmistress, she laughed and looked down at her shoes. They were cheap, rather old-fashioned court shoes with solid heels. Very circumspect. And I received the curious impression that this woman was conscious of them, of her clothes and hair-style, as if they were part of a disguise, or fancy-dress.

As she seemed unable to get herself away, I said, 'Miss Evans tells me your husband's learning French?'

Warmly she came to life. She smiled, and her hazel eyes glowed. 'He's trying, but it's hard for him, I think.'

'Yes, the detail. It's always an effort. If he's short of text-books or dictionaries, I have a few extra ones he could borrow.'

'Oh, that's terribly sweet of you! But I don't think he'd like to be under an obligation. I'll tell him, but...'

14

Where had she found idioms like these? *Terribly sweet*. And *obligation* borrowing a book! This wasn't the language of Stepney. I knew. I'd interviewed there for a public opinion poll.

'Not at all,' I said, confused and a little charmed by the sheer unlikelihood of hearing these sentiments from her. 'No question of obligation. Please tell him.'

I was glad to see her delighted smile, relieved that she had cast off some of that guilt-provoking humility. We exchanged a friendly smile.

'Good night. Thanks for the message.'

'Good night.' Very shy.

As the door swung shut I saw her moving off to the stairs in a most oddly controlled manner, as if she felt the eyes of the world were on her. It was rather pathetic, disarming...I remembered the snow outside, overcoat, library...

'Oh!' I heard a voice call. 'I ought to have said—I'm Mrs Roland. Olive Roland.'

A trifle impatiently—for, after all, who cared?—I went back to say something pointless like 'Oh!' or 'Good!' then added to thin air, for she had leapt off by this time, feeling awkward, too, I imagined, 'And I'm Clemency James.'

Searching through journals and newspapers at the bottom of the bookcase for airmail envelopes later that night, I noticed the surplus French grammars on the shelf above, and sat back on my heels frowning at them.

Why had I let myself in for a conversation with that woman's husband? The irritation of having to wonder when

15

a demand would be made, if it would be! My own fault of course.

At the table I addressed an envelope to Mimi and sealed the letter inside. It was after midnight. The house was silent. Long-distance trucks were beginning to rattle past outside. On the corner, girls would be standing about in the snow, smoking, wearing old suede boots lined with sheepskin, waiting for a man. Prostitutes in *boots*...

As I folded the dark-red cover from my divan I was made to remember, compulsively, as a consequence of those books, the whole ugly heap of distractions mounting in my future: a visit to the bank, stockings to be bought, buses to be caught, hair to be cut. Everything could be postponed, of course, but there they all waited in the future, relentlessly piling up. Enough to make anyone's nerves stand on end.

Out of proportion, I knew, this impatient dread of trivial interruptions to routine. But explicable, surely? All very well for Helen to lecture. All very well for Lewis.

I brushed my hair blindly, resisting the hypothetical abuse of absent friends, and their repeated, 'Where is your common sense?'

Sense could be used up! I argued at them, still astonished to know it. And feelings, and mental stamina, too. One's will could lure one into extravagance resulting in bankruptcy. And finally even that, even one's will, could falter.

For years I had used mine unsparingly, with no sense of strain, expecting always to have further credit on which to draw—mistakenly, I now saw. For I could no longer raise the energy to force myself to be sensible in small ways. So if for the moment I had to be stupid, then I had to be stupid.

The reserves would have to be eked out on essentials for the next several months. After that I might be able to afford the luxury of a return to rationality.

Thus polishing off my jury I filled a hot-water bottle and climbed into bed, pacified.

'Oh, that'll be all right,' said Olive Roland, with a tired smile of relief. 'Chris's clever about fuses. He'll be back in a minute and I'll send him up. He's just gone across to get me some cigarettes.'

It was Friday, three nights after our first encounter, and my night off. Usually my night to see Lewis. But he was in the Midlands somewhere speaking about 'The Real Challenge to the West', so I stayed home, washed my hair and lay in front of the gas-fire, wallowing in glossy magazines piled at my door by Mrs Parry before she left for a week-end in the country. Jan had gone away, too, through the mushy black and white landscape to stay with a friend in Essex.

One moment I was breathing carpet-dust and lemon shampoo, looking inattentively at photographs and print, then the room blacked out. Simultaneously came a loud crack from the direction of the fuse-board, high up on the wall of the landing.

This happened not infrequently. Usually Jan reported and Miss Evans herself came up to restore light. And this was an event, the occasion of much false bonhomie, like Christmas, or a disaster. Everyone emerged and stood about.

But tonight, deriding reluctance, I had had to grope down the shadowy stairs to the ground floor and penetrate Miss Evans's unfamiliar room to demand some assistance.

Olive Roland's smile went girlish, expecting to be drawn out.

'How do you enjoy your job?' I said. 'Do we give you much trouble with fuses and emergencies like this?'

She laughed, looking down. 'Oh, there's always something happening. But I'm not really working here, just Chris is. Except he was sick two nights this week so I was here by myself. But now I just come to keep him company.'

I looked at her with a passive kind of interest, struck by her almost cringing air, by a feeling that she half-expected to be maltreated. And there was something paradoxical about her physical self-consciousness, the careful arrangement of arms and legs and black dress, in a woman whose look and voice and bones said clearly: under-privileged.

Taking pains to seem unalarming, I talked to her for a minute or so then trailed back upstairs to wait in my room, dawdling about, eyeing the macabre patterns cast by yellow street-lights on walls and chairs.

I heard him bounding upstairs and went out.

'Good evening, Miss James!'

My attention did a double-take. He had a beautiful voice. I stared through the dark at him.

'Mr Roland? Good evening. There's some fuse-wire on a hook. The box is up there.'

'I'm so sorry I couldn't find a torch in Miss Evans's box of gadgets—'

I switched on mine and held it up while he stood on the chair. 'These old houses, the wiring...' I said conventionally, remembering what people murmured to encourage electricians.

He exclaimed once with a tense sort of gaiety when he found the right plug. I hoped he knew what he was doing. If someone was electrocuted you were supposed to…

'There! I *think* that's how it should be.'

I smiled at the precarious elation in his voice.

'Fine!' I called from my room, going over to draw the curtains again. 'It works. Thank you very much.'

'Really?' He was at the door, and stood balancing the chair lightly on two legs in front of him, smiling across at the illumination he'd provided, then at me.

And for the second time in a space of minutes he surprised me. For he was twenty-five or twenty-seven, hardly more, and anyway, much younger than his wife. And not only that…He was fair, above middle-height, with a compelling eye and a slightly compelling manner, and he bowed over the chair a little as a token of the deference due from him, an employee, to me, a tenant. It was self-consciously done and ever so faintly, self-protectively, ironic. Certainly he was a most unlikely-looking window-cleaner.

'Where should I put this?' He tapped the chair nervously.

'Oh, over there. Thank you.'

Yes, he was nervous, as his wife was—therefore quite without choice I was on their side. For nervous equalled conscious equalled human, meant familiar, potentially knowable, likeable.

Tucking the chair under the table he said something in a low voice about wires and fuses simply to reduce the silence, to provide a background for the intense and meaningful look he was simultaneously delivering.

19

Like a battering-ram it smashed very successfully the previous moment's erection of sympathy. Evidently it was meant to X-ray me, impress me, reduce me to something or other. Instead it conveyed so comical an effect of over-weening self-confidence that I could have laughed, inwardly, but for his nervousness, which made it seem faintly, obscurely, appealing.

As we talked he was absorbing my surroundings and adding their total to mine: his calculations were very obvious. And yet withal, he had a distracted self-absorbed air.

Was this show of boldness simply a cover? I found it highly resistible. I did not admire boldness. I did not care to be challenged.

And what was this feeling of premeditation he gave off? With what did it connect? Was I simply being manoeuvred to repeat the offer of the text-books? Surely not! Yet an appeal of some sort was nagging at me.

He could appeal away. If I was puzzled I was also very cool, and a fraction malicious remembering the would-be devastation of that stare. And anyway, I couldn't be bothered with all the elaborate Chinoiserie about obligations: if he wanted the books he could ask for them. It was nothing, one way or the other, to me.

Still he stood, gripping the back of the chair. I was in front of the fire. At my side on the mantelpiece was a trailing green plant in a white pot. I pulled off two withered leaves.

With an awkward twisted grin he said suddenly, 'I suppose it must seem strange—working as a window-cleaner? Doing this sort of work?'

It did. What was he? What did he think of himself as? What about the disparity between himself and his wife? No one could look at them without silent questions, astonishment. He must know it.

'I don't suppose there's much wrong with window-cleaning if you can take the heights,' I smiled. 'You see something for your work. I often feel I'd enjoy some physical labour for a change.'

Perhaps it was sickening to have a kind intention, to want to reassure him, but he awaited judgement so stilly, *minded*. And, in fact, I told no lies.

His face changed. He nodded, looking down, saying in a low eager voice, 'That's true! You're right, Miss James. I'm not ashamed of physical work. It's good. Good. But people wonder, you know. Someone like me.'

'Yes, I know,' I murmured, inadequate. He was all to pieces, somehow suffering, his whole attention turned inward. 'But if people are bored they must find some interest. It's not very important—what they wonder.'

Seeming almost inordinately supported by this lame piece of comfort, he said grimly, 'No! I'm indifferent. It doesn't matter what they think, does it?' And he looked across at me insistently.

'No,' I repeated calmly, feeling a little shaken, pressed about by his intensity. 'Of course they wonder why I stay in to study, since it's not what they do.'

'Yes, I've heard about you downstairs.'

And we were silent. We had acknowledged experience in common, given the salute of odd-ones-out. Because it had fallen to me to reassure him, I felt old. Because he was

21

uncertain, I felt wise. Then, he reminded me of someone long ago, at home, perhaps, in Australia. But who? And why there? Because of his un-English quickness to confide? Was it the person-to-person directness of his gaze? No...

I twirled the dead leaves between my fingers. He stood, his head slightly bowed in brooding thought, his face distorted by shadows from the cream-shaded light overhead. A stranger, again, he began to seem. The sense of familiarity trickled slowly out, and with it the mild vicarious nostalgia for the memory of someone I could not remember.

Stretching up to reach the fuse-box had caused the yellow sweater he wore to wrinkle at his waist. Under it he had no shirt. It was light-weight wool. This was January, bleak. Olive Roland's dress was made of crêpe.

They had nothing else to wear, either of them. With a sudden dull shock I knew this. They had no other clothes...

Immediately his head came up, and I was caught knowing. With a great angry gesture his hand went to his side and pulled at the sweater, and very slightly, but quite visibly, he changed colour.

'One thing,' I said blankly, glancing at the tiny ball of brown leaves between my fingers, 'you're helping Miss Evans.'

A pause.

'I'm glad it's Miss Evans. She's a sweetie. No, that's the wrong word. She *is* a sweetie, but I respect her. She knows how to use authority. And she's always gleaming.'

He was staring at me with concentration, and now, again, he was more than composed. He gave a slight

22

reassuring smile and this time I was the one to feel relieved. Mystified by the lightning reversal of mood, I thought: nothing's wrong, perhaps?

'I must go,' he said gently, releasing the chair he held. 'Poor Olive's downstairs coping alone. She's almost sure to imagine I've electrocuted myself by this time.'

He spoke about her so nicely. We smiled and I said, 'Well, thank you for the light.'

He was at the door so swiftly, so almost invisibly, that I was prepared for his total disappearance, but he paused there very briefly and with a devastating look in my direction ducked his head to his lifted hand and smoothed back a lock of hair.

I whirled round and fell into a chair, raising my eyebrows in delighted amusement, feeling stimulated as if I'd stepped off a roller-coaster. So conscious of his appearance! Fixing his hair for *my* benefit. As if I cared!

Jumping up I went to the cupboard and took two biscuits from a tin. Slowly I walked back to the chair. He seemed very odd...So conscious...And how had he looked when he said, 'It must seem strange—working as a window-cleaner?'

Christian Roland. Something to tell Lewis.

CHAPTER TWO

On Sunday we walked round Regent's Park for half an hour, speechless with cold, moisture on eyes freezing, footsteps sounding emptily through the monochrome waste of stone and petrified earth.

The paths, the stone squares, the seats, the rustic bridges—all were abandoned and desolate as broken ruins round which noble walls and pillars had once risen, like the site of some ancient city or battle-field.

Yet even these melancholy associations seemed entirely too gay and civilized to apply to the open waste across which we trudged. More like the derelict ground-plan for a steel foundry at the North Pole, it was.

And here last April we had sauntered under drifts of cyclamen blossom! Flowers had overflowed across the grass. There was transparent sunshine, heat...

'Oh, Lewis, will it ever be April again?'

24

Lewis turned to me, smiling painfully through the cold. 'You're in one of your profound moods this morning, I can tell.' He grimaced and narrowed his eyes at the prospect ahead. The skin on his cheekbones looked a little sore with frost and wind.

Cocooned in clothes, we stood puffing whitely. I blew my nose. My ankles were probably purple. Frowning and breathing steam we stood in the middle of the path.

'How do you feel about lunch?' Lewis surveyed me, mildly anguished and unhopeful. 'Have we ruined our health enough for one day?'

'Were we doing this to please me? I thought it was some sort of punishment.'

Shuddering, huddled in our coats, we turned towards our usual restaurant and belted down the path, all communication cut.

Arriving in London years before I had without enthusiasm made use of one or two letters of introduction pressed on me in Sydney by a friend of Mimi's, thinking it easier to acquiesce than to be pursued across Europe by: 'Have you seen...'

Through one I met Helen Grenville, who was a medical research worker and whose flat in Bloomsbury I later shared for a year. Helen was Lewis's sister, five years older than me, while Lewis was five years older still. He worked for an international welfare organization, and was sent on occasional missions to the east to collect material for surveys.

This slightly chilling misinformation was all I had of the Grenvilles from Mimi's friend, or all I remembered, and

I doubted—for no reason that seemed valid afterwards—
that we would find interests in common.

I was wrong. We soon had a friendship that side-
stepped and superseded acquaintanceships of a lifetime.

Older friends of Helen's and some of Lewis's of long
standing, gazed on this incomprehensible alignment with
amazement. Perhaps *they* were not, but the Grenvilles were,
rather, intellectuals. Was this girl? Was it likely? And an
Australian! Everyone knew...Well, after all...In Helen, in
taking her into her life and home, the motive might be kindness, or obligation felt towards the friend of her mother's
from whom the letter had come. But in Lewis what was the
motive in spending his time and conversation on her? She
was a not unattractive girl, of course, which might have
seemed sufficient motive for some: but Lewis Grenville was
felt to be committed in that direction. (This was no more
than conjectured, for he was a daunting man. No one could
question Lewis.)

The unlikely friendship flourished. In the best sense I
was taken up by the Grenvilles, not covetously as a puppet
or an edible morsel, but with a grand and generous respect
that provided me with earth and aerial.

And this freedom they unloosed in me by *being*. I'd
known few men of principle, and none who combined
integrity with intellect. I had respected almost no one, and
felt the lack.

Then, all my life I had been ill of emotion, had been
much gobbled, prodded. Meeting the Grenvilles I'd wanted
nothing less than to win their interest or liking. To be left
alone, I wanted! Not to have people or things, not to be

had by them. My very survival, it seemed, had hinged on the absence of feeling from my life. How pure was freedom and isolation!

But they laid no emotional snares. Gradually, an extreme of peace and health overlaid the high-pitched silent screams of adolescence. Overlaid? Rather, dispersed, disintegrated.

But now, of course, I knew Lewis very well, and Helen. I was a little restless. I had a feeling of there being somewhere else to go. Was I to be the Constant Disciple? Had I reached the end of the line so soon?

At the end of that first year Helen married Quentin Reid, and went to live in Oxford. I missed her badly and moved to Miss Evans's, to this attic room. Lewis and I continued to meet regularly. And this was possible, and pleasant, because of Gabrielle, whom I had never met and whom Lewis himself saw very seldom, though she still lived in London. I heard about her at the beginning in the sparest possible way. Her husband had been Lewis's professor, and was his friend. There were three children, and Gabrielle's own parents had divorced. So there was nothing to be done. Only the puzzled insistence of his friend took Lewis to their house for dinner once or twice a year.

Respecting fortitude and experience, I had admired Gabrielle's strength of character, and Lewis's: later, in a flat shallow way that was natural to me, I marvelled at their self-sacrifice and deplored it without much thought. For I thought less—quantitatively—of everyone as I thought more and increasingly of work and examinations.

Now we sat on stools in the warm steamy café talking about the crisis threatening in Africa. James Portland, the

27

Labour MP who was most widely quoted in today's papers on the crisis, was a friend of Lewis's.

We'd finished a doubtful chicken *vol-au-vent* and were eating fruit salad. I listened in an amiable stupor brought on by food and heat. Once I looked up and saw our reflections in the misty mirror covering the wall behind the counter. Cheese-boards and mustard pots stood on a shelf in front of it. My spoon was half-way to my mouth. Lewis talked, eating with an attention that somehow belied his faintly forbidding air of austerity. After all these years it still surprised me in a way to know that Lewis ate. He suspected that it even disappointed me a little, and was amused when I admitted it.

Yet I was not exactly wrong, perhaps. In non-action, in the stillness of meditation, in extreme asceticism, Lewis was most truly himself. And even in the interests of survival I regretted—in a purely theoretical way—that a single soul should diverge ever so slightly from his true nature.

At this moment he looked—what? Nothing so vulgar as inscrutable or enigmatic. He had the winter pallor of the man beside him, and dark hair of a not dissimilar colour. But in the bones of his face, there were signs of experience that that other man would never know. A fine and rather frightening face it appeared to strangers.

Two cups of coffee were placed before us. Around us cutlery chinked on china in a soporific sort of way, and a waitress with mousy hair and a black uniform leaned against the wall in a trance.

Suddenly Lewis interrupted himself to say, 'But I forgot to tell you! Last night I rang Helen.'

28

'Oh? How was she? And Quentin?'

'Very well. But the point is—she's writing today to tell you—she's coming back to London in March—March, as far as she knows—for eight or nine months.'

'To work? What about Quentin?'

'Yes, I know. But they're collaborating on a paper. Helen's coming up to do the necessary research, so her absence is—more or less—sanctioned.'

'He'll be lost!—But it's lovely that she's coming. I suppose she'll go home for week-ends. And Quentin's sure to get away from Oxford often. But where's she going to stay?'

'With you. If you can persuade Miss Evans to have a room vacant when Helen gives you the date.'

'Heavens, how do you think she'll like a bed-sitting-room?' But I was delighted at the thought of seeing her again, and we continued to talk about it over our coffee.

We were walking along towards the bus stop when Lewis said, 'You've been very silent today! Have I talked so much?'

'Oh, Lewis! I read one book, then another, and write one paper, then another. I could rattle off some of that for you—I think it's absorbing, but I doubt if you could call it news. What could there be?'

At the edge in my voice Lewis wasn't put out. Normally he had little tolerance for flashy moods and temperament, but in my case there were special circumstances which he knew and approved, so special but not limitless indulgence flowed out to me.

'What about Jan and Miss Evans and all the other...'

'Inmates? Nothing. Strictly nothing.' Was that really so? The tumbled mass of a routine week revolved at the back of my head. Another day I might have distinguished one item to contribute: I had a feeling there might be some trivial tale to tell. But first the cold in the park, then the relaxation of disappearing into Lewis's days, and hearing about Helen, had nervously exacerbated a mind not geared to cope with novelty, and shot into limbo any possible anecdote.

Lewis looked straight ahead, his lips pressed together, his eyes narrowed against the wind and the street, empty of buses. He might have been alone. He had withdrawn from my company.

'But that's what I like,' I said hastily. 'No excitement. At this moment it would be a ghastly intrusion...'

After a pause, Lewis turned his head to regard me with detachment. 'In that case—' he began.

My spirit turned its back.

Music was coming from three separate wireless sets through three open doors: overhead the bare light-globe shone on the dirty pale-green walls of the windowless cubicle where Jan stood cleaning a pot. I paused on my way past to the bathroom, a bundle of washing and a packet of detergent clasped in my arms.

'Sordid, isn't it?' Jan said brightly, wrinkling her nose at the rank smell of drains. 'Like low tide...Oh, Lord! Look how I've splashed my skirt!' Her blonde curly head bobbed up and down over the pot as she laughed. Then she glanced over her shoulder at me. 'I say, I saw the two downstairs arriving tonight.'

30

'Which two?'

'Miss Evans's sitters. What do you think of them?'

'I've hardly seen them.'

'He looks like something from Hollywood. Like one of the Method boys from the New York Theatre Workshop. Can't you picture him as one of these saintly young priests they always have rescuing refugee children, and falling in love with Marilyn Monroe, but getting conveniently killed just before the end?'

I laughed, 'No!'

She swung round neatly, a plate in each hand. 'I can.' She raised her brows. 'There's something hard, something fishy...They're an odd pair. I mean—window-cleaning! And she's old enough to be his mother. And even apart from that...It's rather like seeing the cleaner out with the Honourable Michael Somebody! I bet...I wonder...'

I smiled at her scorn and suspicion, roused at once, on principle. What was it to her? What misplaced energy in that dubiety! What advantage to her if she found a crack in their story, a whispering-point? They were only people.

Jan grinned back, shrugging, 'Trust Miss Evans to get stuck with them!'

Laughing, she lifted the plates aloft as we edged past each other along the narrow landing. Her door slammed shut. Everything shook.

In the bathroom with sudden vigour I drowned a pile of nylon things in sudsy water, holding them under as if they were Suspicion itself, pushing, pushing them down, swishing them through the hot foam. Pleasant, it became, and relaxing. I thought of nothing.

The following night as she advanced upwards like a sleep-walker, I overtook Olive Roland on the stairs. Preoccupied and silent I came up behind the solid black heels, the black crêpe skirt, the broad uncorseted hips, the limp arms hanging vertically.

When she saw me she pushed her dark hair from her face, shyly, and stood aside to let me pass. 'Miss James,' she murmured.

I had forgotten her existence: it seemed suddenly snub-bing in view of that modest glance. Repressing a desire to hurry past, I stopped to talk, then we continued upstairs side by side. But she was meek, her manner insisting that this was charming condescension on my part. I shrank from this interpretation, but how to level out the ground?

Salvaging all the helplessness in my possession I presented it to her. And it emerged that while I could still get lost in London, Mrs Roland knew it inside out. I used a darning-needle for all sewing-jobs: she did fine embroidery. She could knit and she liked to cook: I was not domestic.

We mounted the stairs slowly, for the climb was killing. And I burbled on with a kind of off-beat eccentricity that had the double effect of making me seem not only natural and human but, as well, in consequence, slightly demented and entirely unalarming.

Marlon Brando, Mrs Beeton and yesterday's White Paper jazzed together. Mrs Roland listened uneasily and looked sideways at me to see what I was getting at.

The Welfare State had come too late for her. *Too late*...It was rather sad. Shortly, however, I noticed that she no longer addressed me as though I were the lady of the manor, and I was gratified by the result of these two minutes' labour.

Before we parted—I to climb still higher, Olive Roland to deliver a note to Mrs Slater—she told me she'd found a job serving in the dairy at Notting Hill Gate. The manageress was quite nice, but Chris worried so, she said, smiling a little wearily.

Her face was scored with marks of resignation but, then, she wasn't young. Remembering Christian Roland's probable age as I glanced at her youthful hair-style, I thought her situation pathetic, and her chances fragile. The hope symbolized by that much-combed head of hair!

Quickly, my interest running out, I asked about her husband. My hand was on the railing. What *time* was it?

Chris was ill again, she said, she hoped not seriously. She seemed relieved to speak about it, as I was to have her vague air of unhappiness accounted for.

After that we had chance meetings of a similar sort several times. She wasn't humble any more.

Dora Carlton and her friend, Jean, had slumped over the table for two hours, laboriously exhorting each other to admire the beauties of the Louvre, the Pont Neuf and French cooking. One dark head, one fair, under the centre light, wearily supported. Now they had gone.

From Mrs Slater's room downstairs the nine o'clock news rang out a gale warning to all shipping in the areas...

33

I stood at the kitchen sink and swirled three aspirin in a glass. On the floor at my feet a small zinc bucket stood glutted and festooned with an overplus of refuse, its lid balanced high above the rim on a collection of empty tins, fishy paper, egg-shells and vegetable waste. Something touched my leg coldly. *A mouse?* A long green twist of apple-peeling.

I heard a noise and turned as Christian Roland came slowly up the short flight of stairs to the landing, and over to the side of the sink. 'Good evening, Miss James. Special delivery.'

A pupil would be half an hour late tomorrow night.

'I wonder when they're going to fix that telephone extension?'

He smiled. And his smile was entirely disarming: it admitted that he'd given something of himself away when we met last and didn't mind. He had the look of a truthful feeling person, and in a quite impersonal way this look was tonic to me, gave a momentary sensation of having been translated from sickness to health. For artifice destroyed me, and even in this house I'd witnessed horrifying charades entitled 'Friendship' performed by people who had known each other for years. Arch and brittle as creations of Congreve's: that they refrained from the use of wigs, fans, snuff, titles and Restoration cries, seemed odd.

So there was something here, just now, that was a relief.

He stood by, watching, rather grave, till I dried the glass. 'Headache.' I picked up the bottle of tablets from the draining-board. 'Too much print for one day.'

'What do you take?' he asked looking across at the label with real curiosity. I told him and he gave a shout of amusement and approval, repeating the name, his teeth gleaming. 'Isn't that lovely! Nothing so common as ordinary aspirin!'

Smiling, too, I looked at the bottle again. Evidently he liked to relate people to their accoutrements. All at once the novelty of his attitude made me laugh to remember the marvellous world of idiosyncracy that was still there, outside the house. Life! I'd half-forgotten it.

We had moved from the kitchen and hovered in the few square feet of the landing beside my door, where all was dun, dim and poverty-stricken.

I said, 'Miss Evans told me you're learning French?'

His face closed. He looked away. 'Yes. I've got to. There's nothing else I can do.'

His bitterness—after the gaiety—jolted me. How hard his voice had become!

'Olive may have mentioned I have some extra grammars? And a dictionary? If they'd be any use I'll get them now.'

He was leaning against the wall, arms folded, head down, held by his thoughts. He had a large head, a broad head, with lines that might please a sculptor: it seemed eminently a head to be hewn, chiselled. This feeling surprised me, for I had, in no sense, an artist's eye.

In response to my offer he looked up, not answering, but asking, 'How did you learn?'

'At school, but mostly from my step-mother, Mimi. She's French. She forced it on me though I resisted every inch of the way. Now I'm glad.'

'Intelligent girl,' he said heavily, letting his arms fall to his sides. 'Thank you very much. It's very kind of you. You're very sweet.'

Inside, while I rifled through the titles, Christian was waiting in his own sort of active silence.

'Where are you? What are you doing?'

There was a jerky movement. I had moved out of sight behind the tall armchair in which he sat. Now I returned, dumping the bundle down beside him.

'I was only behind you. Here!'

'It makes me nervous,' he muttered. Then noticing the books, he changed. He looked from them to me with an enormous controlled vitality, as if he couldn't communicate what they meant to him. And, indeed, I found it difficult to guess. He seemed moved. I thought this merely exaggerated politeness but, with reservations, I liked the warmth of it.

'If you could see...I've been using a battered old second-hand thing. Pages missing. Oh, God! You've no idea, but now...'

His eyes blazed at me. Puzzled but pleased that he was pleased, I had to smile as I sat down. What could it be like to feel so young?

Upright and bulky in his chair, he seemed furiously to search the air for a target for all the hope that had been unloosed in him. His hands were planted on his knees.

'Do you mind if I stay for five minutes? Olive won't worry. She likes you.'

I shook my head, making some sort of answer, while he turned with high-pressure intensity to stare at the fabric of the room, thoroughly and without embarrassment, orientating himself. Then he gave a mildly sardonic smile and inclined his head.

'What's the matter with it?' I did think he was young.

'It's a dump, isn't it? The whole place. *This* room isn't so bad—you've got some of your own things about, haven't you? And it's the cleanest room in the house but...' He made a dismissive gesture.

I felt no partisan sense of outrage. I had no sense of identification with my surroundings, but I defended Miss Evans on the grounds of hot water and non-interference.

'No, it isn't for you. You should get out of here.'

'I'll think about it.' This was meant to be ironic, but against all that energy there was no hope. I gave up any thought of competition and sat back, refreshed as though I were watching a spectacle from a Mediterranean beach in summer.

'And speaking of Miss Evans!' he cried. 'I know one must have loyalty, and she's an absolute sweetie. She brings home buns covered with the most lurid pink icing for Olive and me every night. And I wouldn't say it to anyone else—but she's nuts! She's up the wall! Last night she arrived with a ghost at her side! Apparently it followed her from the meeting. I don't say I saw it but...'

He was the best mimic I'd ever seen.

Now Miss Evans stood lecturing the ghost, stern and rhetorical, now Christian was in the chair, giving a shout of laughter at the recollection before he took off again.

I laughed without knowing it, ceased to exist. I caught distant impressions of a broad head covered with light hair, a

37

smiling mouth, and bright eyes which, without exaggerated play, quite mesmerized.

If he changed his position, involved eyebrows or hands in the finished glittering explosion, I saw nothing. The mechanics of his display were invisible, and the words bore no relation to the impact. This must be what they called personality, I thought, coming up for air.

He could have made me laugh at anything. Ordinarily I was capable of seeing pathos and little else in Miss Evans's addiction to ghosts: tonight I knew—but really knew—it was hilarious, and life was funny whatever happened…

'Oh, don't make me laugh any more!'

Christian glanced at me, and was carried on by appreciation. A hand clapped to his chest, he fell back in his chair. 'Then, my dear, Mrs Slater totters in just when—according to Miss Evans—the ghost is persuaded to go home. "I'm afraid I'm terribly drunk!" she says, and walks right through it!'

It was her accent, her theme-song!

I cried, 'She always says that!'

'You can imagine what trouble we had with the spirit after that!' He shook his head, we laughed, he sighed, 'A mad-house!…But I like old Slater and Evans…'

The walls and ceiling returned around us, and the black varnished boards. The divan with the red cover, the table and straight chairs again stood firm. And my left hand was raised as a shield against the fire. I was surprised to see it.

Composed and comfortable, his arms extended along the arms of the chair, Christian watched me with the kind expression of a doctor encouraging a patient out of the anaesthetic.

'You've been nice to Olive,' he said gravely. 'I appreciate it very much.'

'We've talked on the stairs...'

'You've been nice. People take her for granted, treat her like a servant. They make a fuss of me and ignore her.' In the hard controlled tone I'd heard earlier, he said, 'Let's be honest! Olive comes from a poor home. She doesn't know anything. She's had no education. She's older than I am, and looks it. But she's good and they've no right to...' Eloquently he broke off.

I was indignant. Who had affronted Olive?

'She likes you,' Christian said. 'We both do.' He looked levelly at me and spoke without affectation. I was aware that Lewis might call this declaration any one of a hundred unflattering things, but I respected the ability in anyone to speak simply of feeling.

If what he said was true, I was glad. If it was a lie, I regretted his motive. Perhaps it was childish and we were not children: what did it matter?

But this was what it was like to feel young! I remembered. And I felt a defiant defensive sort of happiness.

'Olive told me you'd been ill?'

'No, I haven't! It was the after-effects of flu.' He was smouldering, moody, then he laughed. 'Olive's worried now in case I'm "taken queer" and fall off one of these sky-scrapers.' His hand throbbed in the direction of the window.

'Still, if you aren't well...'

His fist was against his mouth, eyes covered, face closed. 'It's nothing. It wouldn't matter. It's nothing to the mental agony.'

Mental agony. Mental agony?

Shocked and curious, I stared. He had a bitter, private, despairing intensity about him. If I had any judgement, any penetration, this was not attitudinizing. Yet it was the sequel to a splintering, glistering display of talent with a twenty-two carat dazzle. *Mental agony...*

Now, over his hand, without speaking, he looked at me, not blinking, not moving his eyes. I felt a demand in him that commanded a tentative response. What was it? I was confused. There was something strange...The apprehensions fluctuated.

'Oh, listen to me!' he said in disgust, moving restlessly in his chair. 'I'd better go!'

He was off, lightly, silently, carrying the books. Then he stopped, hand to hair in that gesture of vanity and shyness, to say unsmiling, 'I used to play at Stratford. *Hamlet. Macbeth*. Not the lead, of course.' And here he really shrank in horror—as I had only heard that people did—lest I should have been misled. 'But good parts. I was an actor.'

Before I had time to speak he was at the door: there he paused suddenly, his eyes on the small wireless set on the chest of drawers. A finger slid over the green and gold. Approving, as he disappeared, he said, 'Chi-chi!'

During the next week the meetings with Olive and Christian continued. There were brief moments in the hall. If they brought a message up for someone else, they stopped to see me. Or Christian came in to ask about some point of syntax.

Through all my preoccupation with work and the African crisis, I began to be aware of possessing something new, something gay, something shiny and warm. I had a pretty treasure: it was part of me. I liked myself: I was fond of it. In limited moments of leisure—formerly spent in blank recuperation—I would be startled back to life by the movement of this pleasant not-to-be-defined sensation of light-heartedness.

Striking a match to light the gas, cleaning my teeth, I would realize with a shock of relief and comfort that I lived. My blood flowed!

I still knew little about the two Rolands—not where they came from nor where they were aiming, but I was childishly, incuriously, content.

Now, this evening, pausing on the way back from Mrs Parry's room to speak to me, Christian's bright eyes flickered over mine to confirm their capture while the inner spot-light lit up again. His capacity for self-enjoyment seemed endless.

'You said it could be fun cleaning windows, Clem, and it is. I meet all these funny old girls and their lodgers. They ask me to have tea and biscuits. Quite often their windows have just been done, but I flannel them along and they say, "Well, yes, they *are* rather dirty now that you mention it, Mr Roland."'

To himself, rather than to me, and almost dreamily, he said, 'They like to please one.'

One with a capital O.

I felt myself withdraw, withdraw, mentally, from his proximity. I didn't like him! All at once his earnest pleasure in himself was alarming.

'Then after they've asked me to do their income-tax returns—one actually did the other day—they tell me how poor they are. They get out the old purse and try to kid me along. Can't afford! They can't bend their fingers for diamonds some of these old bags!'

As a student of the theatre, I saluted him. As a student of human nature I felt an unprecedented inclination to come down heavily on both sides at once. He was awful! Why did it seem irrelevant?

In the midst of laughing together, our eyes were alert and wary. He watched me with some calculation and drew an astonishing inference.

'Ah...I don't rob old women and widows if that's what you're thinking. We have a natter like that—for a giggle. We have tea, they try to beat me down, I beat them down. They love it. I only charge them the standard rate.'

He spoke doggedly, as if I'd failed to understand his English. And I was ashamed. I was ashamed though his accusation was so far unfounded that I couldn't imagine what words would refute it. But if he was mistaken, somehow I was not right. For I had criticized him: he had seen that in my eyes. And he was not to be judged. Dimly I understood now he was not to be judged.

'And I do a good job for it!' His voice was arrogant, his face set, as though he challenged me to doubt him on this point, the pivot of his pride.

Clearly, he would greatly have preferred me to believe him, wrongly, to be guilty of petty extortion, than to doubt the quality of his work. His work!

My mind circled, circled.

I was baffled by the flat opposition of my feelings.

Olive opened the door revealing Christian in a chair by the fire, his back to us. Then his whole body turned in enquiry, like the automatic turning of a search-light, and he was on his feet.

Miss Evans's sitting-room was pink-walled and cosy. Three chairs were arranged in a semi-circle round the small coal-fire. For a few moments their merits and distribution were hilariously debated. But beyond the sound of our three voices, I had the sensation of being caught in a stampede, of saying good-bye to myself for the duration.

At last we were settled with Olive in the centre; Christian poked the fire then sat forward in his chair, eyes gleaming. I was concentrated on. Under cover of his talk, he and Olive drank me up with curiosity and enthusiasm. They eyed my dark green sweater and straight tweed skirt; they marked the gauge of my stockings and the shade of my lipstick. The smooth folded arrangement of hair on the crown of my head was noted, and the length of my finger-nails. And they seemed to offer themselves for the same kind of inspection. While I told myself that this was the natural result of mutual interest and confidence, I felt slightly abashed.

In Sydney this examination of the surface was habitual, but here of the people I knew, Lewis cared most perhaps for the responsibility with which one lived one's life; Helen for one's awareness and penetration. Jan judged people according to their menu; Mrs Gill, the cleaner, according to tidiness; Miss Evans, according to solvency and a willingness to indulge in amiable gossip...

Now I had a feeling not only of being drunk up but eaten. How friendly! I insisted shyly to myself, still disconcerted.

'My dear,' Christian was saying, 'if you'd seen the three of them setting out for the meeting tonight!'

Olive turned to watch him, half smiling as I was, in anticipation of the laughter that would surely overwhelm us. When she glanced at me the lift of her brows canvassed appreciation of Christian, and I nodded back to show I thought him entirely diverting.

Behind this glittering projection of personality, he sat, seeming confident to the very last degree in his fresh youthful skin. Even now, in the third week of our acquaintance, I was still startled by the variety of his tones and expressions. Without a wrinkle of the smooth forehead or the slightest distortion of cheek or jaw, he was recreated constantly, at will.

It was inexplicable and that was that. But I found such versatility extremely restful, and the overspill of his confidence wonderfully relaxing.

How smug, how mistaken I had been to judge him! All the vanity, the reiterated claims of his effect on other people were deeply ironic, uttered from the safe foundation of his self-awareness. I was sure of it now.

The story broke. The rocket exploded in stars. Our laughter beat about the room. How gay the fire, the clock, pink walls!

Olive, who was turned towards me, speaking, seemed suddenly to nestle closer, girls together, to say with a giggle, 'Last night when Mrs Parry and Ada were down again—oh, someone's down to see us every night—they made Chris so mad. They're always talking about—'

'That's enough!'

She hesitated under Christian's eye, then turned to me again. 'About—you know—the girls on the corner—the—'

'Olive!'

'—prostitutes.'

On his feet, hands in pockets, Christian stormed silently about the room. Olive's expression was pious. At the switchboard in the hall, the phone rang and he went to answer it.

'He hates that kind of talk. You could tell, couldn't you?'

'It isn't very enlivening,' I murmured to discourage her as Christian came silently back to the room.

'You know Olive has a job in the dairy?—It's a wonder you haven't seen her there. *Or have you?*' His voice was bitter.

'No!' In fact I'd been led, rather unwillingly, but guessing at some such reaction in them, to walk to shops ten minutes further away, rather than have Olive face me across a counter.

'No? Well, I mean, it isn't very nice for Olive, is it? Working in a shop? Having to serve all those—' Sitting sideways in his chair, knuckles against set mouth, he stared down at the floor.

But Olive smiled, looking uplifted. 'I don't mind, as long as I can make you happy...' Her words were like a cue: they now gazed at each other in a sudden passion of tenderness.

They acted all the time—with a fervent, slightly feverish earnestness, Olive looking to Christian for guidance constantly, before responding.

'And,' said Christian, returning from the heights, 'while Olive sells eggs and I clean windows, you sit up in your neat little room all day with a private income, studying. This time next year you'll be a lawyer, Miss Evans said. Clever girl. I like intelligent people.' He looked at Olive. 'You like her, too, don't you?'

'Of course,' said Olive, with an indulgent smile.

This portentous attempt at flattery made me look from one to the other without speaking. And how to correct so many misapprehensions? How could a merely truthful statement of mine compete with the implacable confidence of Christian's?

Olive went to stand behind him now, her hands lightly touching his hair. He looked round at her quizzically. She said, 'Did you know he almost fell yesterday?'

'On my head. On my head,' he grinned. 'Would it have made much difference, do you think?'

'That beautiful head,' Olive said in a heavy yearning voice, and we all fell into a respectful silence.

To this point I had resisted embarrassment as an emotion unworthy of a place in (a) natural behaviour and (b) our friendship. If one was sufficiently honoured to be trusted to understand the spontaneous behaviour of others, one was simply not embarrassed. So I had naïvely believed. My head reeled.

Christian lowered his eyelids in a travesty of modesty, then raised them to look directly at me, his expression grave, deliberate and full of meaning. Behind him Olive held his massive head between her hands.

Without moving his eyes from mine he said, 'Sweet, I'm sure Miss Evans wouldn't mind if you made us a cup of coffee in her kitchen.'

It was joy to Olive to be commanded by him. Smiling across at me in a gentle womanly way, she went. And quite beautifully Christian called, 'Please don't be long, darling!' as if the separation might prove more than he could bear.

They astonished me; I sat like a prisoner awaiting events. And whether I would or no, I was insulted by a crudeness in their joint personality: the heaped-up flattery, the pointed demonstrations of devotion, the looks I received from Christian that Olive couldn't see. Yet even as I was repelled I had to relent—for they were so blatant, so poster-coloured.

Christian watched me with his habitual air of electric immobility. 'Olive's been wonderful to me,' he said carefully. 'This may look funny from the outside—other people's love affairs always do—but she's been good to me and I could never hurt her, Clem. You know we aren't married, don't you? Her husband's a great hulking Pole. He wouldn't give her enough to live on. She had to take in boarders—' he improvised quickly 'to keep herself and her two daughters from starving.'

Really?

His eyes darted over mine like those of a story-teller testing a youthful audience. I looked impassive and he glanced away.

But who was I to fade the colour from his fancy? Feeling compunction I said, 'How did you meet?' and he was immediately restored.

A few months before he'd been staying at an hotel on the south coast when he found himself short of money and decided to move to a boarding-house. There were hundreds in the side streets leading back from the sea-front but it somehow happened that he chose Olive's.

Miss Evans's small room was quiet and hot, the fire flaring and cracking. Christian's attention was reflectively lowered on the past.

'It was fate!' he said, turning fanatical eyes on me. 'It was fate, Clem!'

Emptily, aware of a demand in that reverberating cry, I endured his stare and was depressed to the marrow.

He'd always lived with his sister, Stella, he went on suddenly. She was ten years older than him, a singer of talent and very beautiful. Had it not been for the jealousy and machinations of certain people who resented her good fortune—she had generous friends—she might well have been famous.

With strange elation, almost with radiance, he spoke about Stella.

They were never apart till she died, he said. And suddenly his mouth closed on a shocking emptiness.

Without disturbing that air of intense control, he said, 'Excuse me, I must see what Olive's doing.' He made no move. The fire crackled and a spark flew onto the rug. He let an arm drop, slack, to his side. 'It doesn't matter. Sorry about that… Where was I? If this is—tedious—to listen to tell me…'

48

We had avoided each other's eyes. Now, sunk back in his chair the strange man I called Christian looked at me in silence. There was something I couldn't bear. By feeling so much in my presence he seemed to ravage, impose on, my peace of mind.

Abruptly he looked away, going on to say that after Stella's death he'd visited odd people for a few days at a time, but no one had taken charge of him till at the end of several months when he was ill, he'd met Olive. Last autumn. Immediately she began to look after him, kindly, the way an older sister would. Now she adored him, fussed over him, would never leave him. So he mustn't hurt her.

I listened in silence. From the glances he shot me, I gathered that my face had remained reassuringly calm. But because I had the impression that he was beseeching support for his protestations I said, 'I'm sure she wouldn't leave you.'

'No!' He snatched at this, staring to see if I was certain. Then, as if it were a lesson he must learn at all costs, he half chanted. 'I love her and she loves me. She loves me madly. She worships the ground I walk on.'

The desperate extravagance of his language seemed to challenge contradiction, but whether from me or from his own resistant emotions I couldn't tell. There was something here not recognizable...

Now he said with a marvellous alteration from hectic nervousness to gentleness and gravity, and as if it followed, 'But we mustn't lose touch. I like you.'

The note he hit—of one conferring an honour—made me smile, but I said, 'That's good,' and meant it entirely, with a sort of friendly goodwill.

49

My legs were burning. I moved a little away from the fire. He watched intently, thoughtful, then said, 'But you weren't shocked to know we aren't married?'

'How could I have been?'

'No. But you thought nothing of it?'

'No.'

That apparently was me pinned down and found out.

Slightly smiling and frowning at each other, we heard Olive outside in the corridor. He said, 'Don't let her know I told you…'

She stood holding a tray, looking anxiously and obviously into our eyes.

'You were a long time, darling.' Christian cleared a space on the small walnut table, ostentatiously attentive.

'The phone kept ringing. Didn't you hear it? Miss Evans rang from the meeting to say she's expecting someone new in twenty-two tonight.'

As they stood over the tray together, Christian soon made her smile. His back was towards me.

For lack of playing-fields my intuition had been unexercised for years but, suddenly, this evening, it sprang into action again as if the long hiatus had never been. At this instant Christian's back was telling me that while we'd shared a small conspiracy, his loyalty to Olive was unimpaired. (Loyalty, I'd noticed earlier, was a quality on which he placed great value. I couldn't count the number of times it had been invoked during our past conversations.) Even if Olive knew he'd revealed her secret, her love wouldn't falter, my intuition translated in his high-flown style.

How nice for them! I thought airily, feeling gay, wanting to giggle. I ate a sandwich and a piece of cake, so did Olive but more slowly, and so did Christian, but invisibly.

Olive poured more coffee and I noticed the French books on the floor by Christian's chair. 'What progress?' I asked nodding at them.

For a moment he hesitated nervously, seeming almost baited, then with something more than a change of expression, filled by a new and utterly resolved self, he said, 'I'll get on. I must. I'll tell you about it.'

Olive stood apprehensive, the coffee-pot poised. And he must have sensed her reaction for without turning he raised a hand to halt the unspoken protest, saying in a soothing tone, 'Don't worry. Just about the French.'

He looked elated at the prospect of his revelations. Olive sat down, staring at the flat creamy surface of her coffee.

'There are two things I'm trained to do for money: whether you believe it or not—when I'm given the chance— I'm a pretty good Benedict, among other characters, and I play the piano a bit—as Olive told you. But—for reasons that I intend to omit—I can't find that sort of work in this country. And if I did it wouldn't last. So, ultimately, in my old age I shall fix myself in New York. Though the stars say that plan may take a few years. That doesn't matter! I'm prepared to wait. In the meantime I'll get to Paris.

'This is what I've worked out. By this time next year, probably sooner, I'll be fluent. The accent's no trouble and I could recite the contents of the Encyclopedia Britannica backwards in two days if I wanted to...

51

'Then I'll be able to use the old personality and get a job as courier for wealthy Americans travelling over there. We'll live in Paris. I'll establish myself financially and eventually return to my proper milieu. Do you see me at the Comédie Française? It isn't impossible! We'll live a civilized life again. It doesn't cost the earth to rent a place on the coast. Stella used to have...In the summer we could get out of town for two or three months and go down to Nice or Cannes and get brown...'

From ragged sullen nervousness he'd talked himself round to a point where he was portentously happy and optimistic.

I felt myself slide and sink, sink into space. I wanted to reproach him. This was dream-stuff. He was vile. Stupid. How would he feel when he woke? Could Olive believe all this?

He went on with a great air of frankness, 'You know we haven't got any money. You've seen us in the same clothes for weeks, and you aren't exactly simple. I don't mind you knowing—it's these other...It takes us all our time to pay the rent and eat. It's expensive just to exist! We never go anywhere or do anything and we live on eggs. Even you must find it expensive...?'

That there *was* a cost of living seemed to surprise him.

'I don't get much for this job with Miss Evans, but then it couldn't be called arduous, and we don't have to use our own gas-fire—being here.'

Olive poked Miss Evans's coal appreciatively.

Behind his fist, cloudy, dark with contemplation, Christian muttered, 'I must have money. And Paris is

52

the answer. Olive's afraid I'll fall in love with some rich American widow and go off to New York without her. She's a jealous woman...Aren't you, darling?'

'Of course not,' Olive said, modestly reproving.

'Poor Olive. I wouldn't do that to you. You know, Clem, she's jealous even of old Evans and Slater! She'll be jealous of you next, if I talk to you for another five minutes.'

Olive and I exchanged smiles, admitting his hopelessness.

He was saying, 'All kinds of opportunities come if one can talk to people. Influence them...' He gave a shout of laughter. 'Some old Yank might die and leave me all her money...'

Olive and I looked at him. He looked back half-ironic, half-chastened. 'You don't think that's funny?' We shook our heads, but he shrugged us off. '*Anything* can happen.'

It was like enduring a hallucination to listen to the lists of delicious French clothes he would buy for Olive, the delicious Italian shoes, the hand-made shirts, the jewellery.

I hated him for his obtuseness, his dreams, his unwillingness to live in the world. Yet when he stopped speaking and the truth of his situation closed in again, he conveyed such a sense of pain at the deprivation, that I felt, not so much that it was trivial to suffer for the absence of luxury but, rather, that it was wrong that for so negligible a reason as lack of money, he should be hurt so much. Almost, obscurely, I felt it was dangerous for him not to have what he wanted.

At the same time, knowing how little *I* lived on, I wondered how these two could fail to be adequately clothed and fed. What happened to their wages? Had they a debt to pay? Dependent relatives?

As I was leaving he said, 'I don't want you to think I'm nice because we've all laughed and enjoyed ourselves. I'm very likeable but I can be terribly hard. Can't I, darling?'

'Of course.'

'I'm like a tiger.'

I thought: he'll laugh. It'll be all right.

But no, he was really earnest. And because I smiled doubtfully he looked at me in a state of moody flattered exasperation, shooting almost comically significant glances from under his brows.

His face was absurdly young and open, but he insisted wildly, 'You don't know me. I'm really bad. I'm as dangerous as a tiger.'

'He's had to be,' Olive said when I looked at her, bewildered by his vehemence.

I shook my head, gave in. *All right. I believe you.*

But I did not. I felt more than ever charmed and indulgent. Christian's protestations only proved the truth of his face. He was good. Not only that, this preoccupation with his condition, the consciousness of sin—in spite of the histrionics—spoke of sensibility and insight.

True, there were those day-dreams. *If* he was serious… But perhaps he was not? Hadn't been? No, surely he was too sane, too aware of irony!

Collecting myself together I went up to my room.

54

CHAPTER THREE

The long brown envelope that fell into the letter-box held all the visible results of a week's work.

'It won't be so long till you're through,' said Lewis, taking his customary astronomical view of time.

'Only a year this June!'

It was February, bitter. The wet pavements gave up black and shiny reflections of red and green neon lights. We'd dined speedily in Soho and now, after stopping to post my paper, ran downstairs and walked through a long tiled subway to the underground. A sweetish dehydrated wind buffeted our faces mildly: posters loomed. A train swept round the curve.

I said when we were settled, 'How could you wait till we were leaving to tell me? I'd have—'

'I thought if I mentioned it earlier it might hold us up.'

We were going to the Theatre Royal in the East End, and certainly had no time to spare. But I cried, 'No excuses! You finish your coffee, idly call for the check, glance at your watch: "By the way, Clem, I've just heard I'm going to New York next month—"'

Lewis smiled and looked down along his outstretched legs at his shoes. 'How should I have introduced it into the conversation?'

'Just tell me plainly what's going to happen!'

It was an effort tonight to divert him in this manner, but I was genuinely eager to hear his plans.

Seeming reluctant to grant his journey importance he said, 'There isn't much to tell. I'll leave early in March to attend this conference in New York and visit various other cities. It should take roughly about five weeks and if I can work it out with Frazer I'll try to fit in a week's leave.'

'But it's thrilling, Lewis! Please be excited! You assume this awful calm just to exasperate me, don't you? No, maybe it's natural.' Enviously, glumly, looking at the black reflecting windows I added, 'You'll be able to have a shower.'

Lewis laughed. 'It's a long way to go. Why don't you believe me when I tell you that Europeans dislike showers? They're restless. Over-active. Quite inferior to baths.'

'It's ignorance. You are all under-privileged.'

The train rattled noisily for seconds; we swayed, looking ahead at the sparsely-filled carriage, the swinging straps and steady lights.

'I'm more interested just now in what you're doing,' he commented, when he was able to make himself heard. 'When would you take this—Roland—for a lesson?'

'Dora Carlton is finishing. I needn't find anyone to replace her.'

Lewis was silent. Then, 'You would ask your usual fee?'

I frowned at the seat opposite. 'I don't quite see how I could. I doubt if they—he—could afford it. You see—I don't know what's wrong but money is a problem. Oh, yes, I know! Everyone's problem! But a particular one...'

After a longer frowning silence, Lewis asked, 'But how would you manage? You work to a very tight budget.' He paused and went on in a more conciliatory tone, 'I don't mean to discourage you, Clem. If you can help them, and want to, perhaps you should. But think about it. Don't be too impulsive. You've had a struggle to manage. And you don't know much about them.'

Resentfully I said, 'Nothing's decided. I was asking your opinion, that was all.'

I did resent his reminding me of the gulf that separated what I desired to do from what, in the light of reason, was possible. *Was* I pining to increase the austerity of the weekly budget? Emphatically not. The seductive charms of self-denial had recently begun to seem like shackles. The eternal 'no' to all lightness and frivolity seemed crippling now, rather than grand.

Why should I help the Rolands and thus diminish the sum that stood between me and the work-house? That I even wanted to consider it made me feel sulky and ill-done-by. And because Lewis reminded me of it I felt aggrievedly that it was all his fault. He was detestable really.

The train drew in and out of stations, rattled.

I felt Lewis looking at me and turned: his expression was mild, as if he was secretly smiling, understanding my thoughts. I stared at him coldly, feeling a haughty contempt.

It was no use! Years before I had absolutely spent my capacity for anger. *Now* not to be angry was second nature, but it left me short of a weapon. I started to laugh indignantly, and Lewis smiled.

'Would this fellow learn, do you think? And supposing he did reach any degree of fluency—what hopes are there of finding work in Paris?'

'I don't know. I doubt if he could apply himself for long. He's too—strung-up. As for this profitable job I've heard so much about—you know how hard it is for qualified people with French to find anything. But with Christian it's irrelevant—whether or not a thing is possible—as long as it seems so to him.'

Before now I'd noticed a lot of unexplained and inexplicable imperatives creeping into my conversation when I talked about Christian. In case Lewis had noticed too, I hastily mumbled, 'And maybe he's right, anyway. Even about the Comédie Française. I just don't know about these things.'

I glanced sideways at Lewis. He relaxed with me as I did with Christian, and was accustomed to my exaggerations. It would have been embarrassing to have seemed over-concerned. For I wasn't.

To prove the unimportance of the whole thing to him, I smiled, 'I haven't had so many significant looks thrown at me since—probably never! Both Christian and Olive are convinced of his irresistibility. She bolsters up his vanity by pretending that every woman who speaks to him

58

is overcome with hopeless passion on the instant. Even Miss Evans and Mrs Slater! And he encourages her to believe that he isn't absolutely indifferent. It's really weird. But somehow it doesn't matter. It makes me want to laugh. If they knew how I felt they'd be disappointed.'

This had just occurred to me, yet I knew it was true. I said, following it up like a sleuth, 'Unconsciously, if they had the chance, I think they would even entice a third person in. It would reinforce their confidence.'

Lewis's expression made my face fall. 'What?'

'I can't help feeling you'd be better out of this.'

Quickly I agreed, 'Maybe I would…But what I said—enticing—that was imagination more than anything. Or if it wasn't I'll soon convince them there's no danger.'

'Or hope!' said Lewis.

I said dryly, 'Or that.'

For all at once I was irked by them, bored with them. Their company was mentally fatiguing—like wearing trick spectacles, like having one's house walled with distorting mirrors. Debilitating.

I felt very strongly that my gay little jaunt to the kindergarten was nearing its end, and it was a wholesome feeling. Why hadn't I realized how burdened I'd become? How peculiar they were? How much of a strain it was at each meeting to cut my mind loose deliberately in order to make contact? Recalling in the instant of answering Lewis my delusions about unaffected friendship, I felt I must have been ill, and was mortified.

Beside me, the shoulder of his coat against mine, Lewis smiled, seeming to guess I'd undergone a change of heart.

Rueful, shamefaced, I met his eyes. I had interested myself in these strangers to the exclusion of almost everything. So much for spontaneity!

Lewis re-arranged his arms across his chest, looked at a station name. The Rolands were behind me, receding as the line receded from the train, already in the past.

Quite idly he remarked, 'They sound like castaways...'

And, yes! That was it! I had forgotten. That fellow-feeling, the fraternal pull, the need to offer a helping hand. I could see them both quite vividly, standing side by side, arms hanging, waiting...

Reluctantly I said, 'I'm afraid they are. I suppose that's why I've—become involved. It's a reflex.'

'The greater the separation from society the greater the affinity?'

'Don't make it sound so foolish.'

Lewis looked ahead, thinking something impossible to guess. His grey eyes were unreadable, as always. I could only imagine he disapproved.

'I mean—people who've experienced a surfeit of feeling often have thoughtfulness thrust on them. They're aware that soft flesh can be hurt because theirs has been. Conscious that life is more important than its trappings...You don't agree?'

Unwilling to squash me, I felt, Lewis looked down at his hands saying, 'You could be right. But your view is rosier than mine. I haven't found by any means that experience of life automatically turns consciousness in that direction.'

'Oh,' I sighed anxiously. The conversation worried me somehow. 'Oh. Let's forget them. Tell me more about New York.'

Equable, Lewis reached into an inside pocket and pulled out a small bundle of papers. 'I came prepared!'

We held a side each of the typewritten schedule and read it. The prospect of Lewis's absence from my life was daunting. Of course Helen would be here...Not exactly alone.

A sly, smooth, machine-turned, thought slid across my mind. For six or eight weeks I wouldn't have to hurt him if I had to change our Friday night arrangements to see them. My spirits did a loop-the-loop. New York! London! Work progressing well, and my friends, my new friends...

Christian appeared in answer to my 'Come in!' and stood and challenged us with insinuating glances.

With both arms I leaned on the table at which I sat; Jan stood on the other side holding a plate of brown sliced bread. We gazed at the dazzling young man. He looked like the youngest son of the youngest son, destined to die in battle, or like Chaucer's young esquire.

'Thanks for the bread. Now I'll be able to breakfast in the morning!' Jan turned a flat and curious look on me before edging past Miss Evans's window-cleaner with whom I was, it appeared, on surprisingly familiar terms.

'She doesn't like me.'

As Jan closed the door he spoke in a tone that might just have been audible to her, his eyes fixed on mine, and glittering. Taking a step closer to the table, leaning towards me, he gave me a look which, in anyone else would have been unpleasantly audacious, to see how I took the possibility. Could I be discomfited? He wanted very much to know.

61

'Not by you. Not by these means,' I could have told him, but was silent. My instinct was to conserve energy, and I obeyed it, simply watching the malicious curving smile that touched his mouth. I felt exhausted for him. He tried so hard. I wanted to say, 'Relax. Give up. Give over.' But I continued to look at him in silence, trusting that he would abandon these antics of his own accord in due time.

Then it did dawn on him. Still standing, hands on table, bent on winning back my approval, he began to speak rapidly. 'This is just how I pictured you, sitting among your books in this little blue room. I had a bet with myself you'd be wearing that dress...' His tone was gentle, winning and assured. I looked down at that immaculate yellow sweater. Olive must wash it nightly.

At his remarks and manner, I smiled, amused. If he took it as a sign of rapture that couldn't be helped. Besides I understood now that it was natural to him to flatter everyone he met. And I'd noticed that, in fact, he had an enormous capacity for appreciation of all kinds. Colours, textures, the arrangements of line and space, were striking to him and relevant in a way that they had never been to me. What was the secret of that intense and sparkling interest? What sustenance did he draw from faces, places, things?

'Why don't you sit down?'

Now that he was opposite me—books in between, light overhead—he looked so fresh, so ostentatiously fair, that I almost began to understand. A sight for sore eyes. A menace, undoubtedly, but not a very alarming one for, after all, he knew it. It was just part of the game, meant to tease.

62

He half raised a hand in salute and apology. 'I've come for information, Clemency James, and brought my books. Is that all right?' But the books remained closed. 'What've you been doing all day? Working here, like this?'

'Practically.'

We watched each other. His fingers smoothed the corner of one hard red cover: mine touched another in the same abstracted way.

'—don't really understand you yet…a strange girl… very seldom puzzled by people…sort of calm and tolerant… what I like is…out of the world up here in this attic… not spoilt…career at the bar…'

It was after nine o'clock. The room was warm and peaceful. I could see him breathe and pause softly and speak. Since I was two I had liked to hear stories; I listened to this one, lulled by the beautiful voice.

He was asking, 'Then do you often go into pubs?'

'Not very often.'

'There you are! You haven't lived. You're just a child!'

So I was canned and labelled satisfactorily at last!

This came as his opinions always did with an air of tremendous authority. Considering how bizarre, prejudiced and just plain wrong they often were, I thought his confidence all the more charming.

I laughed but Christian said regretfully, 'Oh God, it's refreshing! You've no idea…'

I shook my head, not understanding. He had a way of distributing virtues, vices and histories where and how he would. He rarely asked: he told. And I? Did I contradict,

63

try to straighten out the facts? And if not, why not? Not reluctance, but a feeling of indulgent helplessness, of the uselessness of saying, 'No. That is not the way it is,' made denials peter out on my lips. The accumulation of indrawn breath never translated into language formed a small explosive core of frustration in my chest.

'—and you're always so clean. Ah, *no*. Not everyone is. Your hair shines, and your clothes are nice, and your life is beautifully organized and peaceful...'

But shade by shade the calm of the story-teller was turning to panic. He was wound up, couldn't stop. Brakes slipping on a mountain road. Almost wildly he looked at me for help.

His strangeness jarred me. Lately, I seemed always to be in situations for which I had no precedent, groping for the best word or action, feeling a kind of cold apprehension on his behalf or Olive's.

I picked up one of his safer remarks and talked in a very unstimulating way, but Christian watched me fixedly, concentrating on every word as if I had assumed calm and responsibility sufficient for both of us. I rambled on, eventually asking, 'Did you see that picture yesterday?' It had been his day off.

'No. I lay about. I had things on my mind. Olive washed and ironed and cooked. It wasn't much of a rout for her. Poor Olive. You don't know the awful things I do to her.' His eyes glinted, full of fun. 'I made her cry this morning. Just now I left her crying downstairs.'

There was no doubt he'd recovered from whatever caused that panic.

I looked quizzically across at his foxy smile.

'Why do you look like that? Are you disgusted?'

I turned down the corners of my mouth to indicate that it would take more than he could dream up to disgust me. At random I said, 'No. I was thinking you seemed familiar, I suppose.'

'Why? You don't know anyone who looks like me, do you?'

'No.'

Speculative, brooding, he pressed his knuckles to his mouth and considered me. 'I think I know what you mean...When are you coming down to see us again?'

I heard myself sounding shy, saying, 'I stayed a long time the other night.'

'Don't be mad!' It came through his teeth, with a long professional look from unblinking eyes.

Sunk, half-hypnotized, I wanted to laugh hilariously. He never tired of playing the moustacchioed seducer.

'I must leave you. Olive will be—pursuing me any minute. She knows I like you.'

Shattering exit line: the heroine blushes.

I gave a derisive appreciative grin. At the door Christian saluted slowly. 'Come down and give me a lesson tomorrow night!'

How childish! He'd come to restore himself after a quarrel with Olive the way a small boy glues himself to a favourite aunt if his mother is cross.

I wandered about the room, tidying up, trying to see him in one piece. When he was with me I could never remember that he'd ever been or would be different from

65

this moment. Yet he always was. He was distracting! Why had I ever allowed this much distraction into my life?

No, it wasn't hard to answer. He had spoken of mental agony at our first or second meeting. He fixed his hair like a gigolo, as if it mattered, admiring all that was brassiest in his own personality, and dreadfully underrating what seemed to me to be himself. He was over-wrought to the point of illness. He was tirelessly bold and shocking. He was all that was contradictory, and as if it were part of his sickness calculated the worth of every natural movement of his heart.

How much he might hate me, I thought, and how right in a way he would be, if he knew that without that 'mental agony' all the charms would have gone for nothing.

Work was over for the night. Picking up the *Guardian*, I went to sit by the fire, and started to read, feeling contented but inwardly alert, as if somehow I was on the move and ready for an emergency I'd been expecting for a very long time.

Olive stood inside my door saying, 'When you didn't come down last night Chris wondered if you'd taken umbrage or something. He thought he must have offended you. He's been so worried—it's all I've heard all evening. Could you come down now for a while?' She drooped wearily inside the creaseless black dress, smiling sadly.

'I've just finished giving a lesson.'

'We saw them leaving. Chris asked me to come up.' She gave the impression that it would go hard with her if she returned without the trophy. Poor Olive.

66

I thought of the pile of ironing I had to do, then slid my feet into my shoes. She stood by talking amiably enough, while I put some powder on, but I felt she was uncertain of me again, and mistrustful. As no doubt Christian had intended.

Leading the way downstairs she said without expression, 'I told Chris you'd come.'

I pressed my teeth together.

Reaching the hall she added, 'I've got to make a phone call. Just go on in. He's expecting you.' From the fact that there was utter silence behind my back as I went towards Miss Evans's room, I guessed her eyes were on me. I felt grated and bored. My dear ironing waited upstairs. My life was upset. For what? Why did I endure these loutish insults?

Christian sat solid and four-square in the chair opposite the door. He looked up, a newspaper in one hand, his eyes black with preoccupation.

'Where's Olive?' he greeted me, standing.

'Ringing up.'

'No!...No, don't close the door. It's—er—smoky in here.'

That was a plain lie. This was so lively! These people were incomprehensible!

Sitting down I felt chastened, indignant. Christian looked very grimly about the room and started up a flow of trivial small-talk: if I had been an importunate fellow-traveller in a train, thrusting myself on his attention, he could hardly have been more remote.

I sat back in the old velvet armchair, relaxed with hate. He was leaning over the fire, throwing on a piece of coal, then he picked up the small brass poker.

67

His hand shook violently. He put the poker down and looked across at me haggardly. I had less idea than ever what was wrong, half-wondered if this was some new and intricate act. The chill air from the hall made me shiver.

'This is stupid. There's a draught—isn't there?'

There was, but he closed the door as if on a pretext that made him intensely nervous.

'You didn't come in last night. I wished you had. I was waiting for a lesson.' Against some odds he tried to relax.

'I wished I had, too. But I had other lessons to give, and then it was too late…Could we work tonight?'

'I don't know. I don't think so. I'm in no kind of mood tonight—It's nothing to do with you,' he added quickly. Then with his hands clenched between his knees and staring at the old blue rug, he said, 'I loathe self-pity. But sometimes you can't help feeling sorry for yourself, can you?'

'If you have reason to feel sorry for yourself—do. Self-pity's no crime.'

He looked up tentatively, obviously hoping that I could be believed. I realized that somewhere he must have mugged up on attitudes; he was aware in a peculiarly theoretical way as only an outsider could be, of all that *they* permitted. Self-pity he publicly abhorred: it was a widely-known vice, universally condemned. Or had been when he last glanced through the manual of *Attitudes Accepted in Polite Society*. Visibly he wondered if that view had gone out since his last revision. Then he gave me the benefit of the doubt.

Stonily he said, 'That's right! If you aren't sorry for yourself no one else will be, that's for sure.'

68

'Who should know better than oneself what's deserved?' I said lightly, relieved to see him bitter, rather than defenceless.

Heels tapped along the tiled hallway: Olive was coming. At once he was stern and frozen, his eyes resting on mine and warning that we must on no account let Olive suspect what had happened.

Well, what *had*? I wanted to say loudly. And I felt a spasm of disgust at this sub-adolescent mysteriousness. The pretence he kept up began to seem vicious, perverted, sadistic. Why should I not go? Why not just stand and go?

But here was Olive, her eyes X-raying mine, then passing to Christian with a look of such homage that I felt myself recoil. She was too pale, too old, too fanatical, and Christian also, in an opposite sense, was too excessive.

This was no place for me, yet I was held to the room— far from fascinated now and the reverse of curious—by something I did not believe in: necessity, compulsion.

'Darling,' gravely he held out a hand. 'Why were you so long?'

'I couldn't get on at first.' Olive fluttered girlishly at his attention, then half-nodding in my direction as though I were blind added, 'Can I tell you?'

'Do you mind for a moment, Clem, if Olive and I discuss this—business matter?'

I eyed Miss Evans's few ornaments and her print of Cézanne's apples, absenting myself from the huddle of murmurs and backs. What barbarous behaviour! How tedious they were! I would go...

69

'My dears!' Christian cried, setting himself back from Olive and transfixing us both with a wondrous gesture. 'At eleven this morning I was on a window-ledge six storeys up, industriously cleaning—'

He made us weep with laughter, made us exchange streaming glances as the fantasy wove to and fro. Planted upright on the edge of his chair, he seemed to seek out laughter like a diviner. Here it was impossible that he should put a foot wrong.

We were friends again when we touched down. And seeming still caught in elation Olive said breathlessly, 'Clem, we've been having an argument about you.' Her eyes darted vivaciously to Christian who was shaking himself restlessly in his chair, sliding down, sinking his chin on his chest.

'Olive thinks you like me,' he said sulkily. 'I told her she was mad. *Of course* Clem doesn't like me. Olive thinks because she's in love with me everyone else is too. You. Miss Evans. Old Slater.'

Their eyes would have drawn the marrow from my bones, the blood from my heart, the spirit from my body, had such a thing been possible. Their curiosity was insatiable and incurable. I was a box of tricks they would have dearly liked to pull to pieces. I was friendly. *Why?*

Nicely, even sweetly, I looked from blue to hazel eyes. 'You do like him, don't you, Clem?'

Now what language to speak since words had different meanings for us? Did it matter? I might as well decide not since we all had so little choice but to be ourselves.

'Of course I do. Both of you—or I wouldn't be here.'

'You see!'

Christian groaned and wriggled at that cry. And I, for all my detachment, half-raised a hand to catch Olive's attention. But she looked at me, eyes dark and triumphant—the eyes of a fanatic. The room was like a jungle, no place for speech.

Leaning over her knees towards me, she asked, 'Does he attract you, Clem?'

'Olive!'

Christian and I reacted simultaneously, frantically staring. And hardly seeming to know how she had transgressed, Olive retreated under cover, veiled eyes and appetite, lowered the flame, was extinguished.

'It's rather late.' I rose decisively.

'No, no, don't go yet, please. Don't take any notice of Olive. She's just a peasant. She doesn't know any better.'

How could he insult her so!

'Please don't go, Clem. I didn't mean anything.' How could she lie and look me in the eye! Her face was sallow and waxy. The lines on brow, from nose to mouth, drawn with humility. 'I'll make some coffee.'

They looked guilty, as if waiting to be chastised. Or was the look assumed to make *me* feel guilty? It began to. A natural friendship, after all, was what I'd wanted. I liked natural people and certainly they were that! So was I. But perhaps there were degrees of naturalness? Or something.

And if I had seemed not to resist their ways and questions, had I the right to resist in secret? It was early yet for Olive to have absorbed the idea that one does not necessarily take all the rope one is given, that one does not, in the nature of things, wander like a vandal over another's personality simply because he's erected no fences.

71

Across a rather miserable silence Christian watched me under his brows, dissociating himself from all that had been said, but remembering I liked him. He semaphored a greeting of amusement and interest, conscienceless, incorrigible.

'Clem!' he cried. 'Have you been to Stratford? All our colonial cousins go there sometime or other, don't they?'

Failing to work up an interest in the idea of coffee, Olive sat down again and began to look cheerful at the sound of that 'colonial'.

And I relaxed. It was just a fact that they weren't always conscious of what they did. That was why, must be why, I supposed, every barrier of resistance that rose in me disintegrated gradually, like a sandbank washed by the tide, and eventually disappeared.

In reply to cross-questioning I provided a list of the plays and casts I'd seen. Christian gave a comical growl of disgust and impatience.

'You missed me every time! And I was—' he shook his head, 'I wasn't bad at all. What am I saying? I was great!'

Then he had to stop, at the height of his little act, to stride to the looking-glass behind our backs. Smiling, Olive and I turned to watch, thinking to see a further instalment. But we turned away having seen him run a hand through his hair, straighten the yellow sweater, eye himself woodenly, without life, in the cold looking-glass.

But soon he was transformed again, light-hearted, and we were dragging up childhood treasures, discovering a community of idols chosen when I was ten and he fifteen from the legions of the great.

Olive listened with rapturous interest. 'Chris always lives in the past,' she said fondly. And he looked modest but agreed, 'It's true. I do. And Clem, did you have a gramophone then? What sort of records?'

I laughed. 'How can I explain? Some of them were second-hand and so old and scratchy they practically gave them away. They must have been made in the days of the Roman Empire. And the music thumped out like a brass-band hurrying to catch up with the parade and never making it. Sounding very weak and significant. And the singers! Even through the scratches you could hear the marvellous affectations. Even when they were slightly off-key and breathless. And the greatest of them did scream and go flat now and then. In dramatic ballads and arias they shrieked so seriously and sobbed—I can't tell you how I loved them! And though sometimes their confidence seemed so utterly misplaced it was so complete that you wouldn't have had them know for worlds they had a single flaw. Then, in the end, because they were unconscious of faults, they were innocent, and faultless. Almost geniuses. More than human. And you realized that they were always right. Never their critics...'

This came in a rush. Now Christian was speaking. I had been distantly aware of his entranced attention, saw that he was not attempting to follow—the point I was trying to make was irrelevant: the thing was, for the moment, I created force about me as he habitually did, but in a different way. And he took this in with disinterested pleasure, as in a fellow-craftsman; he had stared into me as people constantly stared into him, admiring, seeming proud of, my difference from him.

73

Seeing the situation I was pleased but rueful for I knew, with me, the capacity to light up fluctuated, wasn't to be controlled.

Miss Evans's coal supply went down. Olive told us about the girl who worked with her in the dairy.

When I was leaving Christian said, 'We didn't do any work tonight. Would you give me lessons?' This was business-like. It was also, subtly, like a dare.

'Certainly—if you want to learn,' I said smoothly, freezing slightly to hear my voice.

The sort of glance I'd only seen on celluloid, in spy pictures, shot between my friends. Aha! That was easy!

'The thing is, Clem, we haven't got any money. I detest people who cry poor mouth, but we are poor. I'm not ashamed of it. And I don't want charity but—what do you think? You don't live on your teaching, do you? You don't depend on it?'

Though we'd remained standing round the fire, virtually I had been pushed to the wall. My thoughts churned in confusion under the pressure of his will.

Evading reaction of any sort, I stone-walled, thinking mildly how weird it was to bludgeon someone as he was, in one's own interest. I felt very slippery, knowing they believed I had been flattered into complaisance, knowing, knowing...

'You don't depend on it, do you? Be honest!'

'Well...' I said doubtfully, feeling it dishonest, imbecilic, to dismiss my need of the fees. A knowledge of this need sat like a cold blancmange inside my brain; a second unpleasantly cold mass co-existing in the same space was my awareness of Christian's intent, ostensibly confident, but in fact speculative dismissal of my concerns. From a purely strategic point of view it struck me that he brushed aside my interests with less than clever perfunctoriness. It was almost beguiling to see how ruthless he could be when he got down to business.

Earlier when I'd discussed this idea with Lewis I half-believed I was indulging my imagination. After all, it was impractical to a degree, and perhaps not wise apart from that. Even now, though the proposal was hung about with inevitability like a Christmas tree with tinsel, I still half-fancied I flirted with it. Of course, he *did* need help, but but but...

'If you're worrying about your money, you needn't bother. When I'm established next year I'll pay you exactly twice your usual fee. You can have that in writing. Then you'll be able to buy a few new clothes and move into a decent flat. You'll get your money all right!' His voice was deliberately insulting, but alarmed exalted glances passed between him and Olive, as it were, in asides, all too easy to translate. How much of this treatment will she take?

With patent insincerity Olive said, 'That's no way to talk to Clem. She has herself to think of.'

Next to having Christian to think of it sounded a small thing indeed. Among conflicting inclinations I wanted very much to laugh.

Chin tilted, arms majestically folded across his chest, Christian was clearly enjoying this role and would, regardless of outcome. He was so gay manipulating me, despising my weak-minded charity, yet counting on it absolutely. He now said in tones of ravishing nobility, 'And I *don't* want your pity.'

Trying to follow his line of thought was unrewarding. The *non sequitur* threw me further off balance but I said, feeling it to be entirely true and entirely false at the same time, 'I've never met anyone less in need of pity.'

Somewhat mellowed, he continued to brood at me over his folded arms. 'You give four nights a week to lessons, don't you? What would be wrong with that? Four. If I took you on I'd want all your time.'

And now without moving he did in essence come closer for the kill. *Reynard the Fox*, I thought, but I could not have sworn with my hand on my heart which of us was the hunter.

'You could manage that. And I think I would make a more interesting pupil for you than those characters I see going upstairs.'

How to win friends and influence people. Lesson one: shock tactics. Stagger them by your boldness. Remember, people love to be bullied.

'You are awful, Chris,' Olive murmured. 'Give her a chance...'

'Is it to be four or not? Nothing less would be much use. *Don't you agree?*'

I smiled what felt like the prototype of a new smile: it felt strange and knowing, bitter and almost loving. And it felt gay, too, for whole-heartedly I admired the complexity of a talent that could persuade me I'd been petty-minded to hesitate.

I laughed, giving up, irresponsible. 'I agree absolutely. Four lessons a week.'

If I added an apology for the delay in committing myself, I realized in a moment of slightly hysterical insight, Christian would spread forgiveness without the least surprise. Somehow, everything was his due.

'Olive!' he cried, grasping her by the shoulders, planting a smacking kiss on her forehead. 'Clem! I love you. This time next year...'

His marvellous plans! With affection, with ironic appreciation, with a sensation of having lifted a burden I was in nature bound to lift, I answered idly, reassuring him.

The gold, the Riviera, the ships, the planes, emeralds and applause! Vividly, unrealistically, he talked as he moved about.

My spirits began to sober. Was I to put all this within his reach? Could he imagine so? My heart smote me.

Out in the hall the telephone rang, and we all stopped talking. 'I'll go,' said Olive, brimming with goodwill, and left us.

Suddenly clinging to his mood of high excitement with pitiful effort, Christian sat down again. 'Don't stand there,' he said almost furtively, smoothing his hair with the palm of his hand, looking up and away. 'I hate people standing over me.'

'I have to go.'

'No. Never mind that for a minute. Sit down, Clem.' Now he poked at the fire, busied himself rubbing soot from his fingers. He was desperately matter-of-fact.

'Till Olive comes back then.' I dropped to the chair.

'When should we start work?'

'In a week's time?—I'll have to organize things.'

'Fine. Fine.' Abstractedly he passed the side of his fore-finger across his set teeth. His disquiet was electric. I stared at the rug and the fire and the brass fender.

There was Olive in the passage again. We both looked up. Encountering that trapped and baited gaze, I saw the shine of tears. Light-headed I stared, and he stared back at me, tormented, fiercely repudiating anything I might feel.

He stood up as Olive entered saying, 'Miss Evans is out in the hall with Mrs Slater and the Commander.'

'Good!' Christian flung an arm round her shoulders. 'Having earned our keep for the night and made use of one Miss Clemency James, we'll return to our humble home. Good night, Miss James.' He extended his arm, watching me stilly. We shook hands, then Olive and I.

'On Monday week, darling,' he told her. 'I start work.'

78

CHAPTER FOUR

An unexpected consequence of this decision was my meeting with Rollo Lawson two days later. Out of the blue Christian rang at three o'clock to tell me that his old friend Rollo Lawson—*the* Rollo Lawson, son of his legendary father—had guaranteed the job in Paris which he *knew*, he said, I had silently doubted. His excitement would not wait on my questions; he talked me down, swiftly, fluently, seeming to listen with fascinated incredulity to the tale of his own good fortune.

He told me how they had met by chance in a club in Soho, and one thing had led to another culminating in Rollo's offer of help. It was, however, dependent on his learning French. Now, he said, Rollo and I must confront each other so that we would both know that he, Christian, was not lying to either of us.

I tried to protest at that but he cut me short again as if, while pardoning my earlier misgivings, he was unwilling to be reminded of the hurt.

At four this afternoon he was stopping work to meet Rollo: would I *please* do the same, just this once?

As Rollo wasn't drinking, we met in a bare scrubbed coffeehouse where he passed most of his time during these phases. He was a brittle-boned, sick-looking man with an air of courteous but profound disengagement from his surroundings. We looked at each other with some comprehension and let Christian talk: indeed, neither of us had power to stop him. But his pleasure was warming.

He elicited from Rollo, for my benefit, the fact that his father had a large interest in an organization in Paris which arranged every sort of European tour for wealthy Americans—just the kind, in fact, that Christian had described weeks before to me. He explained now that he'd known of Rollo's connections and had always hoped for this promise of help.

With glowing enthusiasm he boasted of each of us to the other, trying to make for us the impression that neither Rollo nor I were in the habit of effecting. I knew *that* about Rollo Lawson at once: he was a detached man, with grey eyes, many lives beyond the point where it mattered that his personality should make an impact.

Drinking coffee from mugs, we took in the faces of strangers round about, and the paintings on the wall awaiting buyers. Nearby two bearded men sat playing chess.

Christian and I left together, leaving Rollo, and separated five minutes later at a bus stop. 'This is the first time we've walked down a street together,' he said, after a silence, in a sweet and gentle voice. 'Olive mustn't know about it.'

So we were playing our romantic parts again!

'It's our secret. I'll never forget this moment,' I said in tones of mock-passion.

He looked at me again, brilliantly drawing to his eyes shadows of confusion, of childish trust. 'Neither will I,' he said. 'Neither will I, darling. You make me safe. Every morning I think: I'll see her tonight...But these odd half-hours...'

His voice touched notes so poignant that my heart shifted involuntarily in response. And recovering, I had to concede he was gifted.

We stood at the bus stop. Behind the fond and puzzled intimacy of the look he turned on me I thought I detected a sharp observant glint.

I glanced away, saying almost inaudibly, 'It *is* rather hard...I know how you feel.'

I was amazed to see how dubiously he took it. To help him out I smiled slowly and soon he began to laugh appreciatively, though he seemed slightly incredulous to find himself treated with such levity.

'You were—stringing me along!'

Trifling with his affections! 'Never!' I said, applauding that innocent look in his eye. How many layers were there to this sort of duplicity?

'I didn't think you'd do that,' he said, with that same air of innocent wonder. 'It doesn't seem like you.'

'I know,' I said sympathetically, beginning to feel rather exhausted in the part. 'I know.'

81

The score must be safe enough now: checkmate, stale-mate, anyway, *level*. Perhaps we could leave off? He seemed to think so too, for we turned away from the game and talked practically of his programme of study till the bus came.

'So you see there's no need to lecture me,' I said to Lewis that evening when he rang. 'It's no pipe-dream after all. There's a place coming vacant at the end of the year and it will be held for him.'

While not entirely reconciled on my behalf to the extra responsibility, the loss of income, and the greater drain on my time, Lewis was pacified to some extent to hear that Christian had so unlikely and eminent a sponsor as the younger Lawson. He had to suppose it must be all right. And as I was committed to it, he seemed to decide to give me his support.

'What about Olive?' he asked. 'Will she object?'

'Oh, no, Lewis! I'm sure she won't. And after today, Christian—I have a strong feeling—will come to the conclusion that it's a pity to waste his powers of fascination on me.'

On Monday night on my way downstairs I passed Jan, who was speaking to the new girls on the floor below. Mrs Slater and Mrs Parry stood together on the landing under the bare light-bulb talking in little rushes, stiltedly.

What a pity they were not happier, not like me, not full of purpose, interest, affection, not born Australian and free, not less afraid of themselves and one another! What could one say to make them see that life really was—at least pleasant, if it *was* late February, if it was dank, sulphurous and freezing.

The house was like a self-contained village. They were a community. Then why not be charitable to one another if they could not be fond?

I passed them all, continuing downstairs, warmly contented, feeling clean, straight, shining, scented, accurate as a Swiss watch and as motiveless. I was living in the present.

This was to be the fourth of Christian's lessons since that meeting with Rollo Lawson. He had applied himself with ferocious attention, demanding to be driven, and exerting himself to win praise. I could understand that: once I had been like that myself.

I saw that it gave him confidence in my ability to teach if I was dignified and remote. And indeed for the most part I had no desire at all to seem otherwise. But once or twice glancing up from his books, Christian had drawn back affronted, to say, 'Stop biting that pencil, Clem! Oh, you're childish, childish!'

And mildly provoked by his expectation that I should be unnatural in order to provide him with a smoother picture of his tutor, I was tempted to tease him very lightly from his solemnity.

Under his gaze—a mixture of real and mock severity—I looked at the pencil and all the corrugated marks made by my teeth, pretending myself abashed, while he breathed at me strictly, seeming to say: and so you should be ashamed!

Then I had to smile, and his gaze sharpened, investigating me suspiciously. And over his face came a smile of recognition, half-delighted, half-disbelieving, then finally threatening. Olive laughed with awe to see him in this novel part.

Now he stood by Miss Evans's desk in a blue sweater, not the yellow, which was surprising. What had he been doing? His hands were empty. It was not conceivable that he'd been idle or bored, just waiting.

'Good evening, Clem. You look tired.' He spoke with the air of one taking up a strong position, and with a tinge of very real disapproval.

'Yes. So I was.'

'Don't you mind that I think you look tired?'

'What would be the point?'

Believing in my candour, he was slightly disgusted, yet when he said, 'I just don't understand you,' his voice was warm, relieved.

And dropping to his chair, he leaned towards me across the fire, hands clasped loosely between his knees, temporarily convinced that I wanted nothing from him, therefore free to test my powers of resistance.

How wrong Jan had been, I thought, receiving a full battery of moving expressions, to describe him as some sort of celluloid hero. He seemed the very opposite of all that was implicit and derogatory in the phrase. Watching his face one hazily apprehended that his flesh had intelligence. I realized with the slow and earth-turning sensation of a revelation the difference that existed between that stereotype and this—a face as finely proportioned and outwardly pleasing that possessed the astonishing gift of reflecting thought, transparently, like magic.

The performance over, I half-lowered my lids in a salute to so much virtuosity, and Christian sat back rather disgruntled to find he'd been wasting his time after all. Then smiled.

'All right, all right. So I don't impress you.'

'Perhaps we should get going. I'll check what you've done while you go over some vocabulary for a few minutes then—' I turned to the table where we usually sat, lifting his notebook. 'Where's Olive tonight?'

'Why? Are you nervous?' A pause. 'She had to go out on business for me. She'll be back soon. Poor Olive! She'll have a stroke when she finds out we've been alone for ten minutes.' He said gravely, 'I'm afraid she's very jealous of you.'

Yes, I did feel tired, I did feel irritable now, hearing the portentous satisfaction in his voice. My senses turned over with dislike. I said, 'But that's what you want, isn't it? You deliberately provoke her, so that she can deliberately pretend to believe she has some reason to be jealous.'

'*No*,' he said, his voice low and full of feeling. 'No, it isn't what I want, darling. You're wrong. But what can I do? I can't leave her. She'd kill herself if I did. She's sworn she would.'

I was really taken aback. I sank into my chair, looking at him doubtfully. Had I suggested he should leave Olive? Did he *think* I had?

The foundations began to slide and slip again as, sooner or later, they usually did when Christian opened his mouth. Nothing followed from anything else. I wasn't used to it. Was it impossible for him to leave off the melodrama for five minutes? Feebly I thought: anyway, to say Olive would kill herself...

'I didn't mean...' I began to protest.

'You don't believe me, do you? You don't know Olive, of course. She looks so meek and mild. Everyone pities her.

85

They think I bully her. They don't know anything. She's got me on a chain. Do you know I'm not allowed to see anyone alone? Not anyone? Every minute I'm out of her sight has to be accounted for. You think I'm exaggerating? Tonight she'll almost drive me crazy after you've gone—because of these ten minutes. And yet you'll look at her when she comes in, and you won't believe me.

'Do you know she meets me every day for lunch? At one o'clock she rushes out of that ridiculous dairy and hurtles all over London to check up on me. I start work—at her suggestion—before her, so that she can start *her* day by coming with me, wherever I'm going. Do you understand? She *never* leaves me alone.'

In a daze, and still uncertain of his motives, I shook my head.

'But I mustn't make people unhappy. I must be loyal.'
'I know.'

Feverishly he searched my face to assure himself that this wasn't sarcasm. And now at last I had to trust his strange despair, the strange necessity with which he spoke. I felt an enormous resolution, seemed to discover a vast reserve of strength which was meant to be at his disposal. He *would* be all right.

Yet alongside my certainty I felt a small strain of something like anguish. I was helpless. What could I do? I was like someone who had vowed to produce a solution without knowing the problem.

He was saying, 'I know I can count on you. You're good. You're strong. You're like the Rock of Gibraltar...'

It should have been funny, but wasn't.

86

I watched him stand and go to the mantelpiece where he looked blindly, distractedly, in the cheap mirror. Then he faced me and said without meeting my eyes, 'Clem—the thing is—I'm very grateful to you—and I really like you. So I must be honest. I can't see you night after night—I can't relax with you—till you know about me...'

'Oh!' I said flatly. Constraint and trepidation made my heart beat. I was dreadfully uncertain of my fitness to receive any confidence that evoked that look of suffering on his face. Even, selfishly, I was unwilling to listen. Of course it might be nothing: assuredly he dramatized his every act.

But I shrank from what it seemed to *him*. What affected *him* in this way should not be told, even though I was his friend, even though I wished him well. If emotion was not met with emotion, integrity was endangered.

I wanted to cry: Protect yourself!

But, of course, I was interested...

'It isn't easy to begin,' he said irresolutely, and moved in front of the mirror, smoothing his hair. 'I've never known anyone like you. Oh God! That sounds like the oldest line, doesn't it? You've got a place in the world. You've been sheltered. You know all sorts of things. People respect you. You're a gentle proper sort of girl...'

This dreary catalogue seemed to excite him to despair. And as for me, I listened to these assumptions in wonder and indignation.

'No, no!' he insisted, quietly frantic. 'You really don't know what I mean. My life's been spent with—swine. And I've done things—' He broke off with a hopeless laugh. 'You don't believe me. I don't know how to convince you.

87

That's what makes it so hard to talk to you…You must have wondered, Clem? It's only natural. We've talked about you, and thought about you. Haven't you done the same?'

Frowning, withdrawing myself in every possible way to ward off confession, I said, 'Yes, I suppose so.'

He said, 'I think about you, too, darling. All the time. I don't sleep much any more. I didn't want this to happen again. I didn't think it could…'

I fell back in the chair, grinning and biting my lower lip. He never stopped trying! He really worked hard! Maybe I did seem yielding and weak-willed to him, but I wasn't weak-minded, and only the other when I chose to be. I said, 'Christian…'

'You don't believe me?'

I opened his notebook saying moderately, 'Do let's start now.' And he flashed at me with bright inimical eyes as he took the books I held out.

'All right?' I raised my brows half-apologetically to placate him, for I was reluctant to wound the esteem even of the imaginary character he was playing. Besides, if he felt obliged to stay afflicted all night it would use far more of his concentration than I was willing to spare.

I started to correct his sentences. My left arm hung over the edge of the chair. He lifted my hand, and having caught it, held it in his and shook it very gently, watching me all the while with wary sparkling eyes, his lips slightly parted.

I looked back. If he wanted my hand he could have it. I simply sat and waited for him to return it when he'd finished with it. This he eventually did, seeming slightly non-plussed.

But having retreated to his chair again, and clasping his own hands together, he said softly, 'I wouldn't be surprised if we finished up together.'

Now I have never believed that enough was as good as a feast, but I began to feel hounded by this unremitting pressure.

'Are you jealous of Olive?' Very fondly.

It seemed heartless to upset his preconceptions. Almost reluctantly I said, 'No, I'm not.'

A sharp scrutiny before he accepted this with a puzzled twist of his brows. 'Then, Clem, tell me...Are you attracted to me?'

'No, I'm not.' Very kindly. 'I just like your company.'

'Yes, but *how*? *Most* people are attracted. Aren't you a little bit in love with me? Does your heart beat faster when you see me? When I touch your hand?'

'No, it doesn't. No, I'm not.' I told the truth though it seemed lèse majesté.

'No?' He was almost comically bewildered. But he believed it with the fatalism of one who was always willing to learn. Then he grinned, '*Olive* said...' Then he shook his head. 'You're a funny girl...Tell me how you do like me, then. You mean—as one human being might like another?'

'Is that impossible?'

The fire cracked and sparks flew.

'No. No, I don't say that.' He was silent, seeming struck, even moved by this idea. After a moment he repeated, as if to himself, 'No sex. One human being to another.' And suddenly he smiled and gave a small salute, 'Friends.'

Frequently I'd been exasperated and strained by the effort of keeping up with so much volatility, such violent changes of mood and emotion, the deliberate switches and insinuations. That much trickiness seemed alarming and dangerous, and at a superficial level I was nervously bored and inclined to want to turn my back. Yet whether I liked it or not I was beginning to feel that he was my concern. And what I had to teach him was not French.

How long was it since I had qualified with honours in those subjects he now studied in the dark—perversity and masochism, the art of drinking death and dying daily? They were old hat and more than ancient history to me now. Still, I had to keep pace with him in the shifting present and trust that spontaneity would be rightly guided by the extra consciousness he roused. It gave me a background of strength and reliability which was visible to him, and reassuring. It provided me with new dimensions of versatility and a kind of stabilizing balance to counter his excesses. I thought I could teach him how to survive.

It was half an hour before Olive came in, her black coat flapping and smelling of fog. From the look of clenched inquiry Christian gave her it was evident she'd been on a mission of importance.

'I'm sorry, darling,' she told him. 'No luck.'

He sagged, grimaced at her. 'What are you breathing like that for?'

Olive sought my eyes as she took off her coat with a look of: what would you do with him? 'I'm not even allowed to breathe!' she said.

Rubbing purple hands together she came to join us round the fire. 'How's the French?'

'Fine. But we've been filling in time till you got back. Remember I have to explain about things to Miss James.'

'Oh yes.' Olive looked at me apprehensively. 'It's not easy, Clem...'

'She knows that.' On his feet again, Christian stood by the mantelpiece gripping the painted edge, pulling at his sweater with unnatural jerky movements. Addressing me, but still turned to the glass he said, 'You might be shocked? You might throw up your hands in the air and rush up to your safe little room?'

'That's just possible.'

'Are you easily shocked? You're rather a good girl, aren't you? You might decide you can't give me lessons after all and that would be—unfortunate.' He gave my face a flickering inspection. 'No. You always tell the truth, don't you? You won't change your mind now. One can always rely on your—word of honour.' He sneered at the word 'truth' with the alarm of a child doubting God in His heaven.

I said nothing. The telephone rang and he broke out of the room to answer it.

Olive said, 'He's nervous of you, Clem. He's afraid of what you'll think, but he has to be honest...Tonight when I got home after work he was hysterical because he didn't have anything to wear but that old yellow jumper. In the end he went and borrowed this blue one from Alistair—he's a young actor who lives in the room next door—so you'd see him in something different. He made me swear I wouldn't tell. Don't let him know...

'He wants you to like him. He must have your good opinion.'

'Does he think I like people because of their clothes?'

'That's what I told him—that it wouldn't matter to you. But you know Chris—it hurts his pride…He told you we weren't married, didn't he? I had to go to him, Clem. I couldn't resist. Some people might say I was wicked to leave my husband and daughters, but nothing's wrong if you love someone, is it?'

Love was beginning to emerge as Olive's special subject. At this moment, though she was haggard and sallow, her eyes sparkled. I guessed she was highly sexed. I could see the pinpoint of intention that meant she was ready and eager to cast off all veils at a sign from me.

'Well…' I said vaguely, looking at her with amiable non-comprehension.

She hesitated, signalling busily with the little red-brown pinpoints in case I was simply slow on the uptake. 'Chris opened up a whole new world for me,' she said shyly, lifting her eyes to some spot high on the wall.

I floated for a second neutrally, then I thought: well, it's good if they're happy. What if Olive's way of expressing herself was—highly-coloured, did jar? If the words were second-hand I was sure the feeling was not.

'Chris tells you I'm jealous, Clem. But I'm not really. It's just—I know what he's like. He can't help it. Some of these women! Their behaviour's disgusting! But I was so lucky to get him that I think always when we meet someone new: am I going to lose him this time?'

92

'Oh, Olive…Not this time. I mean—I think you were both lucky.'

She faded visibly under my tactless effort to reassure her, but it was too late to retract. In any case, I reflected, wanting to shed my guilt, she must always have known it couldn't last.

We sank back away from each other as Christian came swiftly into the room again, with his air of being accompanied by incidental music, trumpets, lights. He moved between us and stood before the fire in his borrowed blue sweater, so conscious of the engaging warmth and charm built into his nature, of his vitality and general remarkability, that he was, indeed, truly remarkable.

'What have you been saying about me?'

'We weren't talking about you at all!' Olive said gaily.

'I bet!' he snickered disdainfully, and dropped in a chair.

'Well, where do I begin? With the funny bit about Stella being—'

'It's not funny,' Olive said sombrely. 'It's tragic.'

'Tragic!' he scoffed insincerely. 'Everyone's been in the same boat. You Clem, probably. *Has* your life been full of laughs?' He looked a question in passing.

Non-committal, I said, 'That would have been dull.'

And Christian grasped this distraction gladly, turning to Olive. 'You see!' Then he said to me, 'The other day we were discussing you—*not gossiping*—and I said I couldn't see what type you were. (Everyone's a type. *I'm* a type.) And Olive was surprised.'

'I thought you were—' she began. I looked at her. 'I thought it would be—easy.'

'That's probably what you're meant to think,' Christian said. Then with a grimace he looked down at his hands. 'You might want to back out after this...'

Half-laughing, I said, 'Oh no! Not again! I'm not Little Goody Two-Shoes! Who do you think I am?'

He gave a shout of laughter, relaxed and threw himself back in his chair. 'Little Goody Two-Shoes!' Then sobering, he stared at me. 'All right. If you want to back out—you can. I don't care.'

Christian's father was a successful tenor and, partly owing to a number of recordings made in the early thirties, something of a popular idol in Europe and the United States.

'The critics liked him, too, for his presence, if not for his technique. He was one of those very charming men who could always win people round. It was too easy for him, so easy it was a joke. It was like a trick...'

His mother Beatrice Roland, a small-time actress of no great talent but enormous ambition, 'sacrificed' her career to marry. And though for the first years of her marriage she and her family lived on a sumptuous scale all over Europe, she continued to bemoan the acclaim she might have earned but for Stella and Christian, and their father.

'It was only natural,' her son said softly.

'They both liked to spend. If funds were short they farmed us out in lodgings that cost next to nothing.

We wouldn't see them or hear from them for months, then they'd appear out of the blue and there'd be money again, and clothes and celebrations…Stella was frantic once when they left us in Austria. But I was younger. She didn't let me see…We never went to school. Sometimes we had tutors…'

One season Anthony Roland was ill with some infection of the throat. He arranged with his agent to have his tour of the United States postponed, though money was short and his illness a disaster. Determined not to forego the tour and its attendant luxuries, his wife consulted a doctor, and extracted a prescription for some tablets which were guaranteed to keep her husband on his feet, and capable of performances for the length of the American tour.

'Well, I suppose you can imagine what happened. He sang. He sang his swan-song. He liked those little pink pills more than anyone expected. Poor mother! She got those dollars out of him, but they were the last. He never worked again. But he still got money from somewhere to pay for *it*—from Stella—anyone. All day I was supposed to watch him and follow him so that I could give reports when mother came home. She was working as a receptionist for her doctor. And Stella—Stella came home for a night every few weeks. She was training to sing. She had my father's voice…She wanted to get me out of the spy business, but just then it wasn't very simple for her…'

Beatrice Roland had installed her husband and son in a bogus Tudor cottage in Essex in the hope that his source of supply would be out of reach. But while he was able

96

he travelled to town regularly, trailed by Christian, who was later sent alone to collect the packet of poison that was disintegrating his father's mind further every month.

For two and a half years, till Christian was ten, he and his father lived in this damp plastered cottage—the boy responsible for the demented man.

I pictured the small boy preparing meals, in silence stroking the stray grey cat who'd adopted him, in silence watching his mad entranced father.

'Poor old Tony Roland,' Christian laughed. 'You've got to hand it to him—he was futile! One afternoon he tried to gas himself and failed. God, it was funny! The gas-cylinder gave out, you know, we weren't connected to the mains, and bought it in cylinders...And poor old Tony, instead of waking up in—God knows where—Paradise—woke up in the oven. In the evening I found him. It was summer-time; I was up a tree with the cat most of the day.'

Next time, a year later, when Christian was ten, his father tried again to kill himself and was less futile. He hanged himself from one of the artificial oak beams in the small sitting-room and was discovered by the boy.

'You couldn't blame him,' Christian said softly, looking down.

Two days later, in accordance with plans long made, though unknown to Christian or his father, Beatrice Roland left for Canada with her friend, the doctor, who was a Canadian and allowed to return home in spite of war-time restrictions. His mother told Christian this was all for the best. She had written to Stella, who would probably come and fetch him to London to live with her...

'You couldn't blame her,' Christian said, with soft ambiguous warmth. 'She was a good-looking woman, and not old...'

While he spoke, Olive had watched him with slightly repellent voracity, laughing when he laughed, and at other times preserving that air of almost salacious satisfaction with which people listen to stories of distant disasters.

Glancing across at her now, by chance, he saw what her expression was and ducked his head slightly, turning away, whispering fiercely, 'Christ! Will you *please* not look at me like that!'

And with the martyred air of a dog beaten for no reason he understands, she shrank in her chair.

Silently I exhorted her: Oh, try to understand, Olive! Now that he's grown up that child is Christian's world. He has no duty but to it—to repair the damage, to make happy, to care for, to be kind to. All sympathy, every movement of quick feeling for the oppressed—all for the trapped child he was. Yes, truly, he did laugh, and truly, these events are aeons past. But couldn't you see? He opened his mouth, thinking to toss it off, meaning to laugh at the youthful ghost, to hold him up to mild ridicule, to extract our mild sympathy, and then—I assure you, Olive, for I know the surprise it is—the words fell to pieces in his mouth. He bled inside, still holding the ghost in the air and laughing breathlessly, so that we, too, might laugh with poisonous mildness, and mildly sympathize. Yes, he parodied his father's death and all the rest inciting us to laugh so that we would be worthy of hatred.

Yet all the time he implored through us the world's pity. Temples, churches, sacrifices, masses—what could be excessive reparation? What tears could mend or soothe that child? What gifts, what gentle hands, what puerile heart-whole comforter of foolish goodwill could comfort that child?

I thought: but you *can* recover, Christian. Even very sick children can be outgrown. Truly...

Now Christian leaned back in his chair again, and looking at neither of us said harshly, 'Stella wasn't a prostitute.'

She was twenty when she took Christian to live with her in her Belgravia flat, and had had some years experience of the world. He drew a picture of a lovely girl with a lovely laugh, someone whose face reflected a rich transparent happiness, an uncomplicated love of life that magnetized attention wherever she was seen. And she was much wanted.

'She loathed them all,' Christian said with a smile. '*They* let this happen to her. She was never happy. She was bitter and mercenary, but she loved *me*, she loved *me*, though I was a kid and a mill-stone, I suppose...'

'It wasn't very nice for me, was it?' her brother said angrily. 'I idolized her. It wasn't very nice. And God knows it wasn't marvellous for her either. But she couldn't be poor, could she? What would have happened to us?'

Nor did Christian lack the interest of her friends. More and more often he seemed to say, 'Of course, people were kind,' or, 'People liked one,' or, 'People wanted to help one.'

And I had thought to tell him of kindness and generosity!

But now, though he said so little he implied so much that I couldn't but feel some of it was being lost on me: it was too far outside my range.

99

From time to time he and Stella would have to abandon a luxury flat, stripping it bare of saleable goods 'before it was too late', but when he next spoke it would be to describe their transference to some background of even greater opulence than the first.

How much of this was true? I began to wonder, feeling sceptical. And all these words and phrases—'living on one's wits' (who didn't, after all?), and 'conniving' (with whom, for what?) and 'corruption' and 'promiscuity'—what were they but manifestations of his love of important-sounding words? Some of my engagement evaporated.

'I had private lessons in everything, but everything,' he said, 'then when I was seventeen a friend of Stella's wangled a part for me in a show at the Edinburgh Festival. And I was—let's be modest—only sensational. Don't you believe me? No, seriously, Clem. I did have something...'

He should have gone, he intimated, from success to success, as should Stella on the concert platform and in opera. But she was tied up with people: moreover, he hinted, while she had no taste for the small pink tablets that had killed her father, there were other distractions.

Though they shared a flat, he and Stella, they met very seldom, and when they did it was only to quarrel—about Charles Hargreave, who owned the flat, or Peter, his brother, or money, or other things,' Christian said darkly.

Still speaking in that dry bitter way, as if to himself, and looking at no one, he referred to an incident, obviously of painful significance to him, in so verbose a way, that it was minutes later that I realized he had claimed and denied responsibility in the same breath for the suicide of some nameless woman.

Sometimes he was absent in Stratford for months on end, but he drove up to London regularly: there were affairs there he couldn't neglect. Above all, in spite of their quarrels he liked to be where Stella was. Nothing else mattered—not the broken homes and hearts chalked up to his credit: these were trifling, disgusting. It was Stella who mattered, Stella who'd had loyalty, who'd suffered, who understood him, who had debased herself for him, to save him and give him the chance he hadn't taken...

I could see that cloudy distant gauze across his eyes again, woven of daydreams, wishes, lies...This part of the story about Stella was—he knew, I was certain he knew—a fiction. Yet at the level of speech, from the place where the words and voice originated he did indeed believe his sister had sacrificed herself for him.

His eyes flashed across mine, came back. 'All right,' he said flatly, 'she didn't have to.' And I looked down.

All his life, he went on, he'd had a habit when pressed for a declaration, pinned down to a specific statement, when it was profitable to convince someone of his sincerity, to swear, 'It's true! May Stella die in agony!'

'And she did,' he said. 'I was punished by God. She did. In five months. Of cancer. Disfigured by operations...'

After the diagnosis, after the bloody brutal doctor told Stella and then him, he took care to stay unconscious for the remaining months of her life. The flat was silent, empty, the gay people frightened off by *that* word. And of course they were superstitious. anyone to whom Christian had ever given that pledge ('And I'd used it to kid plenty!') remembered and avoided him. By the time she died he was never sober. To get money he gradually denuded the flat of all valuables. Finally he sold his car and went into the country. The very walls of the flat intimidated him now, and its empty spaces.

From one country hotel to another he began to go, outstaying his welcome, creating havoc, yet so little conscious of his actions that he was only able to deduce what they must have been from the consequences that followed.

Finally, no irate manager, but the astonishing discovery that he was almost out of money, with nothing left to sell, sent him from the four-star hotel on the south coast to the cheap room in Olive's house, where for some weeks he was very ill. Then and during his convalescence he depended on her utterly. In a world without Stella he could not be alone. Moreover he pitied Olive: her husband, this watch-repairing Pole, this pigeon-breeder, considered himself a cut above her, and so did their two daughters. 'God knows,' he said, 'they were ordinary enough!' But Olive had gone from a London orphanage to a dish-washing job in a station buffet, and her ways were the ways of the poor. Christian needed her and was kind; she worshipped him. They decided to go to London together.

It was then, Christian went on, not without a certain unrepentant enjoyment, that a rather bad thing happened. Olive had no money of her own, her husband saw to that. So when they left for London, she took fifty pounds from his shop. Unbeknown to me, he said warningly. Wasn't it unbeknown to me, darling?

That had troubled them both deeply, Christian said, though, on the other hand, when you remembered how her husband had treated her it was, in a way, poetic justice, wasn't it?

In London the money soon went, for he wasn't fit to be left alone, so Olive couldn't work. There was no one to appeal to, finally, but Charles, Stella's friend, who could easily afford to part with a thousand or two. '*He owed it to me*, after all he did to Stella,' Christian said, a slight implacable half-smile coming to his mouth.

Charles was by this time installed in the flat that had been Stella's for many years. He listened sympathetically to Christian's request but was afraid every penny was tied up at the moment. For good measure he added that Peter, his brother, was leaving Istanbul that morning for destinations unknown. After advising Christian to pull himself together he casually asked for the return of his keys to the flat. Christian, who had been on the point of returning them, was suddenly inspired by the refusal and the sound of that sanctimonious advice to say they were lost.

The following night when Charles was out he returned to the flat with Olive. As he had half-expected the lock on the door was changed, so he broke in and left a quarter of an hour later with three hundred pounds. The next afternoon he was picked up by Charles in one of his regular bars, and hustled out, in no condition to resist.

I noticed that, whereas a few minutes earlier, speaking of Charles's refusal, Christian had seemed to take a genuine pleasure in his mistrust and condemnation, had even sympathized with Charles quite fervently for his repugnance and boredom, now the picture rankled. He looked vindictive, oppressed, dangerous.

So there Charles was, Christian said, marvellously got up as usual, all cashmere and Italian suede shoes, with his face massaged and tanned, and smelling expensive, delighted to have an opportunity to moralize and play the wise man.

In view of their long friendship, Christian's talent, and the affection he had had for Stella, Charles said he would give him one last chance.

'The idea was that he would use this—hold—over me to re-make my character. He'd fixed a place for me in a home, a place for neurotics, alcoholics and God knows what, for a cure. Oh, God! He was bloody kind, wasn't he? He could have called the police. Of course he didn't forget to mention that! He said, though he wouldn't drag the law in if I took his way out, regardless of what I decided, he would pass on the news of my latest misdeed to everyone we knew. As a warning. He knew how to finish me.

'I didn't have much choice, did I? He sent me to that… It was horrible, horrible…But, you know, the funny thing was—I wanted some good to come of it. I really did.' He paused, and the look of yearning aspiration melted in malice. 'Just the same I was glad he didn't get any of his money back! I'd paid off all the rent and food bills. People were kind, you know, but there's a limit. And in the morning before he found me, Olive and I went out and spent up. Not much for me, mostly for Olive, wasn't it, darling?'

'He's not mean,' she corroborated.

'But of course that stuff was all sold long ago. It was damn lucky we had it!

'That place, that bloody place...' he moaned and laughed softly. That faint elevated light that I had seen before in his eyes came again as he tried to explain about those weeks in Charles's chosen institution: the conversations with God, the vows, the acrobatic agony of mind and spirit, the degradation and the guilt.

He had suffered, it almost appeared, the birth of conscience, a fall from impervious heights to a tender, new and vulnerable awareness of himself in relation to life. This conscience he held now in himself unsteadily, a fragile device. He was eager, proud, but it was weak, still very new...

'—for what I did to Stella, for murdering Stella...' he was saying, 'I had to pay. I think I did. I am.

'You know the rest,' he said flatly, 'I clean windows.'

'He'll be back up there where he was I keep telling him.' It was Olive speaking.

'Well?' he said grimly to me. 'Have you had enough?' I said nothing.

'Now you're sorry for me, aren't you?' Abruptly his expression became one of almost odious gratification. His smile was small and knowing. 'Now you'll be able to tell everyone,' he said, in a tantalizing voice.

I began to protest but he leaned forward towards me, eager and serious, 'No, no, Clem. I want you to. Not anyone here, of course. But any of your friends. They'll be intelligent. If ever I meet them it's better that they know about me. And besides—I want to know what they think.'

105

In the kitchen the kettle refused to boil: I went back to the gas-fire. Mrs Gill moved large and slow about my room, concentrating on her task with the hairless broom.

'Did you know she's selling up?'

'*Who?* Miss Evans?'

'Yes,' drawled Mrs Gill. 'Some Americans are going to build a hotel. She'll tell y'se all any day now I expect. I think y'se have got to be out in four weeks. And I'll have to go to the Labour Exchange. Dear, dear, I'm not one for changes, are you? You know, you get used to the way of a place...'

I slumped back against the wall with a groan, letting my eyes roam in despair, asking questions, reacting enough to cheer Mrs Gill tremendously. She smiled and clucked as she dusted, agreeing that rooms were hard to find and especially in the winter, and more snow was forecast...

My heart beat with angry distraction at the picture of the mountainous problems suddenly sprung on the future: room-hunting, agents, ink-circles round advertisements, packing, a shortage of suitcases, taxi-fares. Then there was the waste of time, and the loss of all those habits of blindness that made one immune to familiar ugliness and dirt.

Miss Evans announced the sale at a meeting of tenants called by a notice stuck in the letter-rack. Somewhat sheepishly we assembled in her room, and very brisk and blue-eyed, she said she'd be sorry to part with us but the offer was too good to miss. In the summer she was off to Canada to visit relatives, and if she liked it there she would stay. We had a month to find new accommodation.

With her ram-rod back to the wall she smiled at us bracingly, her hands clasped, her plans firm and assured. Next to her the rest of us seemed weak and feckless—not property-owners, not travellers, unrelated to Canada, entirely out of place in her neat sitting-room. But then there had always been something intangibly heroic about Miss Evans: she was brave and intrepid. We wished her well, but wished we needn't go as we fled like competitors to our separate rooms, plotting early escapes from this disintegrating background.

In discussion with Lewis, remembering that Helen was due to arrive from Oxford in ten days' time, I decided to make that date my deadline; with luck I could as easily find two rooms as one. But I was bored to have to bother, not available for these dull and tedious matters.

For seven snowy days, weighed with pennies for the phone, I trudged through a nightmare of bow-windowed slums, developing neurotic fears of washed-out curtains of maroon and shocking-pink. Did the colour signal something to initiates? They couldn't all be brothels and what else was there? London seemed to crawl and wriggle with dirt and cold and marble pig-eyes.

In that first week, Jan moved to a hostel, and Mrs Parry took a room in a house further along the street—a seedy, peeling, unpainted place with empty milk-bottles scattered haphazard at the entrance. It looked an alarmingly downhill step for her to take in middle-age. Mrs Parry was timid, she might never move from there. If she had waited...But she'd been frightened to find herself cast out on London's mercy. And who could wonder?

So now my floor was deserted, the house emptying. The sense of its coming demolition hounded us who were left, sending draughts of cold air from the future to hasten us out, sending pictures of vacancy to replace the present substantiality of the building.

Lewis nobly escorted me through an agent's list on Friday night. Skidding home along bumpy stretches of iced ashes on the footpaths we passed a cheerless frieze of stone, and dead black trees, and purple people—all too sentient, like us. It was dispiriting, but my lack of spirits, it seemed, made Lewis's soar. He left my room predicting success for tomorrow with no justification at all.

Jaundiced, I nodded back at him, with fatigue and irony. But in fact he was right. A telephone call next morning and a bus ride to Knightsbridge produced two pleasantly-furnished single rooms in a clean house in a square. It was owned by a woman called Lucy Turner, a widow, without children, whose hobby it was.

At any time in the past the sight of these rooms, so shiny and whole, would have levitated me with enthusiasm. Now, however, separated as I was from that part of my consciousness which was bent over Christian, I made the arrangements with a lethargic affability that was all I could force through this detachment.

With a tiny elation that I tried to cultivate, I pictured, on the return journey, the square surrounding the old grey church with its trees and lawns. I thought busily of the glossy paintwork in Mrs Turner's rooms, the warm bathroom, how pleased Helen would be, and how the woman sitting in front of me needed a hair-cut. And now I'd be able to work again! It was humiliating to have to admit that I'd sent off several papers to the college that were barely adequate. Next week when we were settled again I would study magnificently. I would understand, remember, analyse, expound...

But really at the source of thought, far below these babbling surface noises, I thought: *Christian...*

'Three of the best!' cried the conductor, accepting some pennies from the boy beside me.

All morning I had washed and ironed and sorted out my belongings. Mrs Gill inherited a few items of clothing and two ropes of coloured shells from Tasmania for her young daughter.

'She'll go mad when she sees them!' she said shyly, tucking them in her leatherette bag.

The doors of what were lately Jan's and Mrs Parry's rooms stood open: I'd trailed past them a dozen times today carrying dishes, and washing, and packets of detergent. They looked bleak; the white March cold infiltrated window-cracks and all the spaces of the house.

Finished at last with pestering jobs in the kitchen and bathroom, I closed my door thankfully, dragged on a loose black heavy-knit over a thinner one and dropped two more single shillings in the meter in the idiotic hope that they would send up the seasonally diminished pressure. Then, eyeing the open suitcases, the barren room, with heavy satisfaction, mentally checking off all that had been accomplished, I went to sit on the rug by the fire.

It was almost four o'clock. Already I had pulled the curtains and switched on the ancient standard lamp. And now, how odd, revolutionary, to be idle like this, staring without occupation at the blue and orange flames of gas. Soon I would be gone from here...

If I felt depressed, turbulent, melancholy, that was the reason, wasn't it? That, and the cold, perhaps, and the denuded room?...

Oh, no, it was none of that! Why try to lie? Self-deception was not one of my talents. All right! *Christian had failed to appear for a lesson on three separate occasions, while he was actually in the house.* Think that out! I hadn't seen him since that night...

Expecting him two nights later I had refused to go out with Lewis, and shut away my work and waited. For he'd sent a note—from downstairs!—to say that he would find it easier to work in my room. I waited. When half an hour passed after seven, a girl who lived on the ground-floor brought up a message: Mr Roland was busy and couldn't come.

The following night Olive rang me on the house-extension to cancel *that* evening's lesson. Considering the lateness of the notice and the inconvenience, she did this with a brevity, with a lack of apology, that was a bit hard to take, I thought now, feeling a sullen sort of anger stir in my chest.

And the next appointment was ignored. No word at all. I'd waited with chilly calm, watching the clock, thinking: it couldn't happen three times! No one would be so peculiar, no one would be so discourteous! By the time I had learned that yes, indeed, someone could be so peculiar and so on, a frozen raging anger made me useless for work.

And think! I might have been out with Lewis on any of these nights. With his customary consideration he'd been prepared to adapt most of his arrangements to mine. And while he would never hear how I had spent these evenings I was still resentful on his behalf. If Lewis's convenience was made dependent on mine, and mine on Christian's, some proper order, some right balance of affairs was sickeningly awry.

On the rug, arms clasping legs, and chin on knees, I cuddled my grievance close as I considered these facts with stormy baffled incomprehension. Admittedly, if I chose to give him lessons I did, and that was that: I awarded myself no halo, but I had thought to receive a certain minimum of co-operation! Let's not harp about it, but...Oh, what was the point! I could have ground my teeth.

But what about this? This morning, this Tuesday morning, I had actually seen the elusive Christian. All hail! I had raced back from the shops not long after nine, and there he stood with Miss Evans talking on the stairs.

At my unexpected entrance he was struck dumb, like a truant encountering a school-inspector. Bland, remote, I glanced away from him and listened to Miss Evans, who was expansive and energetic as ever though knee-deep in packing-cases and workmen.

Instead of getting on with his windows today, Christian had come along to help her with all sorts of jobs, wasn't it lucky? she said. She was certain they would have great fun. Just then the doorbell rang and she went briskly off to deal with the caller. Christian and I stared at each other in silence, listening to her distant voice, he with a kind of frantic resistance. Her desertion had, one would have thought, left him cornered.

His attitude was mystifying, but I was too indignant, too hurt and angry to ponder it. Stooping, I collected my bottle of milk and started to walk past him upstairs.

But, no! That was hopeless! Someone had to speak.

'When *do* you think of having a lesson?' I asked.

Looking haggard, he said uncertainly, 'I'm busy... Olive's coming here for lunch.' And he glanced towards the door almost fearfully, them up over his shoulder he scanned the floor above. No one was about.

What *was* this? This teeth-chattering, haunted sort of fear? Was he lolling and laughing somewhere behind that distracted mask, just seeing how much I would take?

No, I couldn't believe so, whatever it was...More gently I said, 'Yes, I know you're busy, but if you want these lessons we should make some arrangements. If you've changed your mind, though, just say. It won't matter. As long as I know what's happening...'

112

We stood on the same step, I against the banister, clasping it in one hand, he with his back to the wall. His eyes looked very dark and darted from mine continually in so evasive a manner that all my anger and pique dissolved.

'Yes, *of course* I want to go on with them. Everything depends on them,' he said, not looking at me, pushing roughly at his hair, trying hard to sound annoyed and failing. 'It would be a bloody rotten trick on your part, if you let me down now.'

'Which nights then?' I insisted pacifically, mentally holding on to my head. 'We must agree about times and evenings before I leave. I'm moving on Friday...'

'Yes, yes...I'm very busy,' he said vaguely. 'Not tonight. Not this week. I'll let you know.'

Let me know! Helplessly I felt him going, going, gone from me, slipping slippery from this encounter, disappearing with all rational explanations still unspoken, leaving me in the dark, yet not free, still grappled to him by that 'rotten if you let me down—'

'*When* will you let me know?' My voice felt weak.

'Ah...' Moving down a step, he turned his head to look at me, bewildered. Then suddenly an idea could be seen to dawn. Inspired, he said, 'I'll see you the day after tomorrow! We'll fix it all then.'

The day after tomorrow! That was a nice safe distance away. No, much more than that. His feelings of its vast improbability, its Tibetan remoteness from his life, struck me so squarely, so truly, that I backed closer to the railing, as if retreating from a physical blow.

But now at last he blazed out full and warm, his eyelids lifted, his gaze firm on mine: there he was vital and real, healthy to the core again...

And all day till now, even now, I remembered his colossal unawareness of *my* convenience. He was simply using me!

But then I remembered his face, his silly pathetic excuses, his fear, and then I was afraid, and compassion smote me. Something was here on a sterner level than my trivial indignation. If I was useful, he could use me...

See-saw it had gone all afternoon, one version cancelling another, jerking the scales up and down. Was it that he'd regretted his admissions very much, couldn't face me? That would be all too understandable...

Oh, fire, fire, fire, I thought, looking at it, distracted. I wasn't accustomed to this fumbling in the dark.

Oh, I would have to shrug it off! I'd think of nice solid things like tables and chairs, a massive and beautiful thing like Beauvais Cathedral, a bewitching thing like an island with lagoons, a nostalgic thing like Sydney smelling of sun and sea and roast coffee beans...

Though in fact I would be better employed with some work. Neither Christian nor the move justified giving up the good old struggle for existence. But no, I couldn't...

I heard the door open and close. Startled, I turned. Bulky, boyish in that yellow sweater, Christian was half-way across the room towards me, then kneeling beside me on the rug, grasping my hands, kissing them, whispering, 'Oh, I love you, Clem. I love you. Darling, I wanted to see you, but I was afraid. Why do you think I stayed away?

114

Why?...' His head was buried in my hands and vulnerable: I saw the shape of it, the straight flat hair of golden brown.

'Why do you think I stayed away? Oh, Clem!' He pressed his face, his cheeks, his mouth, against the palms of my hands.

'I don't know...'

He gave an impatient groan and looked up, still holding my hands. Our eyes were level and just inches apart. Smiling slightly, shaking his head a little, he looked at me with a kind of loving scorn. His hands were warm and firm and dry: he smelled nice.

He said, 'You smell nice. Oh, Clem, Clem...' He held my hands to his head as if to rest it in them, as if it wearied him. 'I love you,' he said again.

I was softly bemused, but still safe on the ground, deprecating his declarations, his perseverance. To show I understood the spirit of the thing I smiled and shook my head, smiled with a kind of laughing indulgence, as if this was a very tender game.

Feverish, he looked up at me. 'No, you don't understand! And I know you don't trust me. Oh, darling, how do you think I felt when you listened to me the other night? Not a harsh word, not a word of blame, not a shadow of repugnance. How do you think that made me feel? You're good. And you didn't condemn me. I saw by your face. Your eyes were sweet and gentle. You thought of *me*—how it was for *me*—felt sympathy for *me*...Do you know what that means to me? But, oh, it isn't only that. Why else did I have to tell you? It wasn't necessary. I wasn't trying to impress you by—sensationalism, you know that.'

115

He drew away nervously, abstractedly, looking blankly ahead, muttering in a tormented voice, 'That's why I haven't come near you.' He glanced at me almost with hostility. 'Don't you understand? I didn't *want* this to happen. The set-up with Olive—isn't really right—I know that. But I thought it would work because I didn't want anything else. *I've had too much feeling.* For me it's all over. Don't you see? I'm not sick, I'm killed. I can't start again, and yet... I feel like this about you.'

I thought I began to see, yet what I thought I saw was decked with reservations and warning notices here, there and everywhere. Had he simply quarrelled again with Olive? Or had he gone to all this trouble in order, merely, to trap a reciprocal declaration from me? Oh, uncharitable! Oh, cautious! Oh, tremulous and wise!

Again he caught my hands. His eyes burned dark and blue, dedicated, exalted: they glittered with strange exaltation.

Bearing this look, and the sheer load of his concentration on his idea of me, I felt my mind falter weakly.

'Can't you say anything?' he teased gently. 'Haven't you anything to say to me? I don't want to reproach you, darling, but it is customary, you know, to make some sort of answer to a statement like that. Please...Tell me how you feel about me.'

'I like you. I'm fond of you.' Yes, fond, I heard a protective voice in my secret ear. But there's an empty gap in the range of your affections between indifference and fondness. You're fond of everyone you like at all.

I stressed, rueful, 'You worry me.'

116

'*Fond*,' he repeated, smiling, softly derisive. '*Worry*,' he said, gently stroking my fingers. 'Never mind. It doesn't matter. I'll see you tonight. At seven. I'll come up...'

He went on speaking in a murmurous hypnotic tone, leaving so gently, bequeathing such an air of sweet complicity, simplicity and beautiful reluctance to his parting, that I could hardly have said at what particular moment he was not with me.

But, yes, he had really gone and I was alone in the dusky light of lamp and fire. Jumping up I walked about a bit, fiddling idly with the folded clothes of the divan, then I went to the mirror above the empty chest of drawers. My eyes looked dark: I leaned on the chest, staring into them...'

Was that a demonstration of what he called 'the sweetening-up act'? He might well have felt—recalling the absences, the furtive notes, his manner on the stairs this morning—that something of the sort was due. And certainly he had no opinion of subtlety. He had a sort of tank-like directness that always worked like magic: he had said so. Well, he would learn that I had no opinion of pretty tricks, however magical. Flattery was his philosopher's stone. Where had it got him? Did he never connect?

I liked him too well to feed his vanity, or to collaborate with that side of his nature that had been his undoing. Impervious to that much-exploited charm I was and would be.

I remembered the stolen money and Olive saying, 'He's not mean!' and saying, 'He'll be back up there where he was!' Christian listened trustfully to the nearest voice: just

117

now it was Olive's and the stuff she fed him wasn't good. Though she loved him, and would sacrifice herself...

I thought: he recognizes feeling for himself in me, and can only think it must be—what it usually is. Yet I recognize in him that same involuntary commitment that *I* feel—compounded differently no doubt but...

Was he lying then? Not altogether—perhaps some of the time not at all. But if I had loved him and said so in response, then he might have been lying entirely. A trial of strength.

Yes, it was unreal—the thing he said. Couldn't people simply hope not to part company too soon? Of course I liked the sound of it. For the reasons he did, I imagined. In a funny ruined way, in some respects, we were alike—loving love, liking liking, fond of fondness. We shared a mutual love of love...Why not?

I moved away from the chest and wandered back to the fire. But no, emphatically, I did not want to own him. Had interest and possession always been so linked in his mind? His air had almost declared: 'If you want me you can have me. If you like me you must hold me.'

What woke me to him first was that silent call for help from a voice behind the trompe l'oeil façade, the blinding invisible signals of distress. Should I have stopped to ask: who am I to go to the rescue? If you are alone on the landscape where a man lies bleeding you do not stop to debate your qualifications to succour him, support his head, and shield him from the weather. Neither do you rush to aid him for the colour of his eyes.

From the beginning I had been willed, welded, bound to the desperation in Christian. And that night a week ago he had allowed me to know what I faced in him. And truly, he was right. It did affect me.

In a sense I was laid low by his revelations, and humbled. I hadn't expected *this* complexity, *this* suffering. With the will to help had come—I began to see—an altogether unreasonable confidence in my ability, very soon, to deliver him of his burdens by some remarkable gesture which would, I never doubted, come along of its own accord at the appropriate moment.

That seemed less likely now. This aid from the ether that I'd naïvely relied on, might definitely not arrive. That night, a week ago, I realized that. More than I dreamed, much more than I wanted, might be left solely to me: the campaign looked as if it might be rougher and make more demands than I had bargained for when ignorance and confidence were equal.

Now I was on my own. And while Christian understood that I was someone disinterested yet passionately on his side, and was grateful, he wanted to test, trick, trap me into a fall. I could accept that now, and see it as natural and ordinary because it was natural to him. He was naturally in opposition to himself. How else could he be?

Well, well, I thought heavily. We were safe enough. He was safe to try me, test me, and I was safe to take the gaiety he shed. What could be less generous than to refuse the benefits he could give because that other side existed? A little uncomplicated pleasure in familiar company, innocent enough of desire and design, forewarned, forearmed and anyway, impervious, was harmless, wasn't it?

I smiled faintly to remember his reaction to that 'fond' of mine, and then to remember mine to his 'love'. Love…

That was not what ailed me anyway. Nothing did. Switched on, alight, functioning on all levels, living to capacity, confined by subtle laws, yet free, I felt myself to be; more satisfied, more right with myself and the world than I could recall having been. But then, what could I remember before this?

At seven Christian and Olive appeared side by side at my door. The books were on the table open: neat sentences in French and lists of words stared up.

'Miss Evans needs us both to help with an inventory tonight,' Olive said. 'Chris can't have his lesson. He thought you wouldn't believe him if I didn't come, too, to tell you.'

Next to Olive, he stared across the room at me, bold, secret, intimate.

'It doesn't matter,' I said blandly, closing the books, controlling my outgoing breath very carefully. 'After the move we'll organize things better, perhaps.'

'What about Thursday night? Your last night here? Could we work then?' Christian asked, somehow stubbornly, as if I were making difficulties.

'No, I'm going out.'

'We'll see you before you go—to say good-bye?'

'Naturally,' I smiled, suddenly stricken at the sound of that word. Good-bye! Yet, really, I wasn't moving to China! That voice gave him unfair advantages.

We exchanged hard polished smiles. A trial of strength, all right! I found him very dislikeable as he stood there,

120

solid and dazzling in that old yellow sweater. That bold Roman head—not florid, not over-refined—that excessively human head—how nauseating it seemed! And his cunning consciousness of it. And Olive, sallow in black, and knowing of eye, and sly of smile, and curious, and stupid. Oh, God! What had I to do with them?

I picked up my pen to finish a letter to Mimi. 'Then, good night. Thanks for letting me know,' I said, feeling pale, feeling physically sick with revulsion.

With his usual flourish, Christian took off, Olive beside him, simpering in reflected glory, calling, 'Good night, Clem. See you later!'

I shuddered with relief and pulled a face. 'Ugh!'

Restlessly I roamed to the window, with a complete reversal of that soppy sentimental feeling of an hour before, realizing that it would be good to be gone from here, and healthy and sane. I longed to be away.

The restaurant in Chelsea was small, with candles glimmering on red and gold. By day it resembled the Café Rue de la Paix minus mirrors. It was plushy and stagy, and the atmosphere was warm to hot. Of this no one complained—outside snow lay in drifts in the parks, untidily, like the aftermath of some meteorological paper-chase. And while the roads were clear, the footpaths looked darkly normal but were not: camouflaged ice lay all about.

There were four of us at the table: Lewis sat opposite me, and beside him, Helen, in a long-sleeved dress of lovely white stuff. Facing her, and beside me, sat Bertrand Hagon, a grammar-school master of thirty-two, who was a born disciple and who very much envied and disliked me for my friendship with the Grenvilles.

This evening in Chelsea had a dual purpose—to welcome Helen to London, and to farewell Lewis, who was flying to New York the following morning.

'And do you expect to get any sort of assistance from the Treasury?' Bertrand was asking.

In New York Lewis was to meet other delegates to discuss a plan to send working-parties to help under-developed countries. At my request he had explained the details more than once, and once I had even hoped to join such a party after the Finals. I remembered it sounded a very good and interesting idea; it was just that I wasn't any longer very interested...

The candles burned in their silver holders, scarcely wavering. Voices were discreetly muted. Bare arms, rich colours, the flash of cutlery and glass sparsely filled the perimeter of my attention. Faint odours of mingled wine and flowers were pleasant, even somehow soothing.

'*What about Thursday night? Your last night?*'

'*I'm going out.*'

Lewis caught my eye and smiled in connection, I guessed, with some remark of Bertrand's. I deciphered his concluding words and saw that he and Helen were wrangling over—of all things!—the United States' strategy during the latest crisis.

Empty plates were withdrawn, the next course substituted, sizzling, delicious, undoubtedly. And, of course, it was agreeable to eat well. Perhaps it was just that one lost the appetite for rich and largish meals...

122

Bertrand had lived in America for two years, in Los Angeles, on an exchange scholarship. He gave us Adlai Stevenson and Arthur Miller, delinquency and yellow Cadillacs, showers and strawberry shortcake, American universities and the Way of Life. I wielded my knife and fork. Lewis said that he hoped to get out of New York for a few days at the end of the conference. Arizona, he said.

'When I was nineteen this old bag tried to get me out of Stella's flat. Not the right atmosphere for me. Of course, she could supply that. She was about a thousand. I thought: well, I could do worse. Then she started to burble about pocket-money!'

Olive smiled. 'She thought she was hiring a servant!'

'Well, she changed her ideas. I saw to that. But the funny thing was, in the end, Tristan (that was her son) and I went off on a Grand Tour together. We did Europe! She was furious. She thought I would corrupt him. That was a joke. He was neurotic as hell, of course, and it was her fault. When she caught up with us in Vienna she sent him to Arizona. He had an uncle or something there...'

Looking at my watch I brushed Bertrand's arm.

'The time?' he said, with his customary smiling hostility. 'You aren't going yet? What do you think, anyway? You've been denying us your opinions tonight.'

'On what?'

Bertrand smiled again, a pained smile, with his lips closed, from me to Lewis and Helen. Softly he said, 'The Middle East. The Middle East.' He quite hated me tonight.

What *time* was it?

Now Helen was talking about tomorrow morning's move. 'Then it's all set, Clem. We'll meet there at ten. You've given me the address. And her name is Turner. Lucy Turner, isn't it? Could I collect you on the way from the hotel?'

We talked about this for a few moments. But why, I wondered, was Lewis watching me so stilly, with that unreadable expression? Was he thinking of Gabrielle now that he was on the eve of his journey? Did she know he was going?

Bertrand spoke to the waiter. Another bottle was brought. When he approached me with it I refused, answering Helen, 'Yes, everything's provided, thank heaven! No shopping for pots and pans.'

'That's the trouble with you, Clem,' said Bertrand critically. 'You never let go. "No, thank you!" You must drink more! What kind of a lawyer are you going to make?'

What *time* was it?

Would they never want to leave? Were they mad? Were they so afraid of loneliness that we should sit all night?

Animosity continued to rise in me as I turned from Helen to Lewis, who listened, considering everything, eyelids lowered, thinking and thinking about it all. Or was he? With Lewis, unless he was acutely bored—and even with rehashed ideas he was seldom that—it was hard to tell where concentration left off and disengagement began. A good poker face. Dreadfully provoking when all you wanted to know was whether he would prefer tea to coffee...

'—ought to go,' Helen was saying. 'You must have plenty to do, Lewis. Do you need any help?'

124

'No. Thanks to Clem last night. She came round for an hour and we got the packing sorted out. Now I need only check a few papers I'll read on the way over. At least I'm competent to do that!' We smiled. 'Where's that fellow gone?'

The waiter came, a Greek, probably, with slanting almond eyes of extraordinary size set flat in his face. Shortly Bertrand left to bring round his car, and Lewis to find a cab. Helen and I stood inside the small entrance, shivering at the recollection of the world outside this glowing shelter.

It was black and chilly in the back of the cab. I huddled into my coat, turned towards Lewis, catching sight of him coloured now by silvery street lamps, now by blue or yellow rods of sodium lighting.

'It's busy in New York. Look both ways crossing the roads. Don't wander about in a trance, and try to be responsible.'

'Most people assume I can find my way round without falling under a bus. Why do you have such a poor opinion of my intelligence?'

'Because I know you.'

He smiled sadly. He said in a minute. 'You're the one I'd like to warn...

Life went out of me. I shut off the end of his sentence. Tiredly I said, 'Try to understand. I am not enamoured. I do not aspire to take Olive's place—I'm not quite crazy. It's simply—you met them last night when you called for me. You see how it is...'

Lewis said flatly, 'I shouldn't try to advise you. You must do what you think is right.'

(I could have hated him for that. I wanted *him* to think it right as well.)

Resentment, guilt, compunction mingled as we faced each other for a moment before climbing out of the cab.

'Would you like to come up?'

'No thanks, Clem. It's late.'

It was piercingly cold on the wide shallow step by the door, but we stood, and the taxi-meter ticked, and the driver coughed. It was maddening to respect Lewis so, maddening to be so nervous and irritable.

'You're not going to the South Pole, I don't know why...'

'What can I bring you back from New York? What would you like?' And he smiled, relaxing suddenly, looking at me as if I were very young and silly.

'Something frivolous.'

We glanced at the taxi. I kissed his cheek. It was dry and finely lined. I turned the key in the lock.

'Six weeks then,' he said. 'Write. Take care.'

'You, too. Enjoy it very much, Lewis.'

I saw his hand raised at the window of the cab, his head a blur behind it. Suddenly rain blew along the street, rattling like hail. I closed the door.

CHAPTER SEVEN

It was two o'clock in the afternoon and dankly cold. It was even rather shadowy, whatever light there was in the sky shedding itself feebly, somewhere low on a horizon distant from this house. I had switched off the gas-fire. It had taken less than these four hours in Mrs Turner's house to discover that this lady, so jolly, sane and down-to-earth, had a jolly, sane, and down-to-earth regard for household economics— the meters were impressively geared. I saluted her audacity and rose vigorously to the distraction it offered, and the need for rationing.

So from today this room was home, sweet home!

The divan where I sat was new and well-sprung though parsimoniously narrow. I bounced on it gently once or twice and looked at the cold canvasy stuff of the cover, coral-coloured, under my fingers. Opposite, were the double windows curtained in the same material, and encircling

127

me the walls and ceiling shone with glossy paint, pale pink. Clean, unmarred, unlike Miss Evans's it certainly was; I looked at it warily—all that pale pink—thinking: still, as long as you feel well...

Beside the divan stood a small table holding the telephone, a lamp with a white funnel-shaped shade, and on the shelf beneath, the wireless. The gas-fire, with a makeshift fireguard, and the gas-ring, stood in front of a small blocked fireplace, heavily painted over. Above it ran a narrow shelf from one end of which, out of a white pot, trailed my nameless plant. On the other there was an empty jar of marvellous flawed turquoise that had once held Hymettus honey, and which had underneath it Greek letters.

On the facing wall was the gleaming door of a recessed cupboard which held everything—clothes, books lacking shelves, luggage newly emptied. An army it could accommodate in comparison with that small wardrobe I had used before.

Through the double windows I could see a view of bare treetops and similar attics and roofs to those of this house. That table under the windows was where I would work, though, like everything else in the room it was on a small scale, as if it had been constructed for a neat and rather under-sized child. Already books lay open on it, geometrically arranged and minatory, explaining logically how cut and dried life was, and the law. The upright wooden chair was waiting under it, imposing the impression of its emptiness and determination to wait upon me, on my mind.

What else had I? On the fourth wall, the wash-basin with a tangle of hot pipes running into the floor, supplying a fountain of hard London water. Above it was a mirror, undistorted, except perhaps—I'd already noticed—on the side of flattery.

A long straight unit of furniture in pale unvarnished wood, subdividing strangely into compartments for dishes as well as clothes, filled the space between basin and door. It supported a row of books and a vase of anemones, but very indifferently.

Black carpet covered the floor and in the centre there was a padded chair, and a low table. These faced the gas-fire at an angle.

Well, it was an odd little cell, coolly complete without me, snubbingly impervious to my presence, plants and Greek honey jars. A living occupant was as unnecessary, as irrelevant, to its completion as to the works of an alarm clock. I missed Miss Evans's cosy squalor. Here I was like an oyster transferred from its shell to an unfamiliar plate— rather exposed. Or something.

Or something, I thought, chattering my teeth together in jittery exasperation. After *all* I hadn't seen Christian before leaving Miss Evans's, so still there were no arrangements made!

There was a note in the rack for me this morning when I left: *Olive and I are moving, too, to a cheaper place. I don't want to give you the address. I'll ring.*

After he had said, specifically, with that level, straight-in-the-eyes look, that we would certainly, once and for all, arrange a programme before I left the house, and stick to it.

I was disgusted, and I was disillusioned by the fallibility of my judgement. But at last, finally, I was convinced.

129

Promises meant nothing to him. The truth meant nothing.

Now I looked back on myself of two days ago with pity for so much naïvety. And perhaps, in a certain way, the result of inexperience and ignorance, I was partly to blame for my own annoyance? I had pitched my expectations wrongly. Well, obviously. I had been prepared to give Christian lessons several times a week just so long as he responded as I felt he ought. *That* had seemed to be, I saw now, according to some beautifully courteous rule of conduct that had prevailed, maybe, in the Middle Ages, but not now, not here, not in his book of rules.

Now I could choose either to go forward blindly with nothing understood, nothing taken for granted, no rules or treaties, or I could retire from it all and forget it. Why should I be plagued by the man and his wretched lessons, and his wretched past and his obsessions, and his aspirations, such as they were? What was it to me, really, that Rollo Lawson had started wheels turning to find this improbable untrustworthy character an improbable job in Paris?

And *when* would Helen be ready for lunch? I should go next door, talk to her, see if she'd finished unpacking...

The phone rang.

'Hullo, Clem, this is Christian.'

'Oh,' I said flatly, sinking back on the divan.

'You don't sound very friendly. I don't think I like that.'

'I don't *feel* very friendly. I've been fairly patient so far but—'

'You've been patient, have you? And generous—helping me out for nothing? You've been generous, haven't you?'

130

'No!...Yes!...No!...'

There was a silence. I breathed to the bottom of my lungs. No calendar motto, no hoary piece of strategy, was too old or trite for him! As a tactician he disdained nothing obvious. And the obvious was clearly too deep for me.

'I don't think I like you when you talk like this. It's out of character.' His voice was melancholy with reproach.

'That's too bad,' I said through my teeth, seething with anger, aware that I was meant to be on my knees, repenting. But in an instant the anger went. 'I know,' I said, and could have wept for his deceit. 'Christian, all I want to say is—if you intend to learn a language, and want lessons, you must turn up for them.'

This was a rather exhausting statement. Of quite exhausting simplicity. But it had the germ of an idea Christian seemed to have overlooked.

'I don't like to be dictated to,' he said dangerously.

'Truly I don't want to dictate to anyone. But if you've changed your mind just tell me.'

He laughed, not pleasantly. 'You won't back out. You're going to make too much out of me—double fees for every session—*whether I turn up or not*. So what've you got to worry about? You'll get your money.'

The black receiver through which his personality entered my room was alarming.

Weakly I said, 'It isn't money I'm trying to talk about...' But what was I trying to say? He made me feel delirious.

'*Not* the money, *not* the money,' he repeated laughing. 'You're not simple. You don't despise it.'

'Christian—' I stopped and started again. 'It's just—you have plans made. Rollo's trying to help you. You say everything hinges on this. *If* you think that, and want to get the job in Paris—'

'Not the money, you say. But now you're admitting it. You won't answer when I ask if you despise it. I don't like it when you lie to me, Clem. You're thinking of the money you're going to make and you ought to have the courage to admit it.

'That's what you lack, isn't it? Courage. You must be honest with me. Though I may have been occasionally dishonest, and led what you might call a wicked life, I detest lies. I must be told the truth. You think because I'm engaged on humble manual work that there's no need—'

Evidently I could still feel, for I felt bitter. I had acted towards him with a fanatical regard for the truth. But what use to contradict? He neither knew nor cared if what he said was true, only if it served the momentary purpose of distracting his opponent. I was distracted, all right!

'Christian—' I interrupted him. 'Listen!'

'Don't say "listen", I don't like it.'

'All I'm trying to point out is that we're getting nowhere fast. You break appointments. You argue with me instead of coming to an agreement on times. I mean—if you want to call it off—say so. I simply want to know where I am.' I heard my voice getting querulous and stopped.

Hard and unyielding he came in, 'What would you be doing if you weren't waiting for me? Just reading your dull law books. Studying. Can't you just get on with that if I don't turn up? I'm not one of your little schoolboys,

Clem. I'm sorry. I can't just be tied down like one of them.'

'If you're expecting to be interrupted it's impossible to study. You need a settled mind.'

There was a thinking silence. I listened with every cell. When he spoke it was in a voice so changed that it might have been a different man who whispered, 'Oh, darling! I know you want to see me. It makes me unhappy not to see you, too. (Olive's been listening. She's just gone to answer the door.) I can't even speak to you as I want to. She's frantically jealous.'

He switched abruptly to his normal voice, continuing into my stunned ears, 'But it isn't very nice for Olive, is it? To know that you love me, and that we'd be alone together. You have to have pity for Olive. She's not someone like you with friends, and a career, and money—I'm all she's got in this world.'

I said very evenly, 'What do you mean—"Olive knows…"?'

At the other end of the line there was a modest pause: I could see the eyelids modestly drop. And then I *knew*, as if he'd confessed it, that he had reported to Olive that scene in my room and reversed our roles, giving me his dialogue and taking mine.

'Don't you?' he said.

Love? That battered, misused word again! To Christian it was just a lever; to me it was something boring, distasteful, stony. We had both abrogated the right to use it. Everything had curdled—all good intentions, trust and kindness.

'If Olive is jealous you've deliberately provoked her.'

'Oh, I know. I know it's all my fault.' A very public voice. 'I've told Olive that, too. You've said nothing. I told her I made a pass at you.'

Now I understood! He was admitting the truth to me—what he said was immaterial to him—but in agreeing about the facts, he achieved new heights of duplicity by conveying to the listening Olive the impression that this was a lie.

'I told her your behaviour was perfect. And I told her she probably put the idea in my head, being jealous.' He gave an uneasy laugh. 'She doesn't believe me, though.'

'Then you must really convince her, for everyone's sake. She was suspicious of Miss Evans and Mrs Slater, too. It doesn't do any good. Everyone's too old for this sort of game. People get hurt. You shouldn't give Olive reason to doubt you if you don't want to hurt her.'

He laughed. '*You* care if I'm cruel to Olive.'

'It gives me no pleasure to see anyone unhappy! All I want—' Cross yourself! Count to a million! But make him *understand*. '—is to know if you want to have lessons. I simply don't want to waste any more of my time.'

He was silent. So at last it had sunk in!

'You don't want to waste your time...Do you want to give up?'

What did he say? Prison gates open very slightly. Mixed pleasure and fear. Very cautiously I said, 'Well—if you like...'

A metallic crash shattered against my ear. The receiver! Imagine! The first time I'd been hung up on! So people really did it, not only in pictures! I held it away from me and looked at the mouthpiece, hearing the tireless raspberry-bubbling.

With slow numb surprise I hung up, too. My arms felt curiously loose. So great was the flood of freedom to my mind and spirit that it overflowed to my very body. Physically I felt unshackled, mentally still dazed by all that talk, but free and sweet and turning tentative somersaults.

My heart was thumping with the slow aftermath of exasperation. But, Lord, I was relieved! Talking to that man was mental torture, like being brain-washed.

I looked about my alien little room, and rubbed the sleeves of thick creamy wool up and down on my fore-arms. The coral curtains flapped uneasily in a draught. The window rattled. And all was sinister, grey and incompre-hensible. I shivered bleakly, unsure of that recent elation, nervous even of the echo of Christian's mind.

No, it was all too easy, too slick. This sudden release. Could you slide out of involvement as simply as this? Though he might feint a show-down, I couldn't believe he would let go so easily—not to something that could be turned to his advantage. He had counted on me to get this stuff into his head—by telepathy, evidently. And now what? Suppose he had another change of attitude and heart? And it seemed safer to assume he would, in order to be prepared. Suppose he wanted to settle down and work again?

In me something swayed vertiginously. Indecisively I swung between extremes.

What would he do if he changed his mind and I refused, counting this conversation as final? He was desperate, unstable, perhaps ill. And I knew it. Would I be responsible for whatever happened as a result of my refusal? Was I not, in fact, committed, regardless of his behaviour? Would it not be cowardly, pusillanimous, to escape, using his erratic ways as a pretext?

On the other hand—how far could you be prepared to let him go? Where would you draw the line? Were there no obligations to oneself?

There was a light tap on the door and Helen came in, wrapped up in a softy tweedy overcoat, gloves on, her head uncovered.

'It's cold in here! What's wrong? You look a bit forlorn. But no wonder! You must be famished. I'm sorry I took so long. I know I said just another fifteen minutes, but I had to dash off a letter home. Come on, let's find some lunch somewhere.'

'Good idea! No, I was just sitting.' I took my green coat from the cupboard. 'Hang on. I'll get this case out of the way and the place will begin to look civilized.'

Where, oh where, was my ancient routine? The rules of work? Ah, never mind! Nothing mattered. Surely there was a reckless end of the world, decline and fall of the Roman Empire feeling about in the air?

Outside it was grey and clammy cold. We turned in at the first discreetly expensive door we approached, having cast a unanimous vote against sandwiches and Danish pastries.

During the meal Helen filled in the background of her life in Oxford, talked of Quentin, asked about Lewis, and described the research she had come to London to carry out. In return I told her of examinations and study, of plays, concerts, meetings and exhibitions, and finally, about Christian.

The sight of her listening face was reassuring, for it reflected the justified confidence of her mind, the ease and candour of her approach to all problems. Her capability was an immense relief to me: she would be able to advise me.

And then, how solid everything was! The table, the heavy cutlery. How normal and ordinary the world was! Odd to have lost one's sense of proportion over a trifle!

Finally, the coffee poured, Helen lit a cigarette. We stared at the lighter's flame. 'I think you're well out of it,' she said.

'*Why?*' How disappointing that she should be so…

'I'm sure you know all the reasons better than I do.'

'Isn't it feeble to give up half-way?'

'*Are* you half-way? How many lessons had he had? Oh, I know how you feel. But whether it's so wise to persevere on a course that could be disastrous, simply because you've embarked on it…' She scooped up a small spoonful of brown sugar and let it fall slowly back in the bowl.

'Yes. I've thought of that, too.'

'On the other hand,' Helen said, looking at me kindly, 'if you feel bound to go ahead—perhaps his plans will work out as he says, and however it goes, you needn't feel that you've been the one to fail him.'

So tolerant! So equable! Like Lewis. She would never try to influence me, I thought aggrievedly, stuck with my honour because no one would prise me away from it. Anyway, it was not at all obvious how you should set about

137

being useful to someone you never saw. Magic I should have had at my command.

And really, I was revolted by them both: Christian and Olive. Good intentions frustrated, determination thwarted, motives twisted! Why should I allow my life to be messed about? Hanging up on people! And all this ghastly talk of love and jealousy. Who could be so aggravated and still eat? The waiter eyed the plate he took away from me.

As we walked home we talked about Lewis. Helen wondered if he ever saw Gabrielle, whether he was happy. I answered casually, feeling behind the answers and the aggravation and the pleasure of Helen's company, a grim sensation of certainty. Christian would say, 'I wasn't serious. You won't desert if you're my friend.' And I would not desert.

For fully five minutes I sat holding the receiver to my ear, totally silent, while Christian lectured me. I hadn't expected apologies: this was much to be preferred to panicky retractions. Unaware, however, of my preferences in these matters, he outdid himself in his efforts to put me in the wrong, to make me feel vile, and shrill, and cold-hearted. When he'd delivered his set piece, we agreed that we should certainly go ahead as planned, as soon as he could arrange —he said—his life.

Gertie, the cleaner, was sprinkling powder in the basin; I watched her idly.

'Now, the thing is, Clem, I can't come today. You see I've given up this stupid window-cleaning business and—'

'When did you do that?'

138

'Oh, a few days ago,' he said evasively. 'What does that matter? I couldn't stick it any longer. It was—humiliating. I went to a house in Aspley Square—you know, the place with all the window-boxes and brass-work—and I was going to march right round the square, win over all the butlers and house-keepers, and make a good day of it. I had a young kid with me. He's just left school. In fact, he's the son of my present landlady. He was helping me cart all the junk.'

I could see him somewhere standing in a tobacco-smelling phone-box, the sick baited glances flashing round the tight little case of glass and red-painted wood.

'It was a good day: I'd seen you, I was settled in my mind, I'd written some work out for you to correct. Young Rex and I were talking and joking—he wants to act. He's a clever kid, too. Of course, he doesn't know anything about me, but he likes me, he really does. And then, I was away from Olive for a while. Out on a leash. She knows I can't get up to much cluttered up with buckets and the rest of the—paraphernalia...' He made a sound not like a laugh.

'What happened?'

'I told you. Even though I was going about dressed like a clown and cleaning stupid—holding out my hand like a tramp for pennies at the end of it, I didn't mind. I thought it was right that nothing should be easy. You see,' a queer exasperated helpless sound, half-laugh, half-sigh, came through, 'I don't think you quite understand. *Two people have died.* I swore on the life of the only person I cared about, and lied, deliberately. I was a serious actor—more than promising—ten years ago. I was tipped as the white hope of the theatre, compared with the greatest.

Do you understand? It's all gone. Come to nothing. I clean windows, Clem. Go from door to door. And it's my own fault! People tried to help me—I cheated them. You'll never know what I've done...But lately I thought: perhaps it isn't too late...'

'Neither it is, Christian. You're only thirty!'

'Thirty! I'm nine hundred. I should be dead.'

In a moment I said, 'What happened?'

'Oh yes. I was telling you about Rex. The poor kid thinks there's no one like me—and he's right, if only he knew it.'

This was sympathetic, wistful, almost eager. I began to realize that Christian might shake off any tragedy, might rise up from his sick-bed well for an instant, to appreciate the simple human quality of some casual stranger, to be profoundly grateful for the liking of someone whom, nevertheless, he would not be able to refrain from using five minutes later.

'Rex hasn't had a chance. It's a damn shame...Well, it was late in the afternoon, almost dark. We went in—at the Tradesman's Entrance, of course—to this white house: it had monstrous window-boxes—'

I was silent, not tempted at all to prompt him. I was unwilling to know him so intimately, reluctant to over-hear his thoughts. I felt, sickly, that it was unfair to be so connected to suffering.

'In the kitchen we were talking to the cook, a great fat woman with pink cheeks and black hair. She had a deep gruff laugh like a very fat witch we had once for *Macbeth*, but we were flannelling each other and drinking tea. Rex was taking it all in. He'd never seen anything like this

140

kitchen. And then—Mercia came in, Mercia Warren...' His voice was strangled.

'You knew her?'

'Mercia. Lady Mercia Warren,' he said savagely. 'Don't you ever look at *The Tatler*?'

'No. I never do.'

'Oh God! *Everybody* knows her. She had a great thing about me once. We went to Kitzbuhl for Christmas a few years ago, and then later we went over to Monaco. She won about fifteen hundred the first night we arrived...'

I listened naturally, accepting this side of his life on an either or basis. 'What did she say?'

He gave a groan. 'She was having some stupid "At Home" affair. *Everyone* was there. Suddenly Mercia comes swaying into the kitchen with that walk of hers, and stands there staring at me. God knows what her dress cost. She looked terrific, flashing all the family diamonds. She always wore too much jewellery. Her hair's red now.

'She screams, "Christian, darling!" What *was* I doing in her kitchen? Was I making a film? Was I in costume? Then she sends someone to tell a few of the others to come through, so in they troop thinking it's some kind of joke. And, of course, it was. My luck! She probably hadn't been near the kitchen in five years.

'Some of them tried to be nice in a condescending way but—I had no money. You'd have thought it was leprosy I had. They don't know anything! Not that anyone could want to change! It's just money...'

In a minute he demanded, 'Have you thought what it was like for me? Do you see how I felt? I'm not insensitive, Clem!'

141

At once, from somewhere, I dredged up calm and consolation, and infused with energy, forced him to believe in his own worth, in the validity of all his aspirations. Heavily he listened, weighing every word, bound to be convinced and to accept in solitude, but for the moment, equally bound to seem unreconciled. Alleviation of that hurt was not yet possible.

I stopped. We had nothing else to say, were exhausted. He had a pretty habit I was coming to recognize, of dropping the receiver as his farewells left his mouth. Now, blankly, I heard the memory of that tight-lipped, 'I've got to go now. Good-bye,' and slowly replaced the receiver.

Go where? To do what? Drink with old cronies? Or—what was I thinking! It was irrational to try to trick the listening fates by pretending to fear—for instance—suicide, so that what really happened, if anything did, would seem trivial and a reason to praise his moderation. Yes, it was irrational.

Later, Olive rang to ask if Christian was with me. He had flung out of the house announcing he would go to see me. I said we hadn't met for days. When I said, 'What will you do?' she said resignedly, 'Look for him.'

What a prospect! A maze of empty streets stood in my head, and massive, cold, and blackened buildings.

I said, 'Call me if there's any news,' and hung up, feeling shaken and wary, wishing it were possible to unknow, undo, disappear.

The days began to stretch like years. The telephone became my master. Between morning and midnight it was suddenly customary for Christian to ring me every few hours. The calls came like despatches from the front, and like an editor I lived for the telephone and the news.

Every absence from the room was an emergency, full of danger.

The phone might ring. I mightn't know.

Collecting milk and mail from the ground-floor I could perhaps fly without touching a stair to reach it in time, if I heard a sound. But one day I had to shop for food, to leave the house...

I bought enough for a seige: a dozen eggs, a large sliced loaf, cheese, butter, sugar, biscuits, coffee, a monster-sized packet of cereal and a bunch of bananas, rather green.

I didn't miss a call.

Sometimes I was spoken to by a Christian so normal, so gay and settled, someone so assured, reassuring and believable, that I bit my lip, abashed to think I had ever aspired to advise or comfort this man-about-town.

Memories of hysteria, fears of suicide, receded to enormous shadowy distances, unsubstantial as hallucinations.

'Darling, did I sound frantic?' he would say. 'You were *worried*? Why? Never worry about me.' So sturdy, with a smile in his voice, deeply amused and a little moved by my unaccountable concern. 'As soon as—' he had a job, a new pair of shoes, the weather was better—as soon as something was different—almost anything—he would learn his French, climb Everest, perform miracles...

It wasn't possible to disbelieve him. His pronouncements came without a glimmer of doubt. He spoke with a warm impetus, in a way that was quite marvellous. None

143

of the think-thinking, the 'ifs' and 'buts', the alternatives and consequences, that went on in my head and most of the heads I knew.

It was a relief to believe that after all, he was more natural, more spontaneous than I, and perhaps the latest gayest version of him was the real one.

Once or twice he was drunk and repetitive, but often he was more sober than I, as he was invariably more of everything, whatever his mood, than anyone else.

He said, 'This has nothing to do with you, Clem. If I'd never met you I would say it still: I must get away from this woman! She's insane! There's a scene now if I talk to Rex or his mother—and *she's* fifty. I know that doesn't make any difference where I'm concerned—Olive doesn't forget to remind me, either. Everything I ever admitted she throws up at me. Poor old Carruthers is a toothless old bag but kind, Clem. And I like to have a laugh with them just to be pleasant when we're living in the same house. She *is* our landlady. One has to be adult about these things. One has to be civilized.'

From other allusions Christian made I began to wonder if Olive had abandoned her job at the dairy. When I asked, he said, 'I'd rather not discuss it,' so repressively that my mind splintered off, trying to divine what had happened. He added, 'She *is* working, but I refuse to tell you where.'

Did she caretake in a ladies' lavatory? Sweep out trains? Clean office buildings? What could it be to account for that tone? My curiosity lasted just for seconds. Not considerate to press him. Brutal to wound her by being aware of whatever it was...

144

Christian rarely referred to any event or expectation mentioned previously, however recently, or all-importantly. Every few hours a new man talked to me. Continuity would be expected in vain I discovered, and ceased to expect it. I too have volatility! I too can be adaptable!

So where he led I followed, trying cautiously to curb excess, to temper savagery, to reason with arrogance, to inject moderation into that self-lacerating repentence.

No wholesome sense, no liberal attitude, was ever new to him. Impartial and disinterested, as soon as he caught the drift of my argument, he commandeered it and upheld it fluently. For extra measure on these occasions he threw in a few subsidiary attitudes—his disapproval of racial discrimination, anti-Semitism, any signs of neo-McCarthyism—and supported them with anecdotes that proved his good faith. Obscurely baffling as it was to have the ground again cut from under my feet, it was encouraging to know that these sound and liberal ideas did exist inside his head.

Or, a voice queried, was this the living definition of the word 'lip-service'? Perhaps life was a dictionary and one's whole existence no more than a trackless journey in search of the true and felt definition of single words.

Certainly Christian chanted humanist phrases at me like a savage. Behind his almost over-readiness to sympathize with the oppressed I sensed a sort of fundamental derision of the attitude he'd chosen to adopt.

Yet he told me how he had persuaded and badgered Mrs Carruthers into accepting an African student as a tenant—someone called Johnny Matowen, and very black, Christian said, as if that made it somehow much better.

145

Frequently I longed to snatch up the conversation and direct him towards some specific course that would end uncertainty and unemployment. But it would have taken a greater opportunist than I to wrench the talk from his control.

'Don't you miss me?' he asked with plaintive indignation. 'When I get a job settled I'll be with you so often. I want so much to see you. Do you believe me?'

'Of course.'

Pause. 'No. You're saying that—not meaning it.'

'No. Really.' Two can kid as cheaply as one.

'Why do you think I spend all these shillings on phone calls when I'm so broke? Why do you think Olive's so jealous? *She* knows if you don't. I get your name thrown at me night and day.'

'What do you say?' I asked curiously.

'What *can* I say? I'm pretty rotten, but while I'm with her I can't hurt her that much. I say, "No, I'm not in love with Clem. She's useful to me."'

Dryly I said, 'That's a moot point.'

A subsequent conversation turned on highly-mysterious reports of a job with a television company. 'The electronics side,' said Christian. 'I may stay in London after all if I land this contract. The money's good in electronics. I'll let you know more tomorrow.'

'—in television. The electronics side—whatever that means,' I said to Helen triumphantly. 'What *does* it mean?'

She shook her head. 'But that's good, Clem. I hope he gets it. He seems really to have worked at finding something this week. It can't be easy.'

We smiled warmly, raising our brows, respectful and chastened to learn of this unsuspected talent.

Next morning I asked him carefully, humbly, what the job involved. I said I couldn't be more ignorant of electronics.

He gave a shout of laughter. 'Good God! There'd be a nationwide blackout if they let me near any apparatus. That was my first fuse—the one I mended for you in Miss Evans's. What did I tell you?' he asked, still laughing. 'What did I say I'd be doing?'

I told him and he roared with delight, exclaiming, 'I was plastered, darling. But electronics! How in hell did I think that up?'

All week he'd been asked by prospective employers: 'What work did you do last?'

'Of course,' he'd said bitterly, earlier, 'I might have told them I cleaned windows or—'

'—don't.'

Now he said, muffled, 'I had to tell you something. I couldn't give you any more bad news.'

Finally he told me he'd been employed by a hire-car service to act as chauffeur to visitors from abroad. He would start on Monday and work shifts. The pay was only fair but there would be noticeable tips, and 'all in all,' he said excitedly, 'what do you think?'

'It's terrific!'

'But is it true?' Helen asked when I told her.

'*Yes.*' A pause. 'Well, I think so. I know he lied before, but it was understandable. He can't be stripped of his self-respect.'

Helen lowered her eyes.

'I can't be certain yet. I hope it's true, otherwise how will they manage?'

'Olive must earn something,' she reasoned coolly.

I said, 'Oh, Helen, you haven't met either of them. Why are you so—disparaging? You and Lewis both seem to have worked up an extraordinary dislike for them. I know what Christian's done, but he has a great capacity for good—much too much to be allowed to go under. Yet you and Lewis, whom I've always thought of as the most generous people—anything but censorious—now that it's come down to a real person in the real world, start to judge him and make superior faces. This isn't the right time or place or person you say—as if you could save up your principles for people who were worthy of them. You mightn't ever find any! You set a very high standard!'

Indignation and disappointment lent me force: the words poured out. Helen again lowered her eyelids.

'You don't know how silly you sound. No one but you ever talks about principles. As for Christian—I've reacted to the person you've described. You didn't expect me to *like* him? I have a horror of that sort of chaotic irresponsibility, that disastrous energy that barges ahead never thinking of the consequences to other people—'

'The repercussions have fallen on *him*.'

'In what way?…And you've mentioned a few ruined lives in passing, haven't you?'

'Oh! Can't you see? To be the guilty one, the wrong one—and to know it—goes beyond everything. There's nothing worse. There's no consolation.'

'I don't doubt he'd agree with you.'

She went on talking about mindlessness and disasters apparently connecting them in some larger sense with the type of personality Christian was.

Through my teeth I said, 'He *knows*. He has literally no peace. How can you add blame to that? He is trying—to be what he could be...'

'Yet you say he acts all the time?'

'But that doesn't mean that what he acts is false. It's just his way of *being*, Helen!'

That night at eight o'clock Lucy Turner rang through on the house extension to ask us down to have a drink and watch television.

I gave a bang on Helen's white-painted door and passed on the invitation. She was writing letters. I asked, 'Would you like to go?'

'Mmm. Yes. It might be nice. But you're ready for bed,' she said, looking at my dressing-gown.

After another bath I had decided to lie on the divan, warm under the eiderdown and comfortable, instead of pretending to work. But I saw that it could look demoralized, this state of undress at eight at night.

'I'll change.'

When Helen came in a few minutes later I was slamming on some make-up.

She said, 'I'm sorry about this evening, Clem.'

'So should I be.' I brushed my hair down, twisted it round and started to pin it up. I said, 'I hate it, but I'm grateful when you argue with me, Helen—and when

149

Lewis does. He's been—good. I sometimes don't feel safe, somehow. Maybe he knows.'

Helen lifted a little jar of eye-shadow from the chest of drawers and turned it over once or twice.

I said, 'You look a bit glamorous. That's a beautiful blouse. What's printed on it?'

'They tell me they're burnt strawberries.'

We grinned. But as I fastened my belt and switched off the fire I was suddenly angry that Helen could stand there, looking like that, being what she was and—contradiction—content to spend some hours tonight with Lucy Turner. What a waste! What fourth-rate living! Could she love Quentin, whom she had left? It was wicked, dull and stupid of her to stand there at peace with herself and cheerful about it. Life should be intense experience.

'All set?' She put down the jar.

We went out, banging the door. I thought: I'd like to ask you questions. I could make you unhappy perhaps if I did. Which would not be nice. But whether niceness is all...Resentment, anger, restlessness, discontent, are good. Because there *is* something different, something better than this! I despise your contentment with all this...

'Oh, it's gorgeous!' groaned Lucy Turner, retreating reverently for a finer view, then approaching Helen again to examine the material of her blouse.

Was that the upstairs telephone? That double-ringing? Was it mine? Though I listened with all five senses, it was still, incredibly, impossible to decide not only if the ringing phone was mine, but also whether or not it was one of those false alarms that started up in me whenever I abandoned the room.

150

We sat down. Lucy chatted of Knightsbridge fashions. Dimly I could hear Helen answer, as I listened with electric attention to that distant perfect double-ringing of the telephone.

No. It lasted too long. Only in my head. Not real. No need to worry...

'Brandy, please.'

Most people would worry more about phones in the head, I thought, wanting to smile, lightly conceited. My first head noises! Put a cross up. Quite an occasion.

'Cheers!' said Lucy Turner, smiling richly at us.

This was her private ground-floor sitting-room—a long room whose large gold and white lamps illuminated polished floor, white rugs and several oatmeal-coloured chairs and sofas. There was a handsome desk. There were tall spring flowers in tall vases.

'I like people,' said Mrs Turner, comfortably broad-minded. 'Of course in a place like this I meet all kinds—foreigners, all sorts. Often we don't know ten words of a common language, but a smile's the universal language I always say.'

Sunk in the soft cushions of the sofa, Helen and I drank and listened.

'I'm used to them, anyway. I'm abroad every year. And I've found the great thing when you're travelling is to tip well. Really, if you want them to fawn on you, you have to over-tip. But it's worth it every time. I like a bit of fawning.'

More fruity, whisky-scented laughter.

Poor Mrs Turner. Oh, poor Mrs Turner. Madam, if I were available to feel for you I would be pale and shamed.

Lucy, dear be quiet! You know not what you say. You have two niggers in your wood-pile, dearest. You are not agreed with, sweetie. Keep quiet for your own sake, do!

Whether 'tis nobler in the mind to let you ramble on like this, dear Lucy, I am quite unable to decide...

But Helen, with some miraculous sleight-of-hand, was saying what she thought, and lo! here was Mrs Turner contradicting herself in a fascinating bare-faced sort of way.

Now if *I* had spoken, it would have been with terror, lest Mrs Turner should catch sight of herself, be crushed by the revelation and die on the spot. What bending over backwards! What simplicity!

Half an hour later there was a small flurry when Bertrand arrived to see Helen, and was invited in to join us. Mrs Turner bullied him a little and he was charmed. She was Absence personified behind the shiny eyes, and the reflexes which her listener's age and sex and social status governed. But Bertrand obviously thought: she likes me, she cares about me...

The television set was turned on. Legs were crossed and glasses moved from one hand to another. Under cover of a commercial, Lucy Turner was talking to Helen, who sat beside her on the sofa, murmuring questions about her years of training. They discovered a mutual acquaintance, someone with whom Helen had lost touch.

'My dear, she's married *very* well—' I caught and missed a few words. Helen said, 'I'm glad she's happy. She had rather a bad time. I've sometimes wondered...'

'Happy!' said Mrs Turner, almost angrily, looking at her as if she were mad. 'My dear, Derek Awkwright...' Words failed her. 'Derek Awkwright! He's really somebody.'

Bertrand turned to me. 'Have you heard from Lewis?'

Upstairs the phone was ringing.

CHAPTER EIGHT

Exactly at three Christian knocked on my door. It was Saturday, just over a week since I had moved. On some plane far above myself I had roamed all afternoon, attending to bath, teeth, hair, hands and eyes with ritualistic heaviness.

Then he rapped on the door and, disembodied with anticipation, I jumped up from the divan to open it. And there he stood—inevitable yet deeply surprising, grave and dazzling in Rollo's old suede jacket.

'Hullo.'

For seconds we stared without smiling, as if in alarm. Then as though he felt himself to be under the eye of some phantom observer, Christian looked past me into the room he hadn't seen before.

'May I come in? I've brought you some flowers.'

Red tulips in white tissue paper. I took them. He walked in and closed the door. I looked in perplexity at

154

the small vases on the chest and then at the long-stemmed flowers.

Kindly, impatiently patient, he took them from me again. 'In the basin, girl, in the basin.' He let the tap run hard then laid them in the water.

Standing by the single easy-chair, I watched him, relieved to have the problem taken off my hands, amazed not so much to see him as that it was so long since I had. My heart felt gentle.

'Now! Let me inspect your establishment to see if I approve!' He passed behind my chair and sat down on the divan. That is, he gave the impression of rollicking across the black carpet. Ah, yes, he smelled winy.

Acutely his blue eyes came up to mine, and a roistering defensive smile appeared. 'I had a half-bottle of wine with my lunch today,' he announced. 'A half-bottle only.' Measured the size with his hands, screwing up one eye for accuracy's sake, joking.

It occurred to me he expected to be reprimanded, and I smiled again. What was there to blame about this? Except that it wouldn't be simple to pin him down to work, which *was* something.

'Did you? Was it good?'

Indignantly he said, 'It wasn't *rubbish*. Of course it was good. I wouldn't drink just anything.' He went on and on boastfully about his fastidious taste in liquor—how he would rather die of thirst, go on the wagon for keeps, et cetera, than let inferior stuff down his throat.

'I'm boring you,' he said suddenly.

'Oh, no.'

155

'You wretch! You little wretch!' he laughed, sliding down on to the floor beside my chair. 'I *am* boring you. You don't care if I drink turps, do you?…Why don't you answer me? Do you or don't you care if I drink turps?'

Laughter still shimmered over his face, and a feverish theatrical amorousness had come and gone with that insistent, through-the-teeth, 'Do you?' Now he hovered uncertainly over moodiness, pique, disgruntlement. He flung himself back from the chair, still remaining on the floor, to lean against the side of the divan, saying, 'Ah, you don't care about anything! God knows why I get nervous coming to see you! But of course you don't believe that either, do you?'

He said, almost sulkily, looking down. 'Well, I *have* been, whether you're interested or not. Why do you think I stayed away? For ten days! Ten days and nights of scenes with Olive! Wanting to come to you, having to be satisfied with these bloody phone calls, and you're always so cold. And Olive on her knees, and giving up her job to keep watch on me while I was looking for work. And Rollo asking if I'm seeing you for lessons. And *you*…

'When Stella died I swore I'd never harm anyone again. I wanted to do one good deed. I thought I'd make someone happy. I'm not trying to tell you I haven't slipped. I've been unfaithful to her, but I have tried. Till now. And now I want you. But I'm frightened. I don't know what to do…'

He had spoken with mounting desperation. Now, kneeling, face upraised, grasping my hands, he cried wildly. 'Oh, Clem! Are you the one? Are you the one who's going to save me?'

His eyes held mine in frantic enquiry.

'I don't know.' I looked at the shiny walls, numbed by the extent of the demands I had glimpsed in his eyes. 'I don't know.'

'It would have to be permanent—*final*—if you came to me,' he threatened now, with blazing eyes. 'I've had too much of the other thing. I can't take it. I can't go from one to another for the rest of my life. You would have to hold me. You'd have to put up with me forever...I need help. Take care of me...'

'Yes, I know that. Yes,' I said softly to his agitation. After all, though he spoke the truth, all this was more than hypothetical, wasn't it? 'Yes, I see,' I said, supposing in a soft sort of daze that it would never come to a decision, but supposing also if it ever did happen that he should need me, he could have me. Yes, I did accept that.

But now, somehow, for the moment, we circled out and away from this high blinding storm with all that postponed, carefully shelved. The one to save me?...

Christian analysed the room and its contents critically, saying finally, 'But it's like a hotel room. It lacks atmosphere. It needs love,' he said in an altered tone looking steadily at me.

Certainly back to earth! But his quick changes altered nothing. I knew now that every moment was real in its own way, independent of every other moment that had gone, or might come. Mockery now took nothing from the truth of five minutes earlier.

'What it needs is the sound of your charming French accent,' I said.

157

'It needs music, too,' he continued, starting to look about for the wireless. It was beside him, under the table. He found a record programme and, fumbling with the knob, turned it low.

'And you, darling…You should be in black, in a black dress—soft but not frilly—and with pearls, real pearls, with a delicious emerald clasp…'

'It's early in the day,' I said, wanting to laugh.

'No, no,' he corrected me strenuously. 'In a beautiful black dress,' he insisted, 'and much much nicer to me.'

His head was turned. The golden-brown hair grew flat on the broad planes, his neck was strong. And the contrast between his strength and frailty sent a small pang to my heart, of guilt, or compassion.

'Not that I don't like this dress! But wintry things aren't really you.' He surveyed me, seeming to wait for something, then said, 'And what about me? You haven't seen me for ten days. How do you like me in Rollo's cast-offs? Do I look older?'

'Ah! I don't flatter you!'

'No.'

'Would you like that?'

'Doesn't everyone?' he smiled drolly.

'Tell me about your job. You were there all day yesterday, and you start properly on Monday morning: what else?'

Instantly, he brimmed with gaiety. For one thing, he said, after the head-office interview, he'd been invited home to dinner by the manager.

'Why?'

'He liked me. Why do you think?'

'Did you go?'

'Don't be mad.'

Of course. All he had to gain from the manager was a job—that achieved, why spend himself to no purpose?

As if he were a tape-recorder, he mimicked the artless contributions of typist, manager and drivers—astonishing admissions to someone they had known eight hours.

These winning ways, I thought, watching his face. That intelligent sympathy. It was a marvellous façade—or, perhaps, a marvellous effluescence. It made strangers expect not only understanding but forgiveness from him—as if he had some power. If they could win his approval, have the benefit of his directing hand in their lives, there would be nothing lacking. All things to all men.

He was questioning me. Where had I been? Had I met anyone new in the house? Who was I seeing? I answered, and finally asked if he would like some coffee, thinking: strong coffee, sober, French...

'Yes, I would, thank you, darling. I'm cold.' He was suddenly on his feet, staring into the mirror over the fireplace. 'Oh, Christ!' he said; then, 'Can't we put the fire on?'

'It *is* on. It won't go any higher.'

'Here—wait a minute—I've got a shilling.' He was swaying a bit. The coin dropped in the meter.

The room was getting dusky, the gas-fire gently glowed and hissed. Music came from the wireless. Because of the wine, or whatever he'd drunk, the afternoon would be frittered away. But half an hour ago I had learned something; and it was sobering to know just what it was I was trying to handle.

159

Making coffee in the kitchen I wouldn't let myself reflect on the difference between Christian as he appeared, and as he really was. Such pity as he could inspire wasn't to be borne. The respect I had for his potentialities, for the resistance he was putting up, and an intense partisan affection, battled even with my comprehension that there might be cause for pity.

His faults and virtues were on a grand scale, equally. It wasn't possible to pity such a man. Yet, I knew if I had not shunned this profound regret absolutely—'

What I had to remember was that useful involvement and feeling could not go together.

'Sorry I was so long.' I carried the tray in. 'Is it warmer in here yet?'

He was occupied with the flowers. 'Look! I've fixed them for you. I don't trust you to arrange them. You're not domesticated.' The vase teetered on the edge of the chest, unbalanced by the length of the stems. He extended an arm to display his work, rocked unsteadily, his hand flicked past a flower-head and down it all came. Water sogged the black carpet.

Quickly I laid the tray on the table and mopped the floor, jamming the flowers back in the vase.

'Never mind that. Never mind it,' he mumbled, wavering across the darkening room to the divan. Grandly he insisted, 'Leave it!'

I looked over my shoulder at him. He sat glowing on the divan, stolid and solid as an idol. His imperturbability made me want to laugh, but I was feeling faintly harassed.

160

The cloth went under the basin. I washed my hands and going back to the chair, started to pour the coffee.

'Black or white?'

'Oh, darling! I need you so!'

Without warning Christian was lying across the arms of my chair, leaning heavily against me, seeming to have six strong hands. I could smell his warm winy breath on my face.

Surprised, but patient and as though he were a playful bear, I tried to push him away. I started to speak and was enveloped in fresh damp winy darkness. There was his exploring tongue in my mouth. My neck was breaking against the back of the chair. The chair was breaking, I was certain.

Blacked out and breathless, I gave an enormous twisted shove and opened my eyes. Christian's head came up, his eyes baffled, concentrated. 'What's the matter?' he whispered. 'What's putting you off? Is it the wine?...Is it?'

And fiercely I whispered back, 'Just—move! Get off the chair! I don't want—'

He reapplied himself as if to discover where he was lacking. At this moment, by some freak of electricity, the wireless croaked as if clearing its throat and the volume rose.

Mentally I groaned. It only needed this! I thought, pushing against Christian, turning my head from side to side. He came up for air. 'Come on to the bed,' he whispered.

'I will *not*.'

There was another silent struggle. Christian laughed, and his teeth shone. 'I only want to kiss you properly,' he explained, whispering.

'Oh! Will you—*move*?'

He closed in again, and after a moment I gave up. Well, kiss away, I thought. I hope you enjoy yourself.

At first I was nothing in particular, except perhaps fatalistic, niggled by the music and the crick in my neck. Was anyone in to hear the racket? Would Lucy come to empty the meter?

Meanwhile Christian swarmed over me, occupied and slightly groggy, but somehow fresh as the morning milk, demanding and insistent as a child. We breathed the same breath. There seemed no reason why this heavy spread-eagled embrace should end.

But now the very remoteness of my indulgence to the efforts of his lips and tongue could have made me guilty, and I was dismayed by sudden grief, for some quality of extreme helplessness that the closeness of his flesh made manifest.

Dimly, vaguely, I accepted his right to use me, to be aggrieved, to want to break me up, and others like me: perhaps in the closeness of it, accidentally, he would catch some health from me. I wanted that. Next to him I was ashamed of stability, as if of riches, undeserved and inalienable.

At last I became aware that Christian was drawing back from me, freeing my mouth, loosening the clamp on my arms. Though the wireless bellowed there was a sensation of silence as we drew apart. He seemed not to be breathing.

Barricaded into the chair by his torso, which remained across the slender wooden arms, I heaved a few deep breaths,

162

and examined my wrists. I saw that my hands shook. One held a white handkerchief. Dully I started to wipe my face, conscious of nothing but a rather exclusive and self-centred interest in the aches that came to life in my ribs and wrists. Still tasting Christian, inspecting the pale smudge of lipstick on the white handkerchief, I tested my lungs with a few more breaths, and woodenly wiped at my face.

'You *swine!*' said Christian softly.

I looked up at him. He was staring behind me. Turning, I saw Olive standing inside the open doorway, her eyes fixed balefully on him.

Oh no. I didn't believe it. These things didn't happen.

A step behind Olive stood Bertrand. I saw that they had been behind me, and that Christian had known it now, in silence, for seconds.

Slowly he rose upright from the chair and advanced towards Olive, while she came further into the room towards him, grown taller and looming in her anger. Bertrand followed and closed the door. The room bulged with people.

'You rotten swine!' Christian almost sighed with rage.

'I knocked. You didn't hear. You were too busy *enjoying* yourselves.'

'Clem, would you like me to go or stay?' This was Bertrand.

'Oh, it doesn't matter,' I said indifferently.

I was still shaking, but not with shock or temper. It was just a rather affected physical reaction to rough handling that I imagined I could stop at any time.

Christian and Olive were noisy in the corner.

163

Oh, blast, I thought. Go away. I felt nothing at all except a movement of faint incredulity and scorn. Jealous woman throws open the door unexpectedly on love and other woman in heavy embrace! Really! It was too melo-dramatic, too unsophisticated, for my taste.

Their voices clashed. Aching, shaking, I eyed the room: red tulip petals on the floor, the coral cover of the bed contorted by Christian's solitary romp there, cold coffee in the cups—poured and never touched. And both of us wonderfully dishevelled.

> *Well you can cry me a river*
> *Come on and cry me a river*
> *I cried a river over you...*

Oh Lord! The wireless! I snatched at the knob. At a signal, Bertrand turned on the central light and everything became more real—and worse.

'*Do you love her?*' Olive demanded.

He seemed to shrink. 'Don't pin me down, Olive. Don't blame the girl. She wasn't a willing party. I forced her.'

'You see!' she flashed at me. 'He won't deny it. He's afraid you won't give him lessons if he does.'

Lessons!

His powerful frame diminished against the wall, beside Olive, Christian pleaded with her, hands out in apologetic explanation, palms upturned. 'Don't blame the girl!'

'She was enjoying it!' Olive cried, turning on me viciously, and Bertrand, planted by the door, caught my eye.

164

'Do you want her instead of me?' Olive's voice was hammering away at a beaten young man I hardly recognized.

Gone the shine, the gold, the glowing confidence. Hesitant, as if he was suddenly deaf and blind and baited, he slumped against the wall. The broad forehead, even the classical bones of his face, had altered.

'No, of course, he doesn't love me,' I sounded impatient. 'He'd had some wine or it would never have happened.'

'That's why I was frightened of this,' she muttered, mollified in the faintest possible degree. 'Sober, I can trust him, but not like this. But, anyway, I'm going! I'm packing tonight! This isn't the first time this has happened.'

'What did you say? When? When?' he rallied slightly, glancing at me. 'But, no, Olive. You're not to go. I can't manage alone. What would happen to me?'

Olive said, 'This is what I've suspected all the time. This is why I haven't wanted him to come for lessons. So I came this afternoon. And look what I found. Making love! *Was* this the first time?'

'Yes, of course,' he said wearily.

Sallow and gaunt in her black coat, with her dark hair hanging, Olive turned to me again. 'Do you love him, Clem? Do you want him?'

I hesitated, in no doubt, but profoundly unwilling to submit to questioning by that voice, those steamy eyes. However, though I could have shrieked at her for turning him even temporarily into this craven parody of himself, I had no wish for her to carry out her threat and leave him tonight.

'No, Olive. My life is planned. I do have a separate existence, you know. I like Christian, but that's all.'

Her look suggested that this was implausible but welcome news. She murmured with quiet satisfaction, 'So does everyone.'

Indeed? Was that so? I thought, stung by the smug dismissal, the relegation to the ranks, the insinuation that I was one of the crowd. A dozen truncated and edgy rejections of this picture shot in and out of my head.

'You don't want him?' she repeated, staring hazel-eyed with demented solemnity. 'Still, if he wants you, I'll go tonight.'

Christian stammered something, head down, looking at no one, and contemptuously Olive watched him, like a judge and a gaoler.

Bertrand stood with pained discretion, touching his tie.

If only they would all get out! Ignoring them, I went to the mirror, leaned for a moment, teeth rattling in my head, against the mantelpiece, then found my brush and started to fix my hair.

'We're supposed to be looking after the house for Mrs Carruthers this week-end,' Olive was reminding Christian. 'As a favour! And she's reducing the rent for it! We've got thirty shillings in the world between us,' she cried. 'We can't afford to let her down!'

As I turned she was harrying him about the head and shoulders, raising her hands but not touching him. 'Come home! Come on! Come on!'

It was grotesque and pitiful, shameful to see. With one

166

wild look in my direction, Christian submitted, protecting himself halfheartedly.

I subsided into the chair with a groan, stunned and somnolent. Bertrand came back after watching them downstairs. 'Well,' he said, closing the door. 'How are you?'

'All right. Sit down, Bertrand, why don't you?'

He plonked himself on the divan and ran a hand over his mouth. I looked blankly at his brown athlete's face and waited for him to speak. If he took hours or years I felt I could stay there, listening to the silent bombardment in my head.

'Have you got anything to drink? Should I get you something?'

He was romantically supposing me to be upset! I said wryly, 'That was just—a misunderstanding. I mean, I don't need to be revived. But thanks, anyway.'

I was restless. While I smoothed the divan cover, and fixed the carpet and flowers and my make-up, Bertrand apologized for staying.

'But I thought you might need some help. I came up on the off-chance to see Helen, and by the time I found out she wasn't in—this—that—woman—was knocking on your door. I thought Helen might be with you, so I waited. The wireless was making a din and you didn't hear, I guess. But she just tapped once and then she was in before I could stop her.'

His unusual cordiality struck me disagreeably. At once I was galvanized, revitalized.

'It was much ado. You weren't even introduced! Still,' I grinned, 'perhaps it wasn't the time for formality.'

167

Bertrand looked stumped.

At last, after half an hour, having refused his invitation to dinner, I piloted him to the door.

Hesitating at the top of the stairs, he said, 'I think I've been mistaken about you, Clem. I didn't know you were—like this.'

The things people think they can say!

I smiled nicely, 'I'm not, Bertrand.'

I switched the light off and the lamp on, and sat in semi-darkness, looking at the fire in jittery and wordless confusion. I'd been sitting for a long time, not moving, when someone knocked hard on the door.

Jumping with shock, I went to it, very unwilling, and turned the handle.

'Is Chris here, Clem?' Wild-eyed, clasping herself with her arms, Olive came in.

'No.'

But we both stared in alarm at the furniture for confirmation.

'Why? What's happened? Where is he?'

'Oh, Clem!' She started to cry. 'He rushed out. I've been searching for him. I thought he might have come to you. Oh, Clem! He's taken Mrs Carruther's money. It's a private hotel place. We had to take care of it this week-end. We collected the accounts. Fifty pounds, Clem! He's taken it!'

I leaned against the wall. 'Oh, my God!' We stared expressionless. My mind was icy. I looked into the tear-filled hazel eyes. 'But—taken it? You mean…Do you mean he's—stolen it? *Why?* How did it happen?'

Olive shook her head bitterly. 'He doesn't trust me. Since I took that from my husband he won't let me touch any money. He wouldn't leave it in the house with me.'

'Oh!' As I began to understand, I sagged with relief. My senses stopped in flight and started to return.

It was serious enough, but not disastrous. He had taken the money: he would bring it back. About Olive he simply had this sad, unplesant, but understandable kink. Awful for her, I thought, but still…

'Is *that* it? For a moment I thought you meant—'

'But what if he spends it or something? We haven't got anything. There's no one we can turn to. We've got no friends. Nothing. No one would lend it to him. No one trusts him. They know what he's like.'

So much for their fondness! I thought sweetly, with malice. But I said reasonably, to calm her, 'But he *couldn't* spend fifty pounds, Olive. I'm sure it'll be all right. But, heavens, you gave me a fright!'

Of course I was right. Fifty pounds! I lived for two months on that: it couldn't disappear in a night. Besides, that wasn't his intention. And odd though that was, it was not dishonest. I was ashamed of what I'd almost imagined.

'Yes, but where is he?' cried Olive. 'What if something did happen? You don't know the state he's in, Clem. What would happen to him? Mrs Carruthers comes back on Monday night.'

She watched me.

Poor Olive! I stared at her frantic yet resigned expression, thinking slowly with a slowly thawing brain.

169

I heard myself say, 'I would give it to him. Nothing will happen to him.' My voice grew warmer and more certain. 'Nothing will happen.'

'Oh, Clem!' She started to sob, her head sunk in her hands. 'Would you? Would you? There's no one else.'

United with her in fear for Christian's safety, bitten with compassion at the sight—now that I was close to her—of her rough hands and worn face I put my arms round her shoulders. She wept bitterly. I looked vaguely at the threadbare wool of her coat and smoothed her shoulder. She was not young. She was amazingly real. She cared for Christian. I was fond of her, perhaps?

'It's all right. Come and sit down here. I'll get you some Veganin.'

Glancing up suddenly, remembering something, she said, 'Look what he did!' and swept off an old woollen scarf that filled in the neckline of her coat.

Her throat was brutally marked. There was a long scratch or cut running down from her left ear, dark with dried blood.

I felt my heart beat slowly. Standing over her I opened my mouth. 'Oh, Olive.'

'It hurts.'

Mechanically I fetched a glass of water and two tablets which she swallowed. Then, twisting her mouth in a smile, she said, 'And look at my dress. It's the only decent one I've got.'

It was torn across the bodice and stiffened in streaks where the blood had dried.

'Oh, Olive,' I said again, helplessly, leaning forward, hands on knees. 'What *happened*?'

170

She touched her throat delicately with blunt fingers.

'I got him home in a taxi—I *had* to take one—and there was a scene, of course, after what I found here. I suppose I should've let him sleep it off, but Clem, think how you would've felt if you'd been me. Seeing him make love to you. I couldn't stop myself. I said I was leaving. I didn't know what I was doing. He caught my arm and shouted, "No, Olive!" and then he tripped on a torn piece of lino. I picked up the poker by the fire. Everything went funny. I hit him. I could hear him saying, "No, Olive, please, Olive, don't!"

'I hit him on the head. I'd have kept on. I'd have killed him, but he pulled me over. That's when he tore my frock. And he grabbed me then here, at my neck, till I let the poker go. Then before I knew anything he took the money and left. His head was bleeding. I thought he'd come to you.'

Everything went funny, my mind echoed sickly.

Olive added now, with a kind of tragic relish, 'I was mad with jealousy!'

Shortly, buttoning her coat, wrapping the piece of yellow wool round her throat again, she prepared to go. When there was news she would ring me.

'I'm sorry about this afternoon, Clem. Coming in like that. But I'd die if I lost him. I had to know what was between you.'

'I'm sorry, too. It was only the wine.'

I closed the door behind her. And, oh! I could have wished to defend it and the window, even, against a similar invasion. Want him? Want anyone? The room was too small. There was only space for me. Where would anyone fit into my life? Who could recompense me for lost freedom?

What had *I* to do with people who were hit on the head with pokers, who half-throttled other people to defend themselves, and rushed out of houses clutching rolls of money belonging to someone else?

And *why* had Olive spied on him this afternoon? They had quarrelled because he was coming; her jealousy was no doubt what had inspired that great lunge at me. And think! Because she had had to know, one of them might now be dead. Just a few hours later. Money might yet be missing, with what unhappy consequences if I hadn't been able to help? What if he *had* been deep in an affair with me or someone else? Would the confirmation have been worth the damage? With all the vows of allegiance he'd taken, she wouldn't lose him if she behaved calmly.

*Everything went funny...*What they said at murder trials.

There were footsteps in the hall outside. My heart lurched with fright.

'Clem?'

I was at the table bent over a book.

'Oh, it's you, Helen. Wait a minute. I've got the door locked.'

'Not still working?' She pulled off her gloves and her rings glittered.

'No. Just sitting. Let's have some coffee. Was it a good play?'

'Very clever. You'd enjoy it. I loathe matinées, but there was nothing else for it. Alexa had to get this train at eight.'

'Bertrand came to see you this afternoon.'

172

The wireless was switched on, and coffee made. I hurled myself heart and soul into an attempt to amuse Helen—laughed, chattered, did all but swing from the centre light.

'You're very gay tonight,' she remarked, curling her legs up and poking the pillows behind her back. 'Can it be Bertrand's influence, do you suppose?'

'Naturally!'

When Olive rang at eleven I listened and said yes and no. I told Helen it was Jan. She looked at me.

At five past ten on Monday morning I left the Knightsbridge bank with a foolscap envelope in my handbag holding fifty pound notes. And walking in the direction of Hyde Park Corner in a pale bright haze of cold sunshine I remembered it was April. People still wore overcoats, but this morning walked with lifted heads, seeming to sparkle with spring colours and prosperity.

The footpaths glittered and were clean and dry. Suddenly the trees had leaves. A man sold daffodils and tulips and freesias. How busy everywhere! Taxis sped from the rank; a lorry passed laden with fruit and vegetables from the markets. The air smelled heavenly. Women with jewels, women with poodles, women with babies, smooth egg faces and expensive streaky hair, gold bracelet on gold bracelet chinking...

Looking ahead I could see the café sign swinging slightly. This was where we would meet. Inwardly I trembled. I was awed a little, and crushed, even by not imagining what he must feel. It seemed presumptuous to approach him.

With his back to the far wall of the bare cafeteria, Christian sat, monolithic, watching me approach between the empty tables. Theatrical sunshine from a queerly-placed skylight seemed to impart an air of menace, of unwholesome silence and isolation over the quarter of the room where he was.

Dragging back the wooden chair, I sat down, and for seconds neither of us spoke. My gloved hands, his bare ones, rested on the light Formica table-top. I heard Olive's words: found in the street-blind—soaked—blood everywhere—filthy—didn't have sixpence.

I glanced at his face—not a shadow, not a line or a mark. Without evasion he returned the look, his eyes darkly blue and clearer than mine. Seriously, but with no particular expression we stared.

'How are you?' I said.

'I'm all right.'

'Where's Olive?' It was agreed she should be present.

'She'll be along in a minute. She had something to do.'

We were silent again, looking dully at the table.

Last night, Sunday night, Olive had phoned again, much perturbed. 'Something's happened to Chris. I tried to keep him in bed all day, but this afternoon I left him alone while I made some tea. When I got back he was sitting in the big chair crying like a baby. He couldn't talk. I was terrified, Clem. I've never seen him so bad before. And with that cut on his head I was afraid to get a doctor. He'd ask questions. After I got him back to bed I nearly called to get you to come and help me with him, but I didn't dare leave the room...'

Now he said flatly, 'Well? I suppose you think I'm a maniac? I don't blame you. I think so myself. I must be. But I can't apologize to you, Clem. I'm sorry. I just can't.' He gave an uneasy smile. 'I know I ought to feel horrible and guilty and God knows what...I don't feel anything. Nothing at all.'

'Neither do I.'

Olive sat down next to me in time to hear our last remarks. I could feel her hatred. With some surprise I saw she meant to lecture us, to 'have it all out' again. And after all that had happened!

'I want to have it all out,' she said, and Christian gravely nodded, as if this were only right. Fascinated and numb I sat silent while they talked. Christian was to choose between us—as if we were two pieces of fruit, and as mindless. In their different ways they were so strange that I felt no resentment.

Then, as a matter of form, Christian said how much he regretted the scene in my room. At this Olive looked sceptical, and in spite of the rather insincere detachment in his manner, I thought this imprudent of her, considering the results of her last outburst.

'Did anyone see me in that condition?' he asked suddenly. 'Oh, God, yes! That friend of yours was there. Olive told me.' He looked at us wildly across the table. 'What will he think of me? Was I very bad? How did I look?'

A little nonplussed on our side of the table, Olive and I moved restlessly.

'I insulted you and created a disturbance in front of your friend,' he went on, insisting on a full-length

175

confession. 'And after the way I've messed you round with these lessons, too! I don't know why you bother with me.'

I said nothing. When he flashed a magnetic look across the table I looked steadily back, faintly aware that somewhere we were grappling together, silent and intent as killers.

'And did you see Olive's throat?'

Certainly, the bruises were remarkable. Christian looked sentimental, and Olive smiled with stoic pride. Involuntarily I glanced at the dressing that curved from his right ear, away to invisibility at the back of his head.

Coldly Olive followed my eyes. 'Oh, I deserved it!' she said, smiling bitterly.

'Ah, no. Olive didn't deserve that.' Softly Christian reproached my silence. He seemed quite to dote on those bruises.

We let it pass. After all, who got what he deserved in this life?

'That waitress is looking at us. We ought to get some tea or something.' Olive glanced nervously over her shoulder.

'Where?' Christian looked. A few yards away, wiping a clean table-top and eyeing us hard, was a battered warrior in a bright green overall. He took in the grizzled hair, leathery face and toothless mouth.

'I say,' he called in a sweet and bracing tone, 'you wouldn't throw us out, would you?' And he smiled at her with merciless friendliness.

'You can stay all day, love, for all I care,' she told him confidentially, coming over and leaning across the table with the rag in her hand.

They smiled into each other's face while Olive and I looked on with considerable indifference. When Christian realized this, as he quickly did, he detached himself unhurriedly, with numerous gay and sympathetic remarks, from his admirer.

Olive and I breathed deeply. We were all silent for seconds, then Christian broke out eagerly, 'I know it sounds crazy, but I'm glad this happened to me. I needed this knock. There's no reason why you should believe me if I swear to be different—I can only convince you by my actions now... I know you've heard *that* before, too!'

In and out of bars and taxis, caught up in a brawl, and ending on the wet footpath, he had lost the money.

'Fifty pounds!' he said softly, setting his teeth, groaning and laughing in an ecstasy of dismay. 'Till Mrs Carruthers gave Olive that old coat she had nothing—literally nothing but that dress. And I've got this cast-off thing of Rollo's. And I throw away fifty pounds of someone else's money!' He lowered his head and pressed his hands over it.

With the idea that he should not so much hear, as understand, I said, 'Here it is, anyway,' and taking the envelope from my bag, put it gingerly on the chair beside him.

He kept his head down. It was a bad moment. Oh, hell, I said silently, frowning at the table.

'Clem...' He shook his head and grimaced slightly with effort, sounding unnaturally casual and hard. 'Thank you very much. Don't think I don't know what you've saved me from. It's not all that much, of course. You know that. But it's simply a fact that no one else would have given it to me.'

I looked away.

'For once, please try to believe me. I'm not acting now. I'm at rock-bottom. I'm too tired to act any more.' He said, 'But I'll turn up for my lessons. Whenever Rollo wants me in Paris I'll be ready. And then I'll re-pay this and all the time you've wasted on me. Though I'm unstable, from now on I will try.'

He looked at us wildly and brightly. 'But why do I do these things? Could anyone straighten me out? Perhaps Helen—you said she was a doctor—perhaps she would get me an appointment with a psychologist? What do you think?' He tapped his teeth with his knuckles and looked at me.

I took a careful breath. 'If it was someone very good— very good—I'd say yes. Helen would suggest someone, I'm sure.'

I was really terrified to agree with him.

His eyes flickered. He gave a crooked tight little smile. 'You think I'm crazy, I know.'

I looked at him with no change of expression and he muttered behind his fist, 'I'll think about it. I can't go on like this for the rest of my life.'

Possessively Olive said, 'You don't need any psychologist!' and his eyelids came up. 'Hear that?' he signalled defiantly. Yet behind the defiance he looked out, immensely young, immensely frightened of himself, pleading without words.

He repeated stubbornly, 'I'll think about it. No! Ask her if she would fix it up for me.' And he went to get us some coffee and biscuits.

The cafeteria was filling with local business men and office boys. Olive and I glanced about for a minute,

178

then looked at each other. After all, we had much in common.

'Fifty pounds!' she said now in awed and angry tones. 'It seems a lot of money to me. He thinks you can just get it by asking.'

I thought: she doesn't like him. I said, 'He didn't ask me.'

In a low sour voice she said, 'He should've had to worry.'

Not understanding, I gazed at her profile. Christian came back carrying a tin tray, setting in front of us coffee and sugary biscuits.

We broke biscuits between our fingers, stirred silently.

'This has *got to be* the turning point,' Christian said with intense inward concentration, intensely willing idea and intention to connect. 'Thirty's not old! I could still have a good life...'

The failures, the misuse of youth, the irretrievable past engulfed him. He gripped his cup, looking down, agonizingly embarrassed suddenly to feel so much and have our eyes on his face. He was trapped behind the table, could not exit with some shocking quip to throw us off the scent.

Blankly sustaining the overflow of his feeling I heard myself answer him, talking with total conviction, as if with special knowledge, of the good future that would be his.

And gradually he did relax and settle back into himself, and talk about the job which he was now due to start tomorrow, a day late, Olive having phoned to make excuses for today.

'Darling, I wonder if you'd get us some more coffee? I think we all need it, don't you?' He spoke to Olive. She looked at him stilly, hesitating in the act of rising to act on his request.

Lifting his head, he bestowed on her a glance of such understanding, sweetness and familiarity that her face was transfigured, and my heart was moved.

Then he smiled, an intimate tender smile tinged with apology and self-depreciation. 'Don't be afraid to leave me alone with Clem,' he said, not moving his eyes from hers. 'I'm not going to make love to her. You can trust me. So can she. I've learned my lesson. But *please* get me some coffee, darling and—a ham sandwich. I'm starving after yesterday and'—he touched his head sorely—'I'm seeing double, or I wouldn't ask you to wait on me.'

Laughing slowly, melted with loving tenderness, Olive turned away. She looked confident as a queen. Those deep unmoving eyes on hers, the sudden rush of little glances over her face, to her forehead and hair, gave her the look of a woman fresh from her lover's arms.

I looked back at Christian, feeling an almost nostalgic pleasure in his company, as though he had already moved off far beyond me, away from the murky troubled days of the present.

Smiling, I met his eyes. The beautiful expression hadn't gone from his face—rather it had abandoned the trace of teasing gaiety as though that had been an artificiality, and now at last he sat sad and vulnerable and himself.

'What do we do now, darling? She's right, of course. She's right to be jealous. I love you. I love you, but I'm weak and I'm afraid to leave her. I don't know if we'd have any peace. You know what I'm like. My conscience kills me. I don't know if I could stand it. But *I* want to be happy, too. With you. For the rest of my life. Tell me—please tell me—do you love me, Clem?'

CHAPTER NINE

Rollo drew up on the empty square of asphalt. It was very quiet and almost warm. Richmond Park rolled away from us on all sides, palely green under a high and pale-blue sky. May trees stiff with pink and white blossom stood singly and in groups and rows. There was water glinting grey and gold; there were skylarks, and hidden somewhere out of sight a herd of deer.

Looking straight through the windscreen of his convertible, Rollo sat relaxed, his thin white hands resting on the wheel. The breeze was soft and fresh against the skin. The sun hung surprisingly over all, completely round and solitary in the sky.

'Then here it is, if you've never seen it before,' said Rollo idly, in the silent open air.

'It's very beautiful today.'

As tiredly, he said, 'Of course it has associations for me...'

'My father used to bring me,' he explained carefully. 'I've always had a great thing about my father—a love-hate thing, I suppose...Did Christian tell you?'

'No, he didn't.'

'But then there's history here, too...'

'I went to several schools. We were always returning to Ethelred the Unready.'

We sat like Chelsea Pensioners in the sun, fragile, aged and unsmiling.

'Ah, yes,' said Rollo vaguely, 'I remember him. Shall we walk? When I'm—well, I come here most days for an hour or two.' He turned his paper-white Lawson face on me—grey medieval eyes, brittle forehead and nose, dry finely-modelled mouth. And with his permanently unveiled eyes he glanced at me as he reached to take the ignition key—Rollo Lawson, a burnt-out child of thirty-seven, who knew it.

Slowly we climbed out of the car.

It was midday, Tuesday, just over twenty-four hours since the meeting with Olive and Christian. After four hours of work this morning I wandered from the house into the light of day.

The speed and colour of the traffic, the general clangour of commerce and society in the streets made me feel disembodied. It was as though I were taking part by proxy in a pageant that I watched through a telescope, from a vast distance.

Yet in the self-service store, compulsively reading the labels on tins and packets down to the smallest type, I was translated back from airy heights by the commonplace smells of soaps and polishes, by fluorescent lighting, the sticky burning touch of packets from the deep-freeze and the tangle of wire-baskets in the narrow passage-way.

Paying, I was released into the street again where I sauntered in a dream, occasionally, for the benefit of no one, affecting an interest in a flower-stall or shop-window.

An old woman tapped my arm imperiously. 'Someone is trying to attract your attention.'

Rollo Lawson sat at the wheel of a black convertible which was drawn up at an angle that forced exasperated blasts from passing traffic.

'Clemency!' he smiled, holding out a hand. 'I thought I recognized you as I waited at the lights. Would you like to come to Richmond Park?'

Hesitating to think, 'No', I said, 'Yes,' and slipped in beside him while he took the basket and swung it onto the floor behind us.

Soon he was driving through streets unfamiliar to me, and I listened to his soft neutral voice. 'I don't know if Christian told you, my dear, but he's a bad case. Much worse than me.'

I glanced at him. His face and hands were bloodless. I guessed that inside the rust-coloured sweater and drill trousers his frame would be emaciated.

'It was all over for Christian before I met him—that was when Stella was with Charles and Peter. She'd brought Christian from Essex. You know about his father? It was a bit grim. I think no one knew how ill Christian was then. He's always been too damaged to be able to let anyone come too close. You see that? To be known to have borne quite so much is not really bearable—is it?

'Though, ironically, it's what he's needed, above all, I suppose. Lacking a miracle.' He paused. 'I *know*, of course, because I'm not so different in that respect. And the miracle—I don't know if you'll understand quite—would be to start again from the beginning. It is ridiculous, isn't it, for a man of my age—or even his—to need a happy childhood?...

'Christian wanted very much to idolize Stella. But it was beyond him. The capacity for feeling...It's one that damages.

'He and Stella were dangerous, of course. But they had marvellous looks and great charm, and they were tremendous fun, always. And very sweet and generous about drinks and so on when one was a pauper sometimes...

'At the club I often had to ask George to line up glass after glass in the fridge that Christian insisted on buying for me...I was drinking wine, I think, then. At the time I was trying to change the pattern of my drinking. But whatever you were on, he was tremendously sweet and generous...'

For the first time, speaking of liquor, Rollo showed signs of animation and warmed up with horrific sentimentality. Till that moment he had evinced a profound and melancholy understanding of his own and Christian's plight. He had seemed, as Christian sometimes did, quite intolerably clear-sighted.

But now, with an involuntary pricking of my skin, I realized that Rollo, too, had his existence several feet off the ground. And it struck me eerily to see that for all his

184

apparent lucidity he saved his most genuine emotion for the drinks bought, years ago, by Christian, with money collected how? With what result now?

Little by little the idea that here was a normal intelligent neurotic with whom it was possible to speak a common language crept off. He was not entirely, not exactly, sane, and nothing like so honest as Christian.

'How good an actor was he?' I asked to change the subject ever so slightly, fatigued by living, on this level of empathy, by perpetually and wilfully agreeing to take leave of my senses in order to communicate.

Two women in red coats skittered across the road in front of us. I said, 'Did you ever see him at Stratford?'

'Ah...no!' Rollo frowned, lifting a hand to adjust the sunshield, 'But at the Edinburgh Festival, where he was mixed up in some excellent student affairs, I saw him. And, really, he was outstandingly good...

'Then, occasionally my parents supported certain causes that staged plays and so on for charity—I'm so sorry. Let me fix it for you.'

He tilted the biscuit-coloured shade up and out on its hinge.

'Once between seasons Christian helped us and he was everywhere...Organizing...It was great fun. At that time I had an idea that I might paint. I used to help on the décor.'

He shot a glance at me, and went on. 'Yes, I meant to be a painter, but work was unfashionable among my acquaintances and, like most of them, I was too weak to extricate myself from our rather trivial way of life.

'Not having finished anything worth mentioning, I'm free now to think that I wasted my talent. My genius. No one can contradict me. You see how satisfactory that might be.' He added, 'And it's flattering to think, at least, that one committed the worst sin of all...

'We'll soon be there. Do you know Richmond?'

'No, I don't,' I said, then asked, 'What was Stella like, Rollo? What sort of person?'

He thought as the wheel slithered round in his hands turning into the park. 'Like Christian. She was very fond of him, I think. And they pitied each other sincerely. But fondness and sincerity never connected with action. Or influenced it. Perhaps it wasn't a matter of choice...

'Now—with Stella's death—experience has turned the screw once too often. The cumulative effect of Christian's—sins—seems to have overwhelmed him. He's too hot to handle.'

I said, 'What about you? You've helped already by promising to arrange this job in Paris. You're prepared to vouch for him.'

'Ah, yes.' Rollo turned a faint and contemplative smile on me, then looked again at the road ahead. 'But I'm another black sheep. And theoretically I had every chance, so I have less excuse than Christian.'

That was no answer. I insisted, 'Even so...'

After a second he said, 'I thought I'd like to do one good deed before I die. Just one.'

Christian's words.

We drove in silence through the park and shortly left the car. When Rollo started to speak again he told me how

186

he had travelled constantly with his parents when he was a child. An early illness had excluded him from school for a term, and his mother had preserved the notion of his ill-health and kept him with her. Wherever it was gay to be, they were.

'Looking back it seems the parties lasted day and night. They used to let me mix the drinks,' he mused with a quiet kind of pride. 'Soon I was better than the professionals. I'll say that! I honestly believe I do mix a better drink than anyone in London.'

He shrugged with uncertain modesty, walking slowly, staring at the grass. 'An aptitude like anything else. Starting early. I suppose it doesn't amount to much...'

It was half a question. He sounded wistful.

I felt as if I'd been pushed over. I was a little stunned to remember that this man was thirty-seven. He had one life, would walk the earth this once, and that time was half over. Just now he had almost shyly admitted what was his finest achievement. And no! I could not think it did amount to much!

With relief and amazement in equal parts, I realized that I had no sympathy to give, that I could not expect in future to catch every wasted life that went drifting downstream. Who had I thought I was? There were too many. Rollo was drifting away and past—no business of mine. But I thought: it's not human to watch; there ought to be someone...

No, it's hopeless already, I thought. He's really lost.

And I was deeply alarmed to see that some things were impossible.

187

'Oh, wait a moment. I almost forgot.' We were looking at some ducks on a blue-grey stretch of water. Rollo dragged a crumpled paper bag from his hip pocket and carefully took out two slices of stale white bread, one of which he gave me to throw to the ducks.

The careful concentrated solicitude with which he attended to this small operation made me feel weak.

We walked on. He talked of poetry and Fanny Burney. He was very tall. His dark-brown hair was streaked with grey. He kept breaking small twigs off trees and systematically, slowly, snapping them to pieces as he talked.

'But I want to go on living,' he said once. 'I'd like a few more years.'

'Why?' I said before I thought, and shrivelled.

For an instant he stared at me curiously, then answered mildly, 'I'm interested in people. And I'd like to do something good. One good turn...'

Helen was hanging washing on the pulley in the kitchen—delicate hand-sewn things of white and pink, lace-strewn, smelling wet and clean. I leaned against the scrubbed wooden table watching her while she uncoiled the rope from the metal peg in the wall and hauled the bar to the ceiling.

'Now. Do they decide to drip or don't they?'

We stared. She unrolled the sleeves of her blouse and buttoned the cuffs again, then leaned against the cupboard opposite.

'So that's the great Lawson's son. I met him once or twice in Oxford. He sat on various committees connected with the unit.'

'*Rollo* did? Oh, his father! What was he like?'

'Luckier than Rollo! Much crusty charm, much assurance, strong personality. He's been all right. Oh, God, they are dripping! I'll have to squeeze them in this towel.'

Soon we wandered out, switching off the light. I said, fatuously, 'London is no help to someone like Rollo. Or the climate. At home life is lived in the open—I don't just mean the athletic extrovert sort...'

'Heaven forbid!' Helen teased, very solemn.

We laughed idly, lazily. 'Are you taking those sleeping tablets?' she asked as I flopped on her divan.

'Yes.'

'Do they make any difference?'

'No.'

Helen stood by the window filing her short unpolished nails. 'So the appointment's made for him,' she repeated abstractedly. 'In ten days' time. Hamilton's a good man.'

'Fine.' I was to accompany Christian to the psychologist's consulting-room to guarantee his arrival, and to collect him.

'Well, I must have a bath and get into something respectable,' she declared, going to the wardrobe to fish for a dress. 'These annual dinners! Not so very long till Lewis comes home,' she added, in a peculiar voice, disappearing to turn on her bath.

Oh, wasn't it? Hemming me in, thinking at me, both of them!

Sharpened with anger, instinctively resisting pressure, I sat up. And passing Helen in the carpeted passage way,

I said flatly, 'Have a good time!' and half-accidentally slammed the door. Alone, in a quiet passion of exultation I surveyed my room, my cubic feet of privacy.

I had not saved myself from the running stream to be strangled by loving kindness.

Taking off the tan suede jacket he sat down, grave and dignified and sentimental. 'But you offered it,' he repeated gently. 'Olive didn't ask. Why did you do it for me? Why, darling? It's important to me to know.'

And he leaned forward to study me, curious and impressed by what he called his rescue, wanting and expecting to be wrung by my words.

He liked to melt over small gifts, trite expressions of sentiment, conventional pity, a conventional soft heart, a conventional stiff upper lip, over anything romantic, however hackneyed. He liked to be made to melt. I had seen his eyes soften before now with a sort of blind fascination at the sound of a high-flown cliché.

'Why did you help me?' he asked, ardent with the expectation of noble words.

In his face his intention was written: long ago he had discarded responsibility for himself, now he had an inclination to bestow himself on me.

Umm, I thought, boggling slightly. Nothing ever happened for the right reasons. A display of power—power to keep him out of trouble—counted more than most things, after all.

I said it was easy to give what you had, that I'd have done it for any friend in a jam.

He looked down. There was not a single emotional peg for him to hang a sigh on. Had all things been equal, had I been present in my own person, for my own pleasure, I might have been softened by his crestfallen air, his look of hurt at my lack of response. But I was on guard twice over, guarding my disinterest—which he interpreted as lack of interest—as well as his best interests.

We started to work.

Well, I had stuck to the rules. Though these were somewhat fluid and as yet not fully defined I knew that A was: Never argue; and B was: Never judge.

A looser, vaguer, weapon was the kind of mental passive resistance movement I had improvised during the long days and nights when we'd had telephone communication only.

To be of value to himself, Christian himself would have to choose his way. Whatever the provocation I wouldn't move to hinder or influence him. All I was to be allowed was concentrated mental resistance to any schemes and attitudes that were harmful to him. The means as well as the ends should be good.

In effect, I told him: 'Rampage over the country if you must—over me, over Olive and yourself: I won't argue or restrain you, but I will trust and you will slowly stop. And... everyone will live happy ever after.'

That was surely right?

Olive was sucked dry. Out of nowhere the understanding had sprung up that it was my turn to do what I could with him. He would go through his paces, and we would see who won. He *would* break free, grow up, I was

191

certain. But in the meantime, looking wickedly over his shoulder, 'Are you watching me now? You must dislike me for this!' he would never see me shocked or reproving.

I backed myself to stand it, confident that at least some of those disunited states he called 'I' were on my side.

Now, after about an hour's work, in the middle of translating a passage, he looked up, ambiguous and sleepy-sly of eye, leaving one finger of his right hand to keep his place in the book.

'You think I stole it, don't you? The fifty pounds. You think I made off with old Carruthers' money and lied about losing it to get it out of you?'

Sluggishly the meaning sank into my brain.

That he might have tricked me? Lied about it all?

Softly, coolly confused, my mind turned on itself, feeling mislaid. No, he *hadn't* cheated me, but he could *think* of it, and I had simply never...Oh, I was feeble! Nowhere near alert enough! Still too inexperienced...

'Don't be boring! Come on, you're doing well tonight. Let's start at the top of the page again.' And I gave an ironic smile, conveying contradictory messages that would cover every facet of the situation to his acute and wary eyes.

For a moment he seemed to be listening quizzically, then he gave a great smile of approbation. He laughed, leaning across, one hand on the arm of my chair. 'But I *might* have stolen it and kidded you,' he persisted, laughing a little, and watching me closely still. Then he added, seeming vaguely put upon, sad and petulant, 'You trust me, don't you? No one else does. Perhaps you shouldn't either. I don't know…Close that book. We've finished for tonight. I've done—don't tell me—brilliantly.'

'Like some coffee?'

'What time is it?'

I told him, pushing aside the books on the table.

'Ten minutes and I'll have to go. Olive will be waiting. Tonight I'll have to repeat every word we said, say how many lights were on, and what you wore, where we sat… You don't care, though. You aren't jealous.'

I looked at him.

'You don't really love me at all. You couldn't help being jealous if you did. And you aren't. Why don't you admit it? You might as well. I can see it in your face!' He glittered at me for a second in triumph, then the conclusion turned his thoughts inward. His eyes no longer saw. Baffled, wild and blank, they gleamed in his face. He fell back on the divan, half-lying across it. 'Then why…? Why are you so nice to me?'

Not bed? Not money? What else was there?

'Not pity?' He shot up, glaring and rigid.

'Try not to be stupid.'

'Then what? Anyway, you ought to be sorry for me,' he suddenly grinned. 'Olive is. A wasted life!'

'Oh, God!' I groaned. 'It's time you went home. Look at the clock.'

But his face had softened incredibly. A hand came up. 'Ah, darling, don't swear. Don't say that. It isn't like you.'

And I was slightly enchanted. It was ridiculous—the way I was spasmodically, romantically, canonized along with Stella and Olive—but I was a little enchanted just the same. And I smiled at him, and did love him in a way, and did feel irresponsible.

'What will you tell Olive tonight?'

'Nothing,' he said flatly, after a pause, his face sulky and shut. 'I'll tell her nothing,' he said again.

Almost awkwardly, he said, 'What do you think it's *like* for me to go back to Olive after being with you? I don't think you understand how it is. How wrong...'

He looked up, and from his eyes looked out with nervous earnestness, with terrible appeals, the boy he might have been.

So this was where—in discarding charm, and laying weakness, bewilderment and fear before me—this was where his courage and affection were spent.

My expression had petrified some seconds back into one, I suppose, of bright scepticism.

Now, seeing what it was, he seemed strangely to wince, and grow heavier. 'Oh, stop it, Clem!'

Quenched, I stared down at the carpet, then up at him. 'I'm sorry.'

'You don't have a very high opinion of me. Because of what you know—'

'That isn't fair.'

'But you do think I want only to chalk you up?...And it isn't so. You're wrong. All my life, Clem, I've had people wanting me for themselves. They called it love. It suited me. Sometimes I feel I've never even liked anyone but Stella. I don't—relax with people. Yes, there's a lot of gay chit-chat; yes, I have to make them like me, but I don't—' He broke off, head down, hands together.

'Do you know what it's like to lie awake beside someone who's insane about you, knowing they want you? When you feel nothing but pity and sometimes not that?…All right. You don't have to tell me,' his mouth twisted a little in a parody of a smile, 'I'll hate myself in the morning. I know. I'm finished.'

'You'll be late.'

'I'm going.'

Easily, with a minimum of effort, he rose and came to stand behind my chair. I turned quickly to face him, kneeling on the edge of it holding the back. 'Well, good night…I'll see you on Wednesday at half-past six.'

He said nothing. I felt awkward. We were too intimate for this sort of formality, too involved.

'You're talking to me,' he whispered, smiling with a sweet and coaxing familiarity. 'You're a funny girl. Very young. Darling Clem. I've been too nervous to touch you. Sometimes I'm a little bit afraid of you. I don't know what you want. But if you could put up with me, I know what I want. What can I say? "You're too good for me!" Yes, it's funny. It's also true. But I want to be with you, Clem, want us to live together, make love, wake up together. And all the ordinary things…Don't you want that, too? Don't you?' Pleading in a distracted and distracting sort of way. I half-listened.

Now somehow we were standing together, arms loosely entwined, comfortably close: not exciting, but soothing, a relief, I felt our closeness to be. I felt as if something was killing me. The pressure of his personality.

'Couldn't we be happy together? You want that, too, don't you?' he repeated softly.

Did I? I just had no idea. I simply couldn't tell. Trying to edge away from the blank space where some opinion should have been, I said without smiling. 'What difference would it make if I did?'

'Oh, darling!'

Relaxedly, mouth to mouth, we stood, solid and warm, young and alive. It was rather nice. I felt passive and contented. I knew where Christian was for once, and that was a relief. He was fairly happy, too, and so was I. Then, during this long silence I was spared the sound of his voice which, charming beyond other voices though it was, expressed too convoluted a logic too constantly to make a lengthy subjection to it anything but wearing.

'Clem...' For a moment I saw his eyes, large-pupilled, soft and blurred, then we were re-plaited more warmly, more tightly, than before. And there was no more thought.

At length we broke apart in silence, swayed about a bit, leaned against handy pieces of furniture.

He looked down, hesitated, said, 'Sometimes I used to think you saw me just as some kind of psychological case. You know—a rather aged Teddy boy...And then I used to wonder if you could even want to know someone like me, with my sort of history...'

The element of truth in his first suggestion made me confusedly guilty and indignant. Excuses and arguments shot stultified into the air about my head. Mute, I could only stare at him with what I hoped was eloquent reproach.

'Well, I am, I am,' he insisted, leaning back on his hands against the chest of drawers. 'I'm not saying I'm not every kind of delinquent but—that isn't how you think of me now, is it? You do like me?'

'Well, of course! Would I have...Do you think I'd have—'

My voice dwindled.

Christian looked at me, mildly struck. Then he gave a delighted crow of laughter and came to smile over me at close quarters. 'You mean, darling, that you wouldn't kiss someone—like that—that you didn't like quite a lot?'

'No!' It was almost thrilling to be so sure of something, 'Of course not!' I said self-righteously, finding the certainty really heady.

Christian stood against me, suddenly possessed by a private mood of heavy doting admiration. I felt a little as though I were somewhere else. His face looked heavy with thought. 'Yes, you are good,' he murmured to himself. 'That's why I love you. Wonderful and good and clean...'

Feeling faintly baited, I said, 'Oh, Christian!'

He questioned me sharply, 'You aren't promiscuous? You don't lie? You haven't robbed anyone? You haven't ruined peoples' lives?'

So black and white! I protested, 'But—'

'You're good,' he silenced me, with a lowering of his brows. 'Except, of course, that you're hurting poor Olive by making love to me—so perhaps you're a little bit bad, too.'

'Oh, fine! You're going to be very late if you don't go.'

At the wash-basin he stared at himself in the mirror. 'May I borrow your brush?' And he smoothed his soft fair hair, frowning the while and saying over his shoulder, 'But you know, Miss James, you're a complicated woman. Your

197

reactions to everything surprise me. I'm only used to tough or stupid—'

I switched on the light, not answering. He was accustomed, perhaps, to women swooning at his feet? Evidently. I could believe it. For reasons undefined, I felt a confused mixture of compunction and determination.

'What are you going to do when I've gone?' He lifted Rollo's jacket from the divan and put it on in one smooth slow movement.

I shrugged. 'Have a bath. Go to bed.'

He said nothing but looked down rather seriously. 'What can I take? Let me have something of yours…A book.' He lifted a library book, plastic-covered, from the bedside table. 'May I? What's it about? A *library* book?' he discovered. 'Oh, darling!' Very reproachful. Letting the side down. I thought he was going to put it back again.

'What's wrong with it?'

'Oh, darling,' he said gently. 'You should *buy* books.'

I raised my brows. 'Why didn't I think of that?' My fingers turned the brass knob to open the door and pressed up the catch. He was hopeless. I did in a way almost adore him. I could have screamed at him.

'When we're together you'll have an account at Harrods.' This was very stern.

I felt my mouth curl. 'That'll be nice.'

'Don't smile!' he protested, his eyes darting with agitation. 'I hate it when you're sarcastic. It's not you. We'll be together. Don't smile as if you didn't believe a word I said.'

We exchanged a long look—frantic, distrustful, on his part, relaxed, affectionate, on mine. It was an effort.

I put a hand on his. I would feel nothing, but my heart was drained. I said, 'I'm truly sorry, darling.'

I apologized to Christian often—usually, ostensibly, for a word or expression so harmless that once, overhearing, Olive was incredulous, 'You apologize to him!'

But we both knew.

I apologized for knowing him. This was his due and he accepted it.

It was wrong to see through his deceptions, wrong to hold out a hand from a position of strength, wrong to feel compassion, I thought. If he knew, he would want to murder me, and would be right to want to. One might be better dead than known?

He asked now to be dependent, willingly submitted himself to Olive or anyone who would take him—right now, if I wanted it, to me. But I would not be strong at his expense. I would not—to nourish his weakness—take the reins he lately offered, impose order, lead him on strings, humour, belittle, humiliate the adult in him.

In his power equally as he was in mine I would have to be.

Deadly, without feeling, I thought: there is a touch of madness. It rose visibly in his eyes—a weird second self, conspicuous as a harvest moon or a pantomime villain...

Oh, *no*, not madness, but—

A knock. Helen called, 'I heard Christian go. What about some supper?'

I had been standing in the middle of the floor. 'Yes. One minute.'

A face extremely pale, a mouth without a trace of lipstick, eyes so distant that I put up a hand to the looking-glass to orientate myself in space, to assure myself that an arm could reach the shiny surface that reflected them.

The lessons went forward. It was April, now May. Christian came regularly, punctual and sober, bringing homework to be corrected, working like a sixth-former intent on a state scholarship.

Words made us laugh. Once, in the early days, I said, 'Say: "Tell me why you prefer—"' Tired at the end of the night's session, he said defiantly, '*Direz-me! Direz, direz-me!*'

Into the hours of work he infused a carnival gaiety, and behind the serious exchange of glances, his pertinent questions, my reiterated, 'Because—' behind his critical interest in accent and rhythm, and faces too busy to smile, our eyes sent soft familiar messages.

Intense concentration made it seem that syntax and vocabulary flowed automatically from my head to his, suffering no loss or confusion. We became complementary machines. A switch had been touched and a current of knowledge passed between us.

And aeons of time existed contemporaneously with this traffic, it seemed, in which we could sit relaxed, sweetly amused by the carnival of life, and soundlessly laughing...

In a house across the street somewhere castanets clicked inexpertly to the introductory music of some Light Programme feature. I had been working. This unlikely sound had nibbled at my attention—now it made me smile. Castanets in Knightsbridge!

I sat at the table by the windows, looking out, the papers under my arms lifting now and then in the breeze. An early summer heat-wave had closed in on the city, and I was transfixed in the hazy hot blue afternoon, with the headmaster in the school along the street intoning, 'Boys! Boys!' droning out of his windows into mine, 'Silence, boys!' An autocrat. A marvellous man, one could not doubt.

'Now *he* would tell me how to fix my life,' Christian said another afternoon, listening with delighted respect to that minatory voice. '"Roland, go out into the world and forget yourself! Work among the Unfortunates till you have expiated your sins!"'

I had started to laugh at the uncanny reproduction of that distant scholar's voice.

'That's what sinners are supposed to do, isn't it? Serve mankind in some lowly and dangerous capacity?'

'And what would you say to such advice?'

He reflected. 'I'd say, "Perhaps that's a good idea." And then,' falling into a mock-heroic pose, one hand on his heart, 'after years of selfless toil in the jungle I'd come back—a physical wreck, but a *bigger* man—and make an honest woman of Clemency James, who would have waited for me—naturally—sacrificing the best years of her life for our love.'

We smiled very dryly and carefully.

'And then—and then I'd have a clear conscience and we would be very happy.'

'And very old.' It was a game, just a game, but not very amusing.

'Would it take so long?' he cried, shocked, as if I had information denied him.

His hold was precarious! His brilliance made the night about him, into which he might yet fall, seem astronomically dark.

I sighed. The voices faded. I felt hot. My hair was still damp after being washed. I touched it.

'Silence! Silence!' The school-master again. Then the cry of an onion-seller on his bike, riding by. And a hoover downstairs, and trees shifting murmurously, and distant buses. Water in the pipes under the basin, and a single fly sounding half-dead...A plane making for London Airport.

I worked till half-past three. At four o'clock Lewis was due to arrive. He'd returned the night before from New York, and Helen and Bertrand and one or two people from the office had met him, but I wasn't free. When Helen came in after midnight I'd asked her for news, for his letters—frequent and closely-written—I had read, as it were, by radar, and scrapped, remembering almost nothing. Then this morning came his call: the office was closed today. Would it be convenient if he came across at four?

Returning from the bathroom, I hung up my towel, put away toilet-bag and dressing-gown, and went about cool in a white petticoat, collecting stockings from the drawer, and my pink dress.

Not to quarrel with him, not to be flat, not to be rude or bored. What was there left to be? Wrenching my mind over to the idea of Lewis was enormously exhausting.

202

Nevertheless, I plonked my concentration in front of his image and said: *Be nice.*

He was more real than I'd remembered. His face was thin and thoughtful. His look weighed on me with a sort of anxious affection. At once I resented his interest physically, as my stomach would have resented a meal of cut-glass.

'Lovely to see you, Lewis. How was the journey?'

'Smooth. No, it wasn't as hot in New York as here... This is a nice room, Clem. Helen said it was...Here. This is for you. I hope it's all right.'

'What is it?' I took the large brown-paper parcel and held it for a moment while Lewis turned away, wandering about hands in pockets, peering out of the windows.

'—good to be back, especially to this sort of weather, but I'd like to have a few months there with no schedule...'

I wheedled at the knots in the parcel, and in a few moments lifted an expensive-looking black handbag from a cherry-coloured box. It was immensely smart. I liked it tremendously, mentally repented, and repented that I should repent for such a reason.

'Heavens,' I said faintly. 'What initiative, Lewis! I like it very much.'

'Yes, I was pleased with myself,' he admitted, trying not to look too gratified at his success. 'I remembered you wanted one.'

When we were sitting down I encouraged him to talk about his trip, interested to do a little vicarious travelling. And obligingly and well, he did talk. For minutes I was fascinated. Then the walls began to shrink around us. His voice seemed loud, intrusive, each word a small penance to me.

203

In parenthesis I murmured I must turn on the wireless for the time: my clock had stopped. Lewis had the time. He was reabsorbed in his description—an acute appraisal of the people and places he'd seen.

Half-killed by the sight of him in my room, by the strain of unconscious demands on my attention, I went to the basin to get a glass of water.

'—the climate of feeling now...elections...Stevenson...immigration laws...UN and China...anti-Semitic...'

Once I might have been enthralled; now, dully, without reverberation, the words and phrases dropped dead in my mind. I asked no questions, but Lewis, his eyes fixed thoughtfully in space, made point after point in his lucid unselfconscious style, reasoning, contending, convincing, unaware that his expressions were not mirrored in my face, unaware of any impression he might be making, conscious of himself for the moment as no more than a transmitter of ideas.

Goaded, I cried suddenly, 'Your shoes are muddy! How did you manage that on such a lovely day?'

He looked at me without seeing for a second. Then he looked at his shoes—slowly, guiltily, returning to himself. They became visible to him.

'So they are. The road was up outside the flat. I walked across.' Inside his own skin again, he said, 'Was I stunning you with statistics? You should have stopped me.'

'No, no!' I insisted, feeling horrible. 'Please go on.'

'You look thinner.'

'No. It's the heat. But could we get outside? Go for a walk, do you think?'

Five minutes later we were tearing along Knightsbridge in the sun, through the crowds, eyes on the dry white footpath as it shot beneath our feet, suddenly talking like mad and seeing nothing till we passed Green Park, luminous, glorious, banked with daffodils and daffodils.

And now, outside in the air, everything turned inside out. This was healthy—racing through the warm afternoon air, with bare arms, with Lewis talking, hands in pockets, and making the world expand. Yes, this was real life! Where had it been? What had been happening? This was the return of the native, the return journey from the centre of a volcano. I couldn't hear enough. I couldn't hear enough to suffocate the little voice whispering: or is this the way *out* of reality?

Past the Ritz and on to Piccadilly we sped, then stopped, almost rearing at the traffic and the signs. 'Let's not go any further,' I said, and we shot downstairs to the small café of a newsreel theatre.

Lewis peered about in uncritical surprise. 'Do you come here often?'

'No. But sometimes. It's dark, isn't it? Rather holy?' It was impossible not to lower your voice. The four other customers—two lots of two almost invisible in the corners—were inaudible.

Settled opposite, Lewis started to take me in as though I were a barometer. But stimulated by the air and the talk, and the view of the park, I rattled on about the café.

Music was coming from the newsreel. Now I looked up from the red plush banquette where I'd laid my gloves and bag.

Lewis said nothing. He handed me the menu. 'What would you like?'

'What's the matter?'

He looked away from me as if he were bored, as if I were making a scene.

'*What's the matter?*'

Cold, hostile, he directed his eyes towards me with extreme distaste. 'I asked Helen how you were.'

'And she said?'

'Not very much.' He looked at me inimically. 'So you're going on with it?'

I tried to understand. Leaning against the cushioned wall, feebly holding my hands together in my lap, I looked at his averted face.

'Going on with it?'

Lewis scrubbed his forehead with clenched knuckles and said nothing. My blood began to stir. I felt like saying coarsely, 'Be yourself!' For really he was most unlike himself, unused to scenes, bad at them. His failure to do himself justice doubled my animosity.

'Yes?' the waitress waited.

Eyes clamped together hard, quite killingly polite, we discussed the menu. 'Tea and toast is what's customary. Let's have that, shall we?'

Lewis ordered it, repeating after the woman had gone, 'Tea and toast!' with dreadful affected irony. It was awful.

With a muted explosion we were suddenly quarrelling, with rancour, without reason. Bitterly, bitterly, I answered, resenting his having forced this on me, having no interest in, no energy for, this sort of duel.

206

What gave him the right to be so grotesquely censorious? Had he and Helen formed a society for my protection? What was it to him how I spent my time? Certainly he liked a calm and stable life, and for a time, calmly stably working, I'd been a part of it. If I moved, a piece of the pattern broke, but I surely had a right to my own existence if it *was* inconvenient for him? In his mind my image was cast in bronze, hard set: in my own it was fluid. If he wasn't, I was too young not to change. But, also, a youthful manner was as easily discarded as assumed: I no longer craved instruction, if I ever had.

We had talked at once: now we both stopped. I stared at the tablecloth.

What *was* it? Lewis had never loved me. He loved Gabrielle, belonged to Gabrielle, whose husband was his friend, and who had two children, one of whom was his godson. This was one of the reasons I'd been able to like him.

The surface of his mind had been diverted by me undoubtedly—the Wild Colonial girl, the Disciple, the young Court Jester, eventually, the Practical Girl who said, 'Buy some socks!' And there was the girl who knew about Gabrielle and accepted it, which made her pleasant female company and safe—part of the cosy routine of life: so many telephone calls, so many meetings, a week.

If he was afraid for me with Christian, he was afraid for his own convenience, too. His motives were mixed.

Searching the swollen spaces of amazement and dismay for some parallel to drive home my disappointment and incredulity, I said, 'It's like Suez!'

'No, you overrate yourself!' He sounded venomous.

One of us must have missed the other's point.

But just then, in the middle of it all, I could have laughed aloud with a whole heart. For it did sound bats. It was crazy. I had no staying-power. My heart rocked with the desire for the relief of laughter. I longed to laugh and say, 'Have you heard all this rubbish?'

But no. Catching Lewis's eyes, I knew it was impossible. And the laughter curdled, wearily disintegrated to a sigh.

The quarrel fizzled out. We were in public, weren't we? Among respectable people eating tea and toast? With the wretched, harrowed look of convalescents we eyed each other.

Lewis began to present his case again. I smashed nothing, and did neither of us any physical damage. The tea had come; I poured it. We snatched at the toast and stuffed it down, barely chewed; gulping the hot tea.

'How can someone like you admire a fellow like that, Clem? Why should the act of admission—which comes easily, after all, to exhibitionists like Roland—release him from responsibility for his actions?'

Half-strangled with grief, I listened. How could he add blame to that sense of sin?

'Yes, he does admit, Lewis. Sometimes he's unbalanced by his sense of guilt. He doesn't need to be blamed.'

'The point is—you condone his actions. You excuse him everything.'

Condoned? Frustration in me, misunderstanding in Lewis, reached their highest peaks. The very bones of

208

my forehead drew together in frowns. Not to cry, I half-laughed, and took another piece of toast.

A woman appeared in the doorway, pausing to select a table in the lamp-lit gloom. We stared at her for relief—a tall strongly-built woman with heavy black hair hanging to her shoulders, a beige corduroy dress, muscular legs like a dancer. She might have been a Yugoslav. Passing us on very high heels, she dropped her gloves and Lewis lifted them— transparent nylon with frills, like jellyfish, not designed to cheer—and returned them to her in a hand that shook. I stared at it and into his eyes.

'More tea?' When it was poured, though he took no sugar, Lewis stirred and stirred while we tried again, with the simplicity of exhaustion, to explain our separate points of view.

In effect he was asking how I could like what was not admirable, not seeming to understand the subjectivity of admiration, and its irrelevance, anyway, to liking.

I couldn't escape from the awful domination of words he wished on us. My soul was wordless! I might love someone, but what I felt wasn't something to be held in the mouth or head of this man across the table. Not something to be tied down with words or reasons. At no great distance from me, some extension of my being was under torture. And I could not escape.

'You've known a host of people who've overcome hard luck. It isn't an excuse,' he said.

'But people are different, Lewis! Have different potentials.'

'So what do you want me to admit?'

209

'Just that someone like Christian is tried more than most of us.'

'I don't see it.'

'Because people who are *wanted* so much have situations created round them constantly. And important ones, involving lives. They're tempted more. Who can say: "In his place, I would be better!"?'

Lewis noticed what was in his hand—the last strip of toast, and laid it suddenly on his plate. I wiped my buttery fingers on a torn handkerchief, and looked down, sullen.

'That's exactly my point—there always *is* a choice. Though it's smart today to create a little havoc, spontaneously—it's too easy, too simple, to please yourself first, then repent and be forgiven because of your unhappy childhood.'

'You're very hard.' I felt at my side for my gloves. 'There's the waitress, Lewis—You're very hard. People do what they can. Everyone isn't like you.'

'No. People do what they want to do. They follow their inclinations and then say, "Help!"'

'It takes good fortune as well as natural gifts to form a man of enlightened inclinations. If you're one, it seems less than generous to pass judgement on—on someone else who's...You're different, I don't doubt, but I can remember moments when less luck or more vitality would have sent *me* careering off—'

'On the road to ruin!' Lewis exclaimed, inexplicably laughing. And still laughing, he called for the cheque and we left the café. 'I love your passion for identification with villains!'

'Oh, do you?'

Very slowly, not talking, we walked back along Piccadilly, past shops and park, into the pale piercing radiance
of the early night sky.

Without wishing it, I suddenly heard Christian's voice,
gently assured and sanctimonious: *'There but for the grace
of God go I, you must think, Clem,'* himself seated before
me on the floor with the self-containment of a holy man.
Was this what I defended?

'What's wrong?' asked Lewis. 'Look out! We can't
cross yet.' We paused at Hyde Park Corner.

'I didn't speak.'

'You said, "Oh, God!" as if you'd remembered something unpleasant.'

'Oh? No. It's blank now. Look! Isn't that policeman
nice, Lewis? This is the most murderous corner in London
for pedestrians, so you can't help feeling cosseted when he...'

The policeman on point duty sauntered purposefully
out from the island across the street and the traffic stopped
for us. 'But remember, Lewis,' I added somewhat solemnly,
as if it followed, 'that under certain circumstances, at a
certain time, anyone can do anything.'

He ignored me.

And did I think so, really? When I spoke I believed what
I said. But now, already, I was forgetting why it seemed so
true, or so important.

I was a little surprised by the slide of tears across my
eyes, hardly noticeable to me.

That awful smile! The Grace of God!

'Oh, Lewis, thank you for arguing with me! Don't
stop! I don't know what's the matter...'

211

CHAPTER TEN

Voices from the street came through my open window. It was a hot greyish sunny day. 'We'll pay for this. Yes, we'll have a hard winter.'

An English 'character'. Life imitating art in the hair-raising way it did over here. Art limiting life. Impulse moribund...

Lucy Turner was emptying the meter. I had been writing an essay. 'Your Indian neighbour,' she said scathingly. 'He says he's gone to share a flat with a friend. It's always a mistake to take them in.' She closed the meter and laughed sharply. 'He's probably no more a student than I am!'

A short slight boy, he was, a medical student with melancholy eyes and a quick white radiant smile that lit not only his brown-skinned face, but the dark corners of hearts for miles around I would have thought. We had often talked in the kitchen, and several times he'd accepted an invitation to have coffee at night with Helen and me, and stayed to talk for ages.

I said to Lucy Turner now, 'I'm sure he's a student. Why would he try to deceive you?'

'Wait till you're my age!' she cried, laughing in her roguish ribald way, her large eyes darting about on a tour of inspection. Two canvas bags—one for shillings, one for pennies—hung from a milky manicured hand; the other sleeked and massaged Lucy's tightly bound self with a sort of restrained anger. She *did* dislike me. I was so glad.

The essay was finished when I heard footsteps on the stairs and Helen's and Quentin's voices above the crackling of paper parcels. Someone rattled the door-handle.

'Clem?...Do stop. Come and see what I've bought and have some lunch.'

A hot Saturday at lunch-time with everything closing and people making off to the country, or driving up from Oxford, like Quentin, this morning, and flying with Helen to Sweden this afternoon for a holiday. Essays!...Cut flowers overflowing from barrows, and gaudy ripe fruit at street-corners, and newly set hair and scent, and everyone rushing to be happy. Essays!

We had prawns and brown bread and butter in Helen's room, Quentin sitting on the floor and making us laugh, telling gruesome stories with a straight face. I tried to see him as the brilliant diagnostician he was, as he sat, tie askew and shirt sleeves rolled up, eating prawns with his fingers because of our cutlery shortage, and drinking lager.

'Don't do any more this afternoon, Clem. You're not a machine,' Helen said. 'You know what it's like when

213

Bertrand and Quentin get together: they think they admire one another tremendously, but after they've shaken hands I have to carry them. Support me and come out to the airport with us. It's much too nice to be in, anyway.'

'I'm misrepresented but yes, you must come, Clem,' declared Quentin, handing his glass up to Helen.

The prospect of their holiday, the heat and suitcases and tissue paper and suntan lotion, the swimming costumes and new Penguins and sunglasses—all the paraphernalia I eyed without envy—made it impossible for them to stop smiling.

Next to Bertrand, who came over after two, Quentin looked craggy and angular. His black hair fell over his forehead in a great hank; his eyebrows were thick and pointed, his chin square, his eyes blue-grey and level.

How was it that he was more agreeable than Bertrand? For he was conservative, a little bit old-fashioned, eager, yet stern and straight-forward. It dawned on me slowly what a source of rest and good cheer his temperament must be to Helen—never quite knowing, never quite understanding her. The attraction of opposites. Yes, that was really what it meant, of course.

Leaving the airport, Bertrand drove on to Windsor which was full of buses and cameras, then slowly back to London. He suggested dinner and a play but I invented excuses, not liking him well enough to spend an evening in his company.

On the way he told me something I already knew—that he and Christian had had several encounters at the pub near the corner since their informal meeting in my room.

214

I remembered Christian's excitement. Had I discussed him with Bertrand at all, and if so, what did Bertrand think? How clever was he? How much money did he make? I remembered his anxiety to have yet another interpretation of himself. Opinions were like horoscopes—every man his fortune-teller.

Sunday continued hot. At ten o'clock as I sat by the open windows cramming, I heard voices in the kitchen and deduced that Mrs Turner had found a plumber to repair the leak in the hot-water tank. Pitching her voice a tone or two higher, the better to stress her elevation, she seemed to be acting as overseer. How to be very, very popular!

I stared again at the questions set by the college tutor.

How quiet it was out in the bright June street. Even the metallic hammering from the kitchen, competing furiously with Lucy's voice, couldn't make the house seem anything but deserted, full of nothing but summer air and scents. I watched the tree-tops move, faintly aware of the customary activity just below the surface of my mind, the intense busyness.

'Miss James!...I'm sorry to disturb you. It's the plumber—' Standing in the doorway, Lucy explained about the noises.

Oh dear. Since the morning before her hair had become an alarming burgundy. We stood face to face at the door, each with an arm raised to the wall for support.

'No, it doesn't disturb me.'

Under the impression that a smiling mouth hid the rest of her face and intentions, Lucy sent her eyes spying boldly over me.

'I wish I could wear a sleeveless dress,' she murmured, then cried, her manner changing quite radically, 'Oh, Miss James, I'm so sorry! I should have left a note for you but I had to go out. Your Mr Roland rang yesterday while you were away. I happened to be up looking at this naughty tank when he called...'

As self-appointed censor of her tenants' guests, it was inevitable that she should have encountered Christian frequently, if not so frequently as she had. Caught in the hall the two of us would hover in front of her, propitiatory as children about to beg a favour, in the hope of escape. But Lucy was trapped by the illusory built-in messages in Christian's speaking eyes, and would herself stand self-forgetful as a child before a Christmas tree a-glitter with stars and promises of joy.

A conversation would spring up about lazy workmen or cigarette smoking or Swiss hotels. Gradually we'd step back, Lucy following, flustered and voluble. Eventually, cordially, but with regal finality, we would escape.

And Christian would say, amused, sympathetic, 'She's not too bad! I like her!' (The accolade. But he said it, at first, of almost everyone he met.) 'Just the same I couldn't take too much of her. And she shouldn't dye her hair that colour. It's vile! Will I tell her? Do you dare me? She wouldn't mind if I did, you know.'

If a few days passed without their meeting, Lucy would happen to appear when I collected my mail, her hand going to my arm to restrain me. 'Your charming Mr Roland! Is he studying law like you? No?...Such a friendly straightforward young man! I don't think I've seen him lately?'

Even Gertie's tough old hatchet face melted in smiles when he raised a hand in greeting. She mentioned him often, in a rather exclusive way, since he had made some enquiry about her bandaged foot.

I wondered sometimes what it could be like so constantly to be the object of so much expectation. Knowing his situation it often seemed to me unfair and cruelly demanding that casual strangers should command his charm, but somehow, I knew, these were the demands he was made to stand. Frequently when Lucy, or Gertie, or Lucy's 'distinguished lecturer' from the ground-floor, froze in front of him like characters on a broken film, I tried to disbelieve in magic. Though I could feel the stillness in the air, it seemed too strange. Yet it did seem that he was obliged to supply what they were obliged to want, and that each was essential to the other as if it were a minor law of nature.

Now I said to Lucy, trying not to seem anxious, 'Did he leave a message? What did he say?'

Nothing. I went back to my seat at the table and Lucy returned to harangue the unhappy plumber. 'These workmen!'

Christian never rang on Saturdays. What had happened? He'd been working for the car company for some weeks now. Everything there had been fine at our last meeting, hadn't it?

'They love me still!' he declared, gazing about the room in ingenuous wonder. 'The directors are terribly decent types, terribly democratic. We "old boy" each other all over the place. They keep asking me to join them for drinks and—don't worry—I keep refusing. Am I good?'

217

'Wonderful.'

'I'm so grateful to you, Clem.'

'Don't be. How do you get on with the customers?'

'Swimmingly. I'm monotonous, aren't I? But it's true, darling. All these old boys and girls. It's great fun. I salute them, you know, with tremendous discretion, never obsequious but earnest rather—like a student in the summer vacation who wants large tips. "Well, Roland," they say, "one doesn't expect to find a young fellow of your type on a job like this!" That's a bit awkward. I don't like it when they're curious. But then,' he admitted, 'I don't like it when they're not, either.'

'What do you do?'

He shrugged. 'So what does one do? "It's for a wager, as a matter of fact, sir, with one of the chaps at the club. Rather foolish, actually!" Or one gives a gay laugh. "Well, actually, I was unfit for National Service, sir, and the pater thought I ought to rough it a bit, you know, and see life, before I joined him in the City."' He set his teeth together. 'Or you can say—' He stopped with a reluctant, one-sided grin, 'I won't say it! I don't want you to drop dead.'

Between shifts he completed the homework he was set, and drank nothing but coffee. The day when he would go to Paris, a new man, was vivid and real to him. He talked of it constantly.

I'd been working for half an hour when the phone rang and made me jump as if Big Ben had crashed in my ear.

'Where were you when I called yesterday?' He was drunk.

'Out. At London Airport with Helen.'

218

'Enjoying yourself. I wanted to talk. Who else was there?'

'Has something happened? What's the matter?'

'Oh, darling,' his voice mumbled off incoherently. 'If you loved me—if—but you don't, you don't. If you did, you'd be there when I needed you.'

'What happened?'

'Nothing. I'm fired. Booted out. Sacked. That's all. Nothing important!'

Then he forgot what he was saying and grumbled and fumbled and ground to a stop. But it transpired that his firm had asked again for a personal reference. In a moment of panic he'd given Charles's name, trusting that there would be no further check.

'*Charles?*...You mean the man whose flat— Stella's—'

'*Charles*. So it was stupid. We all know that now. But Olive thought it was a good idea, too, at the time. He's what these—little men think of as important. He's used their cars at odd times. I thought—if they did approach him, he might still try to help. Once he would have come back across half the world to please me or Stella. But people change when you're down on your luck and penniless.' He sounded vicious.

'People change when you abuse their trust,' I corrected him hardly.

'Anyway, it's the end of Roland, the chauffeur. Prob'ly told them about the great robbery at his flat. Prob'ly hinted I'd steal the engines out of one of their—I won't say it—cars. Prob'ly said I'd use it to rob a bank...Oh, Clem, they said things, horrible things. They didn't *like* me any more...

219

'—can't fight all this forever—better dead. Better dead,' he said in a dead, sane voice, and hung up.

This wasn't the first time he'd threatened suicide, true. But the fact of his not having killed himself regularly following every threat, carried no guarantee that he might not one day—perhaps this very day—be strained beyond his resources, be pushed—even by pique if he were not granted the respect of belief—into some catastrophic act of defeat.

I sat limply on the bed. What could I do? I couldn't go to him. A meeting with Olive included would bring on any disaster the future held. If he was the man, she was not the woman, in any circumstances, to miss the chance of a great triangular scene.

Besides, where *was* he?

'You look ghastly!' Lewis said agreeably that evening, during one of the interminable quarrels that enlivened our occasional meetings. 'You're not eating or sleeping—anyone can see. If he even made you happy, it would make some kind of sense.'

Unaccountably a wall of tears revolved in my chest. I would not cry. I could not speak. But Christian was reviled. I was anguished. Lewis tortured me! To be so misunderstood!

I cried, '*You* never see me when I'm happy. I'm happy when I'm with him.'

There was no disaster. Christian drank for two days, abusing Olive, ringing me night and day to whisper furtive, incomprehensible plans. In two days it was over, but for that length of time, perhaps to prevent his death, I believed in it as imminent. For it did seem he walked on the edge of an abyss.

But the actual events were ordinary. When his land-lady, Mrs Carruthers, complained of the noise he made, he bellowed insults at her till Rex, her son, and Christian's erstwhile assistant, appeared to defend her and they had a fight.

'Chris hit him,' Olive told me that night when she rang. 'He didn't hurt him much, Clem. He's strong, but he's too proud of his face to fight and risk anything. Anyway, he hardly had the strength to stand up let alone knock anyone out. He didn't know who he was. In the morning he'll be heart-broken when I tell him he hit young Rex. He's that fond of him. And, Clem, we'd been saving up a little bit you know, and got a few things. He's ripped them all up and thrown them out the window. And I suppose we'll have to leave here after this...'

I found I could bear the tragedy of young Rex in a very unmoved fashion indeed, and left Olive, who had the emotional currency available, to hold a sentimental wake for that beautiful friendship.

Mrs Carruthers forgave Christian lavishly and so, of course, did Rex. They had 'a sort of family party to celebrate' with cold chicken and salad served on a red and white checked cloth 'to make it seem like Paris for me. She's corny as hell.' They finished the meal with 'an extraordinary *charlotte russe* thing' and Rex put on his record-player and they danced for a while.

Through a relative, Mrs Carruthers found Christian a job managing a small newsagency and the crisis was over. It was over except for the fact that he borrowed twenty-five pounds from me which was to be repaid in a week by means of another loan from Roy, the painter in the room next door. After his bout they hadn't a penny for food or one article of lightweight clothing to wear in this summer heat. I had reckoned with the need of money for immediate expenses and drawn ten pounds from the bank. But as for the rest...And twenty-five!

'Is it wise to get into debt?' I pleaded a little. 'You have this new job. Why not just save up for clothes? It's what people have to do.'

But I said this as a matter for form, expecting to cut no ice and cutting none. So neutrally and fast to anticipate any opportunities for emotional blackmail—'Don't you trust me?'—I agreed to let him have the money. He was taken aback, suspecting a catch, was half-tempted to argue against himself. I was relentless. I would not sway him. Puzzled, we both smiled as if we had sustained a shock to the system.

Within five days, overcome by his own virtue, and suffering slightly to see the money go, Christian repaid the loan. We were modestly conscious of triumph.

Had he accepted it from Roy, the painter? Yes (very seriously) he *had*, but only after long debates with his conscience, and his nerves were all to pieces because of it. And *so*, I gathered I was to infer, on the most important plane the debt was wiped out.

But indeed he was nervous—like a man in a cage. He would do no work that night.

A call from Rollo Lawson later that week left me with a feeling of having fitted another piece into the jigsaw.

The phone was on the low table. When it rang lately I fell to my knees, folding up Japanese-fashion before it. Not that I felt anything. Not that a sudden slackening of tension, a sensation of my heart having come loose from its moorings, prompted me. Just a habit.

Oh, *Rollo*. And I was no longer anchored to the floor. I sat on the divan and he talked. '—been drinking for days—had a quarrel with my father—feel pretty low—mind if we talk?'

There was a breeze. Clean and cool and shady in here... Coral, coral, coral, curtains blowing in and out...

'My father's a wonderful person,' he was saying. I thought idly: if you say so, Rollo. He's famous anyway—one of the mythical heroes of the day: philanthropist, musician, statesman, great man...

'—very devoted to Christian at one time,' he was saying. '—parents gave a birthday party for him once but he behaved pretty atrociously soon afterwards and after that—'

Rollo's life had been passed among extraordinary people. His world was the place towards which the ultimate in vitality, will, talent and charm must gravitate.

Where, among the wealthy business-men, the doctors, students and social workers I'd always known, was there a place for someone like Christian?

In any other background but Rollo's he was conspicuous as a planet. But quickly he and his kind shot off from their beginnings, taking unfair quantities of glamour with them to succour the great and congregate with their kind.

'—without luck—' I heard Rollo say.

223

Certainly, Rollo hadn't had luck. Look at him! And as for Christian...With luck a planet could be a new world; if luck was against it, it might hurtle off somewhere, be lost, fizzle out. A new world or a disaster.

I thought about this grand thought, the receiver cold on my ear. A calm voice jeered: now let's not be too fanciful, angel-cake! An egotistical glamour-boy with a weakness for weakness and you talk about planets and comets! People are just goodies and baddies: goodies win and baddies lose.

And we laughed again. We were always laughing.

We had been through every stage this evening, that is to say, of nervous glances and flippant conversation to cover the mutual amazement that clanged like a gong whenever a door opened between us. Christian's look of youthful modesty at being himself ('Yes, it's really me!'), his pleasure in having presented himself at the right place and time, amused me happily, for it was consciously done for my amusement, as if he were an amazing treasure that he, the magician, had pulled out of a hat.

I had looked at the written work he brought, and he had read aloud in French and translated. We'd had another conversation during which I was a series of officials from whom he was extracting information. He conducted it with great panache, but seriously, as always, with a tense and total dedication. For he did believe his very life hung in the balance.

We had the usual two-hour session. After that, relaxing, he told me about his African friend, Johnny Matowen. If ever he had money, he said he would pay off the rest of

224

Johnny's university fees. He was so brilliant, had such guts and worked so hard. 'I almost decided to introduce you once, but then I thought: no! She might like him.'

Daylight had withdrawn from the room though it lingered on and on outside in the high cloudy sky. While we read together my chair had been drawn to the side of the divan where Christian sat. Now we talked in the dusk, each with an arm outstretched and a hand held for some kind of mutual reassurance. Half-consciously I felt the need—not so much to hold him to myself, as to hold him to the earth.

There was a breeze. My hair was newly washed. Of my two summer dresses I wore the pink one. Weightless with relaxation now that I was freed for an hour or so from remembering or expecting, I lay back in the chair, soothed to the point of nonexistence by Christian's physical presence in my room.

My eyes were glad to look at such solidity and health, as my ears were to hear that confident and ultra-reasonable voice—that voice which could, if it chose, make the idea of visiting Mars next week so feasible, that one would be inclined to think: what should I pack? rather than: is it possible? Do I even want to go?

But this evening he was gently humorous and serious and wise. There was no limit to the acuteness of his self-knowledge, to the annihilating truthfulness of which he was capable, to the humanity which allowed him, knowing, to give a wry smile. And it was the existence of this penetrating capacity to know himself, this germ of ruthless severity in his bone—the will to have this survive in him and oust the other, that clamped me to him.

225

He was ever so faintly boring, of course, because I had heard this debate on his future and past many times. But how sweet to be faintly bored, to be with someone endlessly surprising, young, to whom you were, yourself, incomprehensible and unknown.

At this moment his eyes were fixed on the future, unfocused, as he argued out in a low concentrated tone the details of his scheme.

'It may be unromantic, darling, but I don't want us to be poor together. I loathe poverty. I want us not to start out with dreary problems. Olive doesn't know any better: she's used to it. But I never want to be, and you never could be. I'll tell you how I've worked it out.' His tone grew warmer and more assured. As he spoke he seemed to be living in an existence that already was.

'It will be—safer if we leave our household arrangements as they are till the day we fly to Paris. We can meet at the airport. I have one or two acquaintances there, you know. And I didn't tell you—I rang Jimmy the other day—yes, in Paris, of course—and he's got his eye on an apartment for us on the Ile St Louis which some friends of his are letting. If you haven't taken your exam you can keep on working for it there just as easily. I've thought of everything! The place has a little wrought-iron balcony and French doors, and inside—everything that opens and shuts. It's been converted and redecorated and its—' he gestured, smiling, 'ideal, Jimmy says. I'll be at work all day, so you'll have peace to study. And at night—we'll eat out, and walk along by the river, and sit in some of the cafés in St Germain...And then—' He looked out at me from this happy life.

226

'And then?' I echoed, smiling.

'And then—we'll go home!'

It was very dusky now in the room. We still held hands, eyes together, smiles fading, fading. Oh, would we go home? The night was dark. We hadn't much power.

'I will be good to you. I'll be so generous to you. And far from you having to take care of me, darling, I'll take care of you.'

It was a charming story—like a song from a charming musical with a happy ending. I cherished my neutrality, attending to him from a part of no-man's-land where I was able to avoid resisting totally, or totally succumbing.

'You do want that, too?' he was whispering. 'If you want it as I do, Clem, we can be so happy. Are you for me?'

That question! My brain woke up reluctantly to the fact that it was being washed again and tried to slink off.

'Say. Tell me. It's important to me to know, Clem.' All the while encroaching on hands and arms. We began to kiss in a slow entranced sort of way. I felt as though I were present by proxy, for the detachment I'd aimed at was complete. He trusted nothing that came to him from any source but love of his personal charm—therefore, that he should have. But to go under to that charm would make me useless to him—therefore, this.

I tried to say, 'It's complicated.'

He was balanced on the fragile chair arm, heavily bearing against my chest. His weight was safe and protective to me. And dimly I felt him to be equally safe and protected by his artless concentration on the business of love. Surely we made each other safe? Anyway, as long as he was, I needn't think. If his brain stopped playing snakes and ladders, mine was free.

This liberty and the contentment it induced made me very grateful. And beyond that I was made aware of an unconscious innocence in Christian; something about his touching closeness surprised my heart.

At first it was not excitement, but a sweet, melancholy, and profound relief from the strain of questioning, from the sickness of the word 'love' that possessed me. The chair creaked. There was no cunning in him now: his head was empty of machinations and I floated in the bliss that would follow the breakdown of some fiendish apparatus of torture.

And yet, and yet...My heart did melt in a way, did beat, and I was fond of him. More concerned than for anyone else on earth...Ah, I could resent his weakness, resent his illness, almost, as though it were his fault. If it were not for that...

'I must be with you, sweet...How am I to get rid of Olive? Think of a way. If you love me, help me to come to you.'

Get rid of! What a sound it had! Reluctant to be disturbed, insincerely apprehensive, I turned my head a bit to see his face.

'Hey!' I could hear him laughing softly. 'Are you still there? Ah, Clem, you've messed up my life, do you know that? Complicated it for me.'

I had a disingenuous way of answering declarations with: 'Do you?' or 'Have I?' as if I was playing for time. What I was playing for I couldn't think—unless it was survival.

228

His voice was in my ear and I knew every shade of it: this mixture of tenderness and trust seemed unfeigned. So I was taken for granted, at last? Leaned on? What I had wanted, but...There was an extra strain somewhere I hadn't allowed for.

'Sweetheart...'

'Angel,' I roused myself to say, adding at the back of my throat, 'This chair's going to break. You must be dreadfully uncomfortable.'

'Don't be so practical! As a matter of fact, I hate to be unpleasant about your furniture—'

'It wasn't meant for two, of course.'

We moved on to the bed, leaning back against the wall.

'Let's try to organize it. What am I to say to her? I mean—I can't just say, "Go away!" can I?'

'I suppose not.'

'Oh, you think I should?'

'No, no.' I thought nothing.

'Well,' he hesitated doubtfully, turning from his inspection of the ceiling, 'you do *want* me to come to you? Knowing it would have to be permanent?'

Had I ever said we must live together? Had I ever been consulted in his plans? No. And no again. Still...How to say 'no' to those guileless deceitful eyes? How to reject him—though this *was* only make-believe?

He pressed his face into my hair, breathing it up, attentive: saying mechanically, 'Mmm? Do you?'

Equivocal, I said, 'But there's Olive...' Given the fantasy we had agreed to inhabit—I was making excuses. But where could I put him, for one thing?

229

He gave a funny cry of comprehension, the small sound of a man lifted out of himself by understanding. Instantly he drew away from me, removing himself rapidly to the far corner of the divan. I felt like a snake.

'You don't care at all! You're just stringing me along, humouring me as if I was some sort of lunatic. As if I didn't know what I was saying.'

'No, no, Christian. Truly, darling—'

'"No, Chris. Do you, Chris? Oh, but there's dear Olive, Chris!" Pretending you care about Olive! I hate it when you're dishonest with me.'

'But I'm not!'

'Then do you love me?' he asked, relentless in his determination to be safe.

And feeling trapped, and terribly sly, my spirit utterly opposed and in horror yet utterly entranced and yielding as to a kind of martyrdom, I said, 'As much as you love me.'

He shifted back. 'That's better,' he said, with gentle reproach. 'Of course you do. And with you I'll be good. On Stella's memory! I'll never hurt you as I've hurt the others. You're gentle and good. For my good. And all that makes you—believe me—not like anyone I ever knew before.' An elevated dreamy note crept in. 'You make me different, because you don't mock me or remind me—of things. We're young together. We laugh. And—very important—we want each other. Though you still insist on—But I don't have any doubts about what I want.' He turned away as I had seen him do sometimes when he spoke about Stella—sitting slumped on the edge of the bed, round-shouldered, head down, examining his fingers, sounding gruff and

230

bad-tempered. 'You make me feel—I feel—all the rest—doesn't exist.'

There was a silence. Neither of us moved. The white enamel clock ticked on the table. Under the basin water gurgled in the pipes. Outside the tree-tops shifted, shifted...

My heart beat. Obligations lay heavy on me. There could be no slippery escaping, no getting out from under—I realized that. I would never say now, 'It's too hard for me. This wasn't ever what I intended. I didn't understand it would be like this. Must I give up my life to him?'

For after all, why not? Life had to be passed in some way. And if that child was comforted and made secure, if he was not treated like an object, if gradually he could reach the maturity that was rightly his—what happier life could there be?

'Give me your hand.' He turned to face me again, lounging across the divan 'Oh if only she would leave me! Olive. But she never would. Should I save up and pension her off?...What's the matter? Why do you look like that? You think I should send her away without a bean?'

'For heaven's sake, no! I don't think that at all. Just—' There was no way of saying what I felt. 'I was thinking of—the promises you made. They were important to you. How will you feel?'

He made a careless gesture of disgust. 'When Stella died I was insane. I'd have sworn anything just so that someone would hang on to me. Why weren't *you* there?... All right, so I'm breaking a promise. It's not the first time, and it won't be the last. Olive means well, but I just can't live

231

with her for another thirty years. I'm sorry, I just couldn't do it, darling.

'And, anyway, *does* she mean well? Look at the way she's performed about these lessons. How many have I missed? And don't think it's just because it's you: if I was seeing anyone it would be the same. It would suit her if I never escaped from this filthy newsagency. I'd have nothing and no one but her: no real security, no friends, no money, no outlet for my talent. She's a vampire.'

The range of his voice was so varied and expressive that it heightened now, as it often did, my sensation of unreality, of being at one remove from responsibility. All he said about Olive was true. But there was another side. Not counter-balancing this, but still—there was another side.

Never mind! I laughed aloud indulgently. Why not be reckless? All right! So he was weird and ruthless and a broken-up baby who loved no one but himself. And he took no trouble to hide it, and made me uneasy sometimes, as he did now. But could I, eternally, stand with a cane in my hand: 'Now, Christian, dear, there is something basically strange about the way you look at life...' No, I could not. Who was I to divert a river single-handed? Who, tonight, anyhow?

He had caught my mood and jumped up and walked across the room, roaring with laughter. When he came back we stood together in the dark.

'I'm still a little bit nervous of you,' he bantered nervously, his arms wrapped round me. He was familiar to me as my hands, as packed with power and warmth as a chunk of uranium. 'This—this sort of difference, you know—it makes me nervous. My conscience again...

232

I say to myself, "I'm unworthy! Have I the right to touch her lilywhite hand? She's always said not."' He struck a theatrical attitude. We laughed not happily and stopped.

I sat on the bed while he fixed the door and drew the curtains. Silently he glided back to me in the dark, kissing me, drawing me to my feet. 'Clem?...Clem?'

Automatically I undressed in the dark, draping my clothes on the chair. Till now I had given him words, comfort, tuition, advice, will-power. I had trailed with him through many a weary maze, had praised, admired, encouraged, exhorted, chastised. I had wept. I had insulted my friends. I had lost the enthusiasm of my college tutor. I had lost weight, gained two grey hairs. I had been wrung and near-demented for him. And had understood.

Now this. Till tonight I'd evaded this for reasons: now I accepted it for reasons that outweighed the others. Like anyone who takes a risk I hoped more good would come of it than harm.

'You're not very nervous.' He was a black shape against the wall by the basin.

That was true. At a great distance a kind of calm lay like snow on the layered mountains of my motives. I slid into the bed saying, 'After all, I'm not seventeen.'

But my mind grew wings and flapped away, and my will. If either of us was to survive, these must not be subject to him.

Very quickly, silently, he was beside me—long and warm and smooth. I was astonished and yet not. And my heart turned over, and I thought, surprised: perhaps I do love him. And might have been frightened.

In ten minutes he would have to go but still we lay lazily, clasping hands, fixing arms and heads and pillows, kissing a cheek or eyelid absent-mindedly, with perfunctory fascination.

He had switched on the lamp, now he leaned up over me to say, 'Darling, you would make anyone happy.'

Could I deny it? 'Not anyone would make me happy,' I said flatly.

'Does it have to be me then?' His face had a fresh wild gleaming look under the long fair hair.

'Yes,' I said, firm and disengaged as someone drunk.

After all. Words. What were they? And whatever one said one might sooner or later turn out to mean. Or alternatively not to mean. When one connected up again sometime with oneself.

'Now this is not exactly a question. I'm interested to have your opinion, that's all,' said my lover, to the ceiling, guardedly. 'Understood?'

'Absolutely. Not a question.'

'Do you like the idea of marriage?'

'What?...No!'

'No? What do you mean: "No!" Have you tried it?'

'No!'

'Well, then, how do you know?' he asked reasonably, peering over at me with a surprised, curious and gentle smile. 'I know we've talked about this before, but you mean if I said ...Ah, you mean me, of course! The reprobate. The sinner.'

Tossing round I buried my face in the mattress and against his shoulder, groaning, half laughing, 'Ah, no, angel! Anyone.'

234

'But why?' Christian asked, bright eyed with interest and tenderness. 'I mean—I'm glad you're not! But why? It would be a way of making sure you stayed with me.'

He tried to lift me by the shoulders to turn me, see my expression. We were laughing. I rolled over, looked up at him. And my heart quaked. His face was among the least of his possessions to me, nevertheless, as it hung above me, burning with gentle fanaticism, my heart quaked.

'When should you leave?' I asked the dazzling eyes.

He breathed and altered, falling several storeys, saying, 'Now. But I don't want to. Make me stay. Hold out a hand.'

I held out a hand.

'It's as easy as that.'

After a few minutes with a rueful laugh to cover an emotion that was not resentment quite, and which I would not call chagrin, I said, 'You *must* go. I'll see you tomorrow. It isn't so bad.'

I didn't sigh or look reluctant.

He dressed swiftly. From the bed I watched him leaning back—knees bent a little to catch his reflection in the mirror—brushing his hair. It was my brush he used, having asked permission—a very ordinary artifact of dull blue plastic. I was watching him, swept and dully ravaged by anonymous gusts of feeling that were rendered harmless by non-recognition, when suddenly he cried, 'I love it!' and looked at this inanimate blue brush with such gay and vital affection that its continued lifelessness hung for a moment in doubt.

'Everything of yours. Everything, everything,' he whispered, coming back to kneel beside the bed.

235

'Don't ever let me go. On Stella's memory, I love no one but you. Please, please, believe me, darling.'

'Yes.' I stared ahead at the softly shining pale-pink wall lighted by the lamp.

'I'm going now,' he said, gravely warning, as though I might leap from the sheets like someone possessed and tear him from his place by the door. He gave a comical, self-mocking grin. 'Exit the Golden Boy! Can you bear it?'

'Only just.'

'Good night, darling...' Lightly we kissed, and open-eyed we stared at each other with tender fear and ambiguity.

CHAPTER ELEVEN

From the space beside me where he so often lay, I heard his voice again: 'I'm sure your clever respectable friends want you to stop seeing me in case I corrupt you, don't they?'

And gratified to think of himself as the villain of all time, he delighted in having brought off a coup, having caught me, spited those Insiders who thought him dangerous, depraved, beyond the pale.

Yet, straightaway, at the thought that someone 'good' had been weak enough to fall under the influence of someone like himself, was, after all, no better than the rest, without virtue, the rigid puritan behind the noisy self-confessing sinner gave a hollow unhappy laugh and covered his eyes. Should he despise those who would not despise him? He was inclined to want to.

Inwardly my spirit had groaned at this indication that in choosing not to make him doubt what he was sure of in himself, I had still not found the wisest course.

I remembered. And I remembered other times, no better, when he was uplifted with reverence and humility, eyeing me with glowing fanaticism, building a pedestal, begging me to stand upon it.

I thought of the times at first when there were poisonous words and phrases stealthily inserted in my ear, of the still electric smile that covered his face to hide the fact that he waited in bright terror for my reactions. A clay-foot hunt. What is she really like? Just promiscuous after all? Another in the line of wanting ones?

And his face looked large and smooth, and different again to his many faces that I recognized. I was vaguely appalled and repelled, yet charmed, to see what I was responsible for. As if I had made a pet of, grown fond of, a snake or a fox.

But now it seemed he did trust me—in so far as he was capable of trust. And if I could now steer between snake-pits and marble pedestals, survive the eternal third degree, and continue to hold revulsion and attraction equally at bay...If I could find intuition, some high understanding... Oh, my caution wasn't excessive! His soul was sick. He watched me and my actions like a spy. He always had.

I remembered the times he'd come in smiling like young Lochinvar, confessing to jealous scenes with Olive, during which, under provocation, he had ill-treated her.

'She likes me all the more,' he smiled peculiarly, and mourned, 'But it's uncivilized, darling. I loathe it. With you I would never be like that.'

238

And the atmosphere was vicious, and I was at a loss.

I remembered his reports on Olive's plans for my murder. 'I don't *think* she would ever try to harm me,' he said. 'But if and when we go away, darling, we must arrange it very carefully. She's not a sane woman where I'm concerned. Don't look so sceptical! I'm not trying to amuse you. I'm warning you. I want you to stay alive.'

It was true she paced the streets waiting for him at night when he was with me. I had even seen her standing across the street to watch the windows.

I remembered the library book he took away and returned. Olive read it, finding the one great love scene, crying, 'There's your marvellous Miss James! That's the kind of sexy book your sweet teacher likes to read!'

He said, 'That's Olive. At least I know it's a classic. I liked it a lot. It's a funny thing—a funny thing—the way that everything that comes from you to me—small things— I don't know...

And under he went to his great need to be enchanted.

I thought: if he believed the world was peopled by noble puritans, he might be happy.

Oh, well! Perhaps it would work out in spite of my deserting instinct, and even though I could feel a kind of indifference creeping over me now and then, and though I did feel less and less able to influence what happened.

And then, though it wasn't in the rules that we should be happy together, we were. If he flirted with the idea of giving himself to me for the rest of his life, and if I flirted with the idea of taking him, wasn't it harmless? We pretended, perhaps, to love each other?

239

Perhaps sometimes we almost did. But that was never what I had intended...

On Friday night Christian rang just at seven when I expected him to arrive to say he couldn't come, he would be along tomorrow night instead. As usual, no discussion.

I said all right, though in fact it was awkward. Lewis had tickets for a concert and I'd agreed to go with him, but now...

When I apologized to him, adding, 'Helen would go. I've asked her,' Lewis was very angry. But he had justice on his side—should he not disdain to feel anger?

About the concert Helen had said, 'Yes, I'd enjoy it. But Lewis will be disappointed. Aren't you treating him rather badly?'

'Oh, *how*, Helen? Don't pretend that there's anything— that I'm anything but a sort of toy to Lewis. Oh, I know—a respected human sort of toy—but just that.'

One arm slung over the back of her chair, she drank and put down her cup, saying mildly, 'You could be wrong. You don't think that Lewis might have been waiting for you to get through these last months before your finals—'

'Before what? No, I don't! And please don't say it! What about Gabrielle? And what about *me*? No, please.'

Now it was Saturday. And Lewis brought me roses and two new paper-backs and sat in the black chair talking about one of them while I leaned against the cupboard door. Christian was due in ten minutes. On the divan Helen looked glamorous in black; she was smoking busily and frowning.

Lewis had decided to interest my mind in something, to make me think, crackle, objectify. His manner was so thoughtfully guarded that I felt as though he were visiting me in prison or in a mental institution. The kid-glove treatment.

'—mass entertainments on the working-class mind,' he was saying.

Mass entertainments on the working-class mind, my head echoed, unintelligibly, and closed down.

'Yes,' I said, trying not to seem as glazed as I felt, 'It does sound—er—'

The phone rang and Helen caught my eye, then Lewis. They were guessing.

Hell! I thought, moving from the cupboard door. He isn't coming, I suppose. And they'll know.

'Clem? It's Olive. I'm ringing for Chris. He isn't coming tonight. He's in bed. He's upset. His nerves are bad.'

'Oh.'

'So he'll get in touch with you later.'

Carefully I replaced the receiver, breathing carefully. With a shrug I smiled at Helen, turning down the corners of my mouth. 'He's not coming...Do we need a light on?'

She leaned across to the lamp, depressing the switch with her thumb. My feet took me to the basin where I washed my hands in warm water. 'I've been trying to get this ink off my fingers all day...So, Lewis, I'll be able to study the effects of mass entertainments for myself tonight.'

'Now, look here,' Helen stood up smoothing her skirt. 'Both of you go to the concert as you originally planned. I ought to stay in tonight. It won't take you minutes to dress. I'll give Lewis a drink while you're getting ready.'

'No, Helen!' we both exclaimed. And Lewis went on, standing up and turning on me where I stood behind him drying my hands. 'How often does this happen, Clem? Last night he broke your appointment, and now again tonight. How can you allow yourself to be treated like this? He hangs up on you, humiliates you, and you say nothing. It almost seems that you invite insult.'

I watched him calmly.

'Would you criticize anything he did?'

'No.' I folded the towel and hung it on the enamel rail under the basin, so indifferent to all the anger and incredulity in the room that it was almost outrageous to lift my eyes from the neutral surface of the furniture.

The moment before a clap of thunder.

'You're afraid of alienating him, aren't you? You pretend that you want to help him, but the fact is you would let him walk on you without asserting yourself. Haven't you any pride? When I think of the way you let him use you, and that woman...'

My spirit winced a little on Lewis's account. Nevertheless his crass misinterpretation goaded me. I cried, 'Oh, for God's sake! Afraid of alienating him! Pride! Humiliation! You understand nothing. Whatever I do, I do for good reasons, and that isn't one of them. I appreciate that you're both thinking of my welfare, and I know that all you can see of this situation isn't exactly cheering, but you do only see a fraction of it, from the outside. I know what I'm doing.'

Helen was looking at her long suede gloves: no challenge there. And Lewis seemed to have left the mountain peaks of whatever emotion had driven him to that overbearing speech. More calmly he said, 'Yes, all right. I can see you may have some more complicated motives than I admitted. But the point is, Clem, that those two see only the result, and not your motives. They probably think that you're no more than soft. I grant you,' he said, seeming stunned by the effort of putting his horror into words, 'I grant you he's a poor lost object, but he's worthless, Clem. Useless. It's too late. He's irredeemable!'

A silent shriek rose from my heart. We stood staring, blind and blazing. I seethed with screams and unshed tears.

To say that! How dared he? Who was he to speak like that of—someone who meant so much to me? I would not have heard Lewis abused. How could he imagine that even years of friendship permitted this? You're speaking of the man I love! How ludicrous and unsayable! Perhaps not even true. Almost certainly not quite true, but—

'Lewis,' said Helen, 'don't hurt her. This does no good at all. Clem's grown up since we've known her. She isn't twenty any more. But she humours us both politely when we still treat her as if she was. Clem,' she caught my hand pacifically, but I shook her off, untouchable with emotion. 'Lewis, why don't you wait in my room for a minute?'

But he opened his mouth to speak at me again. I covered my ears, shouting at him, 'Go away! Get out! Leave me alone! Don't talk to me!'

With the fringe of our attention we were all aware of Lucy Turner talking somewhere outside in the hall. Our voices were raised. The room was explosive. She would hear. Let her!

243

Hearing Lewis's voice again I turned my back, crushing my hands against my ears. Go, go, go, go, I willed him.

Helen's dress brushed against me. She held her black jacket on one finger. I looked at her.

'He's gone. It's all right. Would you like me to stay with you?'

'No!...No, thank you very much, Helen.' I leaned against the wall. 'Go to the concert.'

'We'll do something.' She shook her head slightly, then raised her hand to signal good-bye. Her dress made a soft rasping sound. I stayed where I was, not moving a muscle. The door closed with a click. And then I slowly took a step away from the wall. The room smelled of cigarettes and Helen's perfume, of roses lying in pink paper on the table. The air-waves rippled, rippled, rippled, quickly. My heart banged in my chest.

I will *not* be broken.

I was conscious of breathing. I went to stand by the windows, clasping my bare arms. I kept repeating, 'Truth is relative and subjective,' but I could no longer remember what it meant, or how I knew.

For some weeks Christian turned up with regular irregularity, the visits interspersed with phone calls. We moved jerkily towards the end of the set lessons, and according to mood, he seemed to have progressed brilliantly or to have learned nothing at all.

And love was a see-saw.

He said, 'No one else would have put up with me and persevered the way you have. No one else would have cared

244

whether I landed Rollo's job. And if that hadn't turned up and I hadn't met you I'd have left Olive anyway, and found some rich old woman to keep me. No, I mean it. And that would've been the end of me.'

And he said, 'This newsagency job terrifies me, darling. I don't want the responsibility. There's money in the register. I won't take it, but should I be left there with it? Some mornings I have to have—I won't tell you how many drinks to get up courage to go—but I think: she'll be disappointed if I don't. Do you understand I've never tried so hard in my life to do the right thing?'

And saying this, he studied me with a devotion and dependence that made me cast about in panic. For I was unsupported, and had given out, it sometimes seemed, almost more than I possessed.

I sat in a deck-chair in Green Park, like an invalid, eyes closed to the warm August sun, breathing the grassy wind.

If I had a house, a country cottage, of my own... If examinations didn't loom...If my own survival didn't depend on them...A house, and just enough to pay for food and heating...

It was bitterly frustrating to be so helpless, like trying to plough a field with a toothpick. I could do *nothing*. I was powerless, bound hand and foot, helping to send him, ill, to a job in Paris, instead of finding for him the peace, the green summer fields, sweet air and quietude, the man of gentle genius who would find the only cure, and calm and heal him.

A leaf blew into my open hand—a tender cool and succulent leaf which I examined and discarded.

Dear God, I'm very sorry it's impossible to believe in you. Everything's falling to pieces...

'When it's quiet in the shop after they've all bought their birthday cards and daily papers, I get a chance to sit down and read a bit,' he said. 'But they terrify me, you know that? The newspapers. Let's face it! At thirty you're an old model these days. Look at me—I'm out-moded! The Boy Wonder!'

High-spirited, he leaned back away from me, extending his arm to an invisible audience, and sang a few bars of an ancient popular song about an old-fashioned boy. Laughing and breathless, he pushed back his long hair. 'Sometimes I wonder if they print the Positions Vacant in English! What do all those initials stand for? Am I just dumb? What kind of people do these things? Remember, wireless was hot stuff when I arrived on the scene.'

'I'm old-fashioned myself. I know how you feel, believe me!'

More lazy laughter and more kisses and love. Bed seemed the sanest place, the warmest and safest place, when it was raining outside and the curtains damply blew; with daylight palely spilling through their closeness, sending peachy-pink light to the corners of the room. Love was the only anchor when the world turned too fast.

He sat upright in the black chair, drinking coffee, sedate and proper as an early Victorian, being prodigiously, priggishly proper. He said mildly, using his most pompous accent, 'If it weren't for money! It isn't that I want millions. Just enough to buy Olive off. Just enough to live modestly in the country—I like to hunt, I like to shoot. Just enough

246

to have a flat in town, and travel about a bit in a civilized fashion like everyone else. Is it too much to ask?'

I felt myself retreat. To demolish him? To say, 'Frankly, yes!'? To force him to look at reality? Or to accept it as part of his necessary fantasy?

My mind stood in fatal hesitation, seeing long vistas of unfortunate repercussions attaching to both responses. But it felt, even more, a profound reluctance to function any longer as a sledge-hammer. Besides, how deadly to be so literal! He had to have dreams. Why shouldn't he have dreams?

So when he said, 'Now, when we're installed on the Ile St Louis, you'll have finished your course and you'll find some marvellous job, and I'll be at the Comédie Française. We'll drive to the coast for swimming and sun,' I agreed, hugging my knees. 'All right. That'd be fun!'

And when he said, 'In New York I'll break into television. They'll love my accent there: actually I have got a particularly good voice, and though I'm thirty, getting on for thirty-one, my face isn't a ruin. Is it?' I waited and he continued, 'Delicious clothes for you darling, from Fifth Avenue, and some really rare steaks. I am so tired of boiled eggs! It's all we eat! What? Is that what you have, too? Oh, God! We've got to get out of this. I'll talk to Rollo again tomorrow.'

And I said, 'Yes, all right.' And, 'Yes, it would be wonderful.'

'Tell me what you would like best,' he said once. 'It's your turn.'

So I thought, and in a minute resurrected a picture-postcard dream of the simple life among the Polynesians.

There were blue lagoons, golden beaches, leaning palms, shells, bread-fruit and yams, sarongs, fishing, festivals, folklore and traditions. It wasn't so hard: I'd read Margaret Mead on Samoa, and Robinson Crusoe.

And yesterday's panic was silted over and lost in today's milk-and-honey wholesome simplicity. Why had I worried? How happy, young and healthy we both were, after all! Slightly battered plants, perhaps, without supporting stakes, and due for a short season, possibly, but still!

'Isn't it lovely—falling in love?' he murmured, coaxing in my ear. 'The nicest nicest feeling...' reminding me of all our meetings from the first.

'Yes. Yes, it is.'

'Soon we'll be together all the time. I can't bear to have Olive near me any more, touch her...You don't think about that, do you? You don't suffer. You don't say: "Come away next week!" She would die if she knew about us, but you...'

I said nothing. Did I conjure up torturous pictures during the long waking nights? No, no I did not. My mind could not be made to manufacture the most innocuous picture of them together. It was too unlikely.

But in Christian's eyes we were competitors for a prize which was himself. He often seemed to suggest that as a sportswoman I was disappointing, refusing to vie with Olive in threats and hysteria. I wouldn't excite him into a passion of sympathy by recounting sad stories: I wouldn't flatter him, or encourage the vicious boy who sometimes stared out from behind his eyes, and it rather sapped his confidence in me.

248

'Anyone else who's ever claimed to love me,' he said more than once, 'has been extremely jealous.'

Was the old magic going? Was this age? Uncertainty in his eyes: eyes stalking mirrors: ironic apologies for his appearance, 'Sorry I look so bedraggled, darling!'

Lewis and I stood in the entrance hall of the block where he had a flat. We looked out at the street, the rain pounding down warm and grey.

Lately we had a new and rather less strained relationship. I felt myself regarded as something almost lost to sight, a ship leaving the wharf, all streamers broken. Tonight we had listened to music.

'Look, there's a taxi! I'll come back with you, Clem.'

'No, really, it's quite late. Don't come across the street. No use getting soaked. Good night.'

A taxi. How many shillings? Was I quite mad? But the preservation of some physical energy now was the one thing of importance.

On the wide curving step Lewis watched me dash across the road. The taxi-driver had a red face and looked out in the taciturn way of taxi-drivers. My hand was on the door of the cab, shining with water.

'Where to?'

But I'd forgotten something. 'Just a moment! I have to go back!' And back across the road I ran, splashing across puddles, blinking in the rain.

Lewis caught my arm. 'What's wrong? You're drenched.'

My hands whipped a few wet strands of hair from my forehead. 'Quick! What's my address? I can't remember.'

Lewis had come out onto the step to meet me. Standing in the warm soupy rain, in the late summer evening, he regarded me uncertainly, with a world of reserve.

I was daunted, felt guilty, wanted to laugh.

In the cab I found two handkerchiefs and started to dry myself off. Perhaps some people were like this all the time? Like being someone else altogether. *I* was temporarily missing from my body. Oh yes. And there was another way of saying it, too.

We see-sawed up and down: when he fell over into love, I was free. But the timing was tricky and our gazes often intertwined in fearful question.

'They say it's bad to be obsessed,' he whispered, smiling. Gone was the noble Roman tonight; he had the pink and chubby cheeks of a very young boy and his transparent earnestness. 'They say it's not healthy to be obsessed,' he murmured, 'but I like it. I like it. What about you?'

'So do I,' I whispered back, kissing his cheek, surrendering all pretensions to responsibility. *I* had to live too! And we were happy now, at this minute. If someone chose to drop a bomb we could be something less than dust tomorrow. How misguided, how tragic, how foolish, not to be happy!

Decline and fall...Civilizations crumble...The populace of the city...

Of course it didn't have a good sound: *I like to be obsessed*. But hardly the deadliest words ever spoken between two people? And honey in the mind, anyhow, and honey in the heart.

Behind Christian on the table the lamp was alight. He selected a long strand of hair from the pillow, tugged it a little and wound it round and round his finger. 'Have you been obsessed like this before?'

Like this? 'No,' I smiled, feeling the softness of the pillow against my mouth.

He accepted that, still watching me, winding the length of hair round his finger, turning it for an instant into a monocle and peering through it, laughing silently. But under this flippancy he was deeply serious, slowly breathing, brooding.

'Can I trust you, darling? You wouldn't have had enough of me in two or three months and want to leave me flat? Would it last forever?'

'Yes, it would last,' I said stoically, marvelling at his doubts, feeling older than the Great Wall of China.

As if love ever lasted! As if it could or should! Of course it *might*...

'If you talked about it less,' I added.

With a critical eye for effect he laid the handful of hair back on the pillow. Reproachful and tender, but having to laugh, he said, 'You'd say anything. Anything. You don't believe a word I say. You kid me all the time.' And his eyebrows shot up in laughing indignation. 'Darling, I'm *serious*. This is important. You don't seem to understand.'

My heart opened and was still. There was a pause. I said, 'There's such a thing as self-defence.'

Christian looked at me along the pillow, nervous and demanding, the way a child looks at an adult who is bound

251

to take the initiative. He wanted to follow the leader. I felt my own expression was much the same.

In the end he said, 'It's no good. This sort of double life is killing me. We'll make a complete break or you must come away with me.'

This was Friday night. He would give notice to Banks, the owner of the newsagency, give notice to Mrs Carruthers and tie up all the loose ends with Olive by next Friday night. Then, if I chose, we would leave London till the job in Paris was available.

'Where for?' I asked faintly, as if it made all the difference.

'I know a couple of old pros. They used to look after me when I was a kid. They've got a market-garden outside Dublin. They'd love to put us up for a while. They were always mad about me. What do you say?'

We stood on either side of the windows, leaning against the wall, fantastically solemn as if we were discussing prepositions. Yet we stared with mutual astonishment.

I wondered who was this stranger, the weight of whose gaze on me was almost physical? Aghast I took in the lines of his face, the firm but curiously adolescent mouth.

'Will you come with me? Or must we say good-bye tonight? Because I tell you quite simply that I'm *breaking up*. It must be settled once and for all. If you love me, come with me on Friday.'

'Yes. All right. Yes,' I heard my voice, and felt like someone reading of an earthquake far away—very little, almost nothing.

Christian exclaimed. We caught hands, leaned against each other talking nonsense.

'Darling, have you got anything to drink in that cupboard of yours?'

'No, and if I had I wouldn't give you any.'

'No?' He smiled uncertainly, examining my expression, then was immensely relieved. 'I don't believe you would either! That's one of the reasons I love you. You're good for me. It doesn't matter.' We swayed towards each other. 'You make me feel drunk without brandy...'

'I'll try to get a short let for your room and then if your friend in Stratford gets better quickly it will be here for you to come back to.

On Monday morning encountering Lucy Turner on the first floor as she inserted the key in the lock of an empty room, I gave notice.

'Well!' she exclaimed, eyeing my pink dress and straw basket stuffed with brown-paper parcels. Then frowning actively she began to examine ways and means of receiving me back.

'Well, no,' I broke in. 'When I leave Stratford I'll visit other friends. I'm not coming back to London.'

'Oh. Well,' she said again. 'I'll be sorry to lose you. We must get together for a drink.' Expensive in mud-coloured shantung, Lucy turned the key again and opened the door. I noticed her hair was now rather a becoming shade of chestnut, instead of the burgundy that Christian had deplored. Had he told her?

253

I went up to the kitchen where Gertie was on her knees slowly scrubbing at the immaculate inlaid linoleum. While she told me about last night's quiz on television, I unpacked the food for dinner: fillet steak, spinach from the deep-freeze, butter, fruit, cream and cheese.

'Mr Roland coming tonight? You don't do much cooking in the ordinary way, do you?' Gertie enquired, not entirely without malice, though she liked me well enough, I knew. But I lived a lady's life, sleeping late, reading books just, didn't I? Now and then she gave me a jab and watched in vain for a reaction.

'Ah, yes, you've got to eat,' she said, getting up off the floor and wringing out the cloth over the bucket. 'Look out for your health.'

Gertie, whose face was yellow as cheap batter! I left her shaking coloured powder into the sink and scrubbing away with that patient right arm.

The week-end had been quiet: Helen went home to Oxford, and Lewis was preparing for a conference that had opened this morning. We walked in Regent's Park for an hour on Sunday morning but I hadn't been able to say to him: 'I'm going to Dublin with Christian at the end of the week.'

I hadn't seen Christian or heard from him since Friday night, but he had warned me not to expect a call, saying that he might have to take Olive to one of her daughters, who was in Bristol, or find a room for her. It was impossible to anticipate the unpleasant tasks ahead. On Monday night, though, we'd have dinner together and make arrangements.

So it was done. One life was over. I would never be that person again. The mysterious future was now resolved into, at least, a certain uncertainty. Would I ever take the Finals? It was unlikely. I would never be a snug Insider, never be a useful, respected member of the community, never be secure, never have lasting friendships.

So it was good-bye to friends and relations, good-bye to aspiration—of a sort, anyway. Who asked about free will? Don't smile when you mention destiny, stranger!

All right, and I did love him. So we would be together, might come to no good. It was just possible he would drive me insane. Or I might still, with luck, help restore him to himself. Anyway, we would laugh sometimes, and now and then be truly happy, and even at worst be real. My heart would beat. Yes, it was right for both of us, if not safe or comfortable. He was someone's life's work—mine it seemed.

And yes, not to worry, a kind insidious voice insisted in my ear, you can always die when it's too much. Both of you—you're quite likely to die young...

In the evening I dressed about an hour and a half too soon. Tonight he would have his black dress, and the nearest I possessed to real pearls. For once I would allow myself the joy of trying to please him.

Helen came in for five minutes, and throughout the house doors opened and slammed, baths were run and cutlery and china chinked and banged in the kitchens on all floors.

Now it was seven I saw by my watch. I stood in the kitchen rechecking the preparations for dinner. He was critical; I was no chef, but as far as my remotely functioning brain could gather the meal was ready to assemble itself at a single gesture.

The spiky heels of my best shoes tapped on the linoleum as I made for my room. I felt really ill with tension. At a noise I turned in the hall and saw Christian coming up the stairs. And I stopped. In silence I fell through a vertical tunnel, I was falling, clammy cold.

The girl who had taken the Indian student's room, a tall red-haired girl with a hard confident air and a loud confident voice, preceded him. She looked at me curiously. He was very drunk.

'Hullo, darling.' I put a hand on Christian's arm as he barged past on his way to my room.

His eyes couldn't focus. They seemed to be fixed on a mountain five miles behind me. But, 'Darling!' he cried gallantly, and leaned against the wall, eyelids drooping, beginning to heave the sighs that are a preliminary to sleep.

On the divan he lay face down, and I stood watching him for a minute from the middle of the floor. He dragged himself to the surface to mumble, 'Sorry about this. Forgive me, darling. Please, bear with me...'

'Yes. It doesn't matter.'

'Bear with me...'

And after a breath I found it easy to do just that.

I sat by the window, looking out. It's all right. You feel nothing. It's all right. Steady hand. Steady heart. It would take a lot—I hardly know what—to make you suffer. Remember? You were immunized long ago.

Next door Helen's wireless was playing. Smells of someone's dinner—fishy and oniony—came under the door and through the cracks. Christian breathed and grunted.

256

Then suddenly he jerked awake, quivering, jerking, looking about in terror—alive, but no one in particular. Wary, trembling, he looked about. Gradually his life inhabited him again till all at once he knew everything, was tricky, petulant, defensively aggressive.

'Well, what'll we do? Will you prove yourself by walking about the streets with me drunk? Will you come to dinner? *Please*...No! You'd be afraid I'd embarrass you, wouldn't you? That's not love. I dare you to prove you love me...Oh, please, come!'

Slumped he sat on the bed, looking heavy, dishevelled, wanting with a dreary sort of viciousness to avenge himself on someone for something.

I let him go away alone.

The red-haired girl knocked on the door. 'Have you finished in the kitchen?'

'In a moment.'

With a blank thoughtfulness I dropped steak and vegetables and strawberries into the polythene kitchen-bin. I poured away the cream and ran the tap in the sink.

Then, unable to think of anywhere else to go, I went to bed, and cried a surprising volume of tears without much emotion. It was hard to stop, that was all, like any bad habit.

Next day I told Lucy Turner my sick friend in Stratford had been taken to hospital, so I would stay in London where I was.

Dublin was not mentioned again.

Christian had charged from my room into a Soho club where young Rex Carruthers found him much later, much the worse for wear. For thirty-six hours he was ill and in bed. Then just as he was returning to normal he persuaded Rex to smuggle in past Olive's eye two bottles of brandy. 'Trying to lay off it?' Rex said, when reproached. 'Don't be mad! Anyway, he needed it. I couldn't say no.'

Once again in a violent quarrel their room was wrecked, and once again, this time for Olive's sake, Mrs Carruthers forgave him.

But Olive had long felt signs of change in Christian and hounded by her suspicions, travelled half across London in her lunch hour the day he returned to work—according to his version—to spy on him.

'She suspects me of carrying on six separate affairs at once, including one with the girl in the cigarette kiosk. She stood in the doorway like a tragedy queen, all out of breath. Shockingly untidy. No make-up. Her hair uncombed. She looked about eighty. Frightful!'

Gordon Banks, the owner of the shop, had come in for some special stock-taking. There were several customers waiting. The presence of employer and customers, as audience, inspired a ferocious quarrel between them.

Fired, of course, and lucky not to be arrested, he said.

But two days later he said, 'Why should I do menial work, anyway, for a creature like Banks? Slave for a few miserable pounds? I'm thirty. By this time I should be well-established and comfortably off. I should have something of reasonable importance to do.' Voice pompous, eyes fanatical, frightened.

The public humiliation of Olive in the shop had been the touching means of a reconciliation. 'I hurt her. Poor

258

Olive. I mustn't do it again,' he said as we lay side by side one afternoon. 'She'll be my nurse and housekeeper, and I'll be unfaithful and abuse her, but she'll stick to me.' And he smiled at me grimly. 'I'm not for you. We're too late for each other.'

And because we were both so relieved to be relieved of the awful decision, we stared at each other unblinking—with so much old and knowing disenchantment, not so much with one another as ourselves—that tears came to my eyes. And his expression softened with compassion. Then as we looked, and the easy tears slid across my temples and into my hair, minor clashes of anguish and rebellion began to sound distantly in some deep recess of my being.

'*Don't* cry. This isn't the end. I'll see you for weeks and weeks yet, and after that—we'll think of something.' His eyes investigated the future for loopholes then slewed round to me again, very kind. I was seldom as pathetic as this. Clearly it was rather a treat, gave him sad pleasure.

But soon he stopped smiling and we stared almost resentfully into each other's eyes. For renounce one another as we would, and as we were relieved to do (there was something too demanding, too hard and exhausting asked of us) there was still a sort of obligation between us, that seemed not to be ours to dispose of.

'There is something...' he said reluctantly, frowning now.

I heaved a great breath. 'Well, it hasn't worked out this time whatever it was. But another time, darling, we'll fix it better and arrive on the scene quite early, won't we? At the right time for each other...'

So touching, smiling wryly through the tears! And yet…

I had never been romantic. It was a grievance between us. My few words to him were chosen carefully as if I was a secret agent. Might he not repeat them to Olive? Now this sudden appeal—shameful and pleasing to me—pierced him, deflected him entirely. I had forgotten his extraordinary responsiveness to words.

'Clem. Clem.' He caught my arms and almost shook me, saying my name in a toneless whisper, as if I had deceived him. 'Why haven't you spoken like this before?' He had a blind wounded look. I wasn't sure that I did not hate him.

Not then, but later when we were silent after desultory talk about—of all things—grammar, it came to me that I might never experience this identical moment of contentment, or forget it. It was lasting, lasting, and did last a long time. A light sweet happiness.

But finally as if a match had struck against my heart and lighted, lighting up the bleak, unavoidable future, it all changed.

Not desolate, but aware of a future desolation that would come and certainly go, I started to cry heavily and without hope. Groping for a handkerchief under the pillow I was vaguely aware of Christian drawing himself up to watch me. Well what if I did look two hundred—all tears and long tangled hair! He'd soon be gone. He couldn't hurt Olive. I couldn't hurt him. Who couldn't hurt me? Why shouldn't *I* make a commotion for once? Everyone else did. No one else went round suffering in silence. Seeing was believing was it? Well now he would see I had tears to shed, too! I was bloody well mixed up and unhappy!

It seeped slowly into my consciousness that Christian was peculiarly still. Half-resentful, half-fearful, I turned to look across my left shoulder at him.

He was stretching up beside me, supported on rigid arms, stretching up towards the blank wall, his face contorted.

'I'm afraid. I'm afraid,' he whimpered very softly. 'I love you. But I'm afraid.'

My tears were dashed from me. I went cold with fright.

He teetered on the edge of destruction. He could break. A wrong word could murder him.

'No!' I said strongly. 'No, it doesn't matter. Tears are nothing. It's all right, darling. Look, I've stopped. Nothing wrong. I want nothing from you. Sweet…Listen. Nothing's wrong…'

Wildly repentant, and with a force that wasn't mine, I talked to him, gathering his head between my arms with some mad idea of protecting it, and covering up those strange blue eyes. It felt big and hard, yet fragile as an eggshell.

'I don't know what to do, Clem. Please help me. Tell me what to do.'

'Listen…I'm not hurt. You've done no harm. It doesn't matter. Everything's all right, truly it is…'

'No, we *must* be together. It's no use. I can't be strong. I can't help promises. It has to be you.'

Chilled to the heart, I half listened, holding him and being held, clasping shoulders, arms, hearing his heart, murmuring, 'No. It doesn't matter. Don't love me. Don't think about it. Don't love me.'

261

CHAPTER TWELVE

The sun shone. There was a breeze on the river. And in the air was the freshness of a hundred London parks—the blazing flowers, the cut grass, the leaning lucent trees.

We continued to walk along the Embankment in the direction of Westminster, perambulating slowly. It was Thursday afternoon about half-past two.

Free of Olive's regulation during working-hours since he had no job, Christian had dared to ring and ask me to lunch before he went for an interview at three.

According to the advertisement an administrative assistant was wanted to supervise the management of a chain of restaurants in the Piccadilly/Leicester Square areas.

I asked cautiously if he'd had any experience of that sort, unwilling to have him apply for a rebuff. But he was patient and explained good-humouredly, 'I've eaten in every decent restaurant in London, darling. I know how all these people act. It's not experience in serving or washing dishes you need for this kind of work. They're ordinary places but the job's at rather a high level.'

We crossed the road at Westminster Bridge, stared at the red double-deckers, snubby dark English cars, sleazy blue blasts from the exhausts.

He continued to talk. I caught fragments now and then, 'Did you see Olivier in *Carrie*?...No?...

'I like to look at you in the street,' he went on saying. I heard the searingly intimate voice rise deliberately when anyone came near. Just testing again. I took not much notice.

'You ought to feel wonderful walking in the sun with someone you love, but you don't, do you?'

I gave him a dry look. But I had thought of that, too. Streets and passers-by were visible about me: it was quite unlike the blind juvenile joy of other existences I could remember. But a simultaneous awareness of the world and Christian seemed not, to my purely mechanical dissatisfaction, to guarantee the absence of love, or anything else.

'Leave it. Leave it. Have some mercy.'

He was trying to make me look at him. 'Have I given you hell? You'd be better off without me.'

'No doubt.'

Slowly up Trafalgar Square we walked, his voice boring away at me.

'If you really wanted me, you'd fight for me and show some signs of jealousy. Like Olive. You'd suffer. Then I'd know.'

Inwardly I smiled with hatred. 'I could say the same to you. I'm a pacifist. Fighting doesn't appeal.'

'No,' he said heavily, frowning at the footpath. 'You're not exactly the fish-wife type. You're sweet and gentle. That's why I love you.'

'Oh, leave it! Leave it!' I begged without expression.

Sitting in the bus to go home I watched him turn away and walk along the street towards his appointment, optimistic as a lion in a den full of martyrs.

Helen's room was larger than mine with an extra armchair and a stuffed blue window-seat on which she sat now, leaning an arm on the window-sill, tugging occasionally at her short yellow skirt in an absent attempt to cover her knees.

I lay on her divan clicking the spring of a ball-point pen to the general irritation, sitting up to gulp a mouthful of brandy and soda which was warm and too wet.

Lewis was between us in the big armchair.

'Perhaps you're right,' Helen was saying. 'Are we cushioned, Lewis?'

He glanced over at me and I jumped quickly up, shocked to find him watching me. I jammed my teeth together and clicked the point of the pen in and out.

'I don't quite know what Clem's suggesting we should do,' he said to Helen. 'She seems to feel that anything as conventional as contributing to the general well-being is rather crude. So I suppose, for the sake of our characters, we should abandon work and aspire to become addicts of one sort or another.'

'Let's begin with alcohol. Have another drink,' Helen said, rising to fill his glass. 'Clem?'

264

'No thanks.' I clicked the pen with concentration.

'Yes, we should copy the parasites and criminals and mental defectives. Dead beats, that's what we should be.'

Oh dear. I looked at him. He had lost the control, lost the direction of me, and I had been soft-seeming, pliable. Now he was angry and unhappy, perhaps. Incredibly. But I wasn't sorry.

'I'll certainly commit a crime if you don't stop that!' Helen whipped the pen from my hand as she passed with Lewis's glass. And I frowned to see it go—the nice noisy gadget that tortured the nerves of those who tortured mine.

On the window-seat she said, 'I don't think Clem's sentimental about neurotics.'

'No? Surely, Clem, you find their lives exciting and colourful? It's vogueish, isn't it?' He raked my face for a sign of anger, willing contradiction.

Very blandly I stared back. He emptied his glass and clamped it on the bedside table.

'Well, as I understand it,' Helen said, rumpling her hair, 'the charge is that people like us build a personal system of values and claim to live according to high-sounding theories which are—Clem says—never put to the test. Right?'

I shrugged. 'I suppose so. Intelligence can make you cautious. A worthy career and a reasonably high standard of living do protect you from a wider kind of self-knowledge.'

'There would have to be some advantage in being a layabout,' Lewis said smoothly. 'So they monopolize self-knowledge?'

Helen said temperately, 'You say we're protected from the pressure of circumstance and tend to judge the range of

265

our possible behaviour, theoretically, in the light of what is relatively a narrow range of experience—and I think it's true enough.'

'And of course if we agree to that,' Lewis said, 'we must be very tolerant indeed?'

'I don't know,' I said vaguely, feeling baited by that word 'tolerant'. It expressed an idea I had once believed in wholeheartedly, but an army of reservations rose in silence at the sound of it now. 'It's just—we seem to adapt away from what's most human in us—like new-type dinosaurs. But the ones who don't deliberate, though they might go under in one sense, mightn't be successful, for instance—stay closer to themselves than most of us. They can afford to be human.'

My voice! Their voices! All these words! Chains of words!

Helen started, 'But can they benefit from that freedom—'

The phone rang. An extension served the three rooms on this floor.

'Most likely for you.' Her voice was casual. I walked casually round the bed to pick it up.

'Darling, I'm going to ask you a favour.' His nervous manic high spirits glinted and laughed in his voice.

'Oh?'

'I want fifty pounds. You to lend me fifty pounds.'

'*What?*'

He was so excited he seemed to restrain laughter with difficulty. 'Yes, I knew you'd say that. You'll think: "What's he up to this time?" But it's not like that at all. It would be for three days at the most. You wouldn't be giving it to me. Listen: I'll explain from the beginning.'

Snow was falling on my mind. It was blanketed in snow—soft, cold, clear, frozen.

'About the job. I didn't get it. If you'd seen the other applicants, darling, you'd have understood. I wasn't exactly the type. Ordinary, I said it was! My God, that was an understatement.

'I left there and went into a place in Soho. Yes, for a drink. They rattled me in that crumby hole. You know how I dread the routine—applying for their menial filthy jobs... Are you there?' He laughed nervously. 'Don't go away!

'Well, in the club over against the bar I saw Rollo quietly drinking himself to death. He told me some—piffle about an argument with his father. And I told him about you. You and me. And he respects you, you know that? Says you'd be good for me...Oh, for God's sake! I'm not flannelling *you*. You know me too well. Even if I wanted to I'm too clever to be quite so obvious. Ask Rollo. Check with him.'

'Go on.'

'I don't much like the way you say that...Well, I'm sorry to *bore* you like this. I won't keep you much longer. I'm just speaking about a matter that happens to be of some importance to me. I don't expect you're really very interested.'

Coldly he continued, 'We discussed my work in Paris. The job will be vacant in a few weeks, and I put it to Rollo that I needed money to—furnish myself with a—minimum of necessities. One can't quite arrive in Paris to take over a

267

responsible post looking like a dustman. So Rollo agreed to come home with me to assure Mrs Carruthers, my dear gentle old landlady—' his voice was suddenly soft and fervid, growing tropical plants, 'that I'll be well-placed in Paris to—repay her loan. Rollo couldn't help me himself, if that's what you're thinking. He exists on a pittance from his father.'

'Mrs Carruthers?' I said now, at last.

'It happens that she trusts me,' he said relentlessly. But then he forgot he was punishing me and being wounded, and shouted gaily, 'You'd have laughed like hell, darling. Before we'd put the proposition to her she was telling us she had fifteen hundred invested in the City. Saved up for her retirement. God, she can afford a rotten fifty. And the rest. But I won't cheat her—may I drop dead tomorrow!... Well, what do you think?'

'Nothing. You know what I think.'

'Ah...You...Now the thing is—she's all tied up with stocks and shares. Tomorrow she's giving instructions to have some sold but it may take a few days to get the right price and I want the money now. Right away. So will you let me have it, darling? Just till I get it from her? You don't want me to be a disgrace to you when we're walking down the Champs Elysées?'

I said nothing.

'But what do you think of old Carruthers? Pretending to be poor! Holding out on me.'

A ticker-tape played through my brain: the gambling losses, the cars wrecked, the cruises, the staterooms on Atlantic crossings.

'So she earned it! That's what you're thinking, isn't it? I'm not asking you for anything you've earned. Your father worked so that you can sit and study all day. You should have a job like everyone else. I've worked bloody hard in three jobs at least since I've known you!'

Well, well. Was that so? Did he want a VC? I smiled slightly with hatred, feeling my heart beat slowly.

'That's true,' I said nicely.

'Oh, Clem, I shouldn't have said that I suppose, but will you *please* help me out for exactly three days? Then as soon as the oil's converted into cash it's yours again. Three days. Ring her and check. Ring Rollo. I'm not trying to trick you. I love you, though you don't believe me. What do you say?'

'Yes.'

No! I didn't want to! But my will was sweetly bent and said, 'Yes,' as if to murder one of us.

Silence. And then incredulous delight. 'You mean it?'

'I'll meet you tomorrow morning—ten-fifteen—that coffee-bar in Charing Cross Road.'

'Darling, I knew you'd trust me—'

Replacing the receiver I shivered and blew out a deep breath. 'My knees...Where's Lewis?' Limpid and casual, I turned to Helen as I rose from the floor.

'I asked him to get some cigarettes. We'd both run out.'

'Oh.' I dropped onto the bed.

'What was that about?' Helen had a relaxed and unsensational approach that made it possible to speak to her without feeling that one was in the middle of the dance of the seven veils.

269

When I'd told her she closed her eyes, shook her head, and came over to sit in the chair by the bed. '*Why*, Clem? This is foolish!...But you love him, of course, so—'

'No, no. I don't feel anything for anybody. I feel nothing at all.' I bubbled very brightly. 'That's strange, isn't it?'

'Oh, you're wrong,' she said, smiling at me with compassion.

'No, Helen. That isn't why I agreed to this.' My mind still bubbled with strangely neutral high spirits. I groped about in an effort to explain. 'You see, he knows this is a bad move—taking more money—and from old Mrs Carruthers. And he knows that I know it, too. And it isn't essential that he should have it *now* from me. But, just the same, he must have the initiative left in his hands...If love were all that had to be considered, I would probably have refused.'

'I don't know if I follow.'

'No...I don't always follow very well myself.'

Helen rubbed the skin on the back of her hand, eyelids down, then looked up, quizzical. 'Sometimes I wonder if you're practising *Satyagraha*.'

'What's that?' Sullen, I frowned at her. 'I'm not practising anything. What do you mean—"practising"?'

She shook her head. 'It's the name Gandhi gave to non-violent resistance. It's a Sanskrit word, a compound of *satya*—truth—and *agraha* which means adherence, insistence.'

'Oh. I'm not practising anything. Why does everything have to have a name?'

Names made things too deliberate, and somehow small, and very distant. Names took things away.

Weighed down with worry and abstraction I lay on the bed, pressing my teeth softly into the cushion of my thumb.

Helen was saying, 'It's a philosophy of life: the search for truth through love or non-violence. Someone who practises it accepts wrong cheerfully and bravely—I'm quoting—and tries in this way to reach the heart of the opponent with the intention, not of defeating him, but converting him. A weapon of the strong, not the weak.

'Wait a minute.' She went over to the book-shelves in the corner, found a book, and came back, flicking through the pages. 'Yes. Here it is. Gandhi said, "Man and his deeds are two distinct things. Whereas a good deed should call forth approbation and a wicked deed disapprobation, the doer of the deed, whether good or wicked, always deserves respect or pity as the case may be. Hate the sin, and not the sinner is a precept which, though easy to understand, is rarely practised, and that is why the poison of hatred spread in the world."'

I was sitting up. 'Did he say that, Helen? Is that what he said?'

He sat in the coffee-bar like a hunted man waiting for a gun. His manner was both elated and cowed. Intense nervousness made him talk even more volubly than usual and he could think of nothing but Mrs Carruthers' belief in him. The tone of his conversation was prophetic, biblical, elegiac.

We sat against the wall, dipping spoons in and out of the creamy froth of coffee, while he talked about the Day of Judgement, and the Day of Reckoning.

Having seen the envelope in my hand, he wouldn't meet my eyes except for occasional glazed glances of fright that he disowned by assuming an air of desperate patronage. You'd have thought I was his conscience.

Not unkindly I said, 'Here it is.'

He winced away, muttering, 'Oh, God, it spoils everything, doesn't it? Though it's just for a few days, it ruins everything—money between us. And I still owe you that other. When I was working I *thought* of repaying some of it gradually, but Olive...I suppose you're adding up how much I've spent on whisky?...Darling...' he cast about, hating to appear in an unfavourable light. 'I don't *want* to do this. You know that.'

'Then *don't*,' I begged him. 'I believe you don't want to. Debts prey on you. Wait till you earn something. Clothes... They're only things. Futile. Not worth your peace of mind.'

Was it hopeless? Could he be swayed? Yes...

But he made a noise of disgust, looking at the table, touching spoon and saucer, deciding. 'You'll like me better when you see me well-dressed. For my self-respect I must have them.'

I was free to relax. I smiled, feeling tired. 'All right. Don't worry. Yes, I do trust you. Yes, probably you're right. I'll see you tonight, yes.'

I felt like a skeleton in a green dress, peculiarly light-limbed.

But now Christian was a dazzle of blue and gold, a victorious banner, a generous victor with God on his side. Benevolence and wisdom shone in his face. He knew it.

We parted cautiously as if each of us was afraid the other might wake.

'Mind if I come in for a last cigarette?' Helen was ready for bed in a dressing-gown of olive silk, white spotted.

'Help yourself!' I said, waving my brush at the divan and turning back to the mirror.

But I did mind. I did resent her physical presence in my room, her words in my ears, her breath on that air. My heart revolted at the intrusion. I brushed my hair venomously. Unbearable to be looked at! To have to look at her. Yes, I did resent the thoughts in her head. Her kindness did provoke in me a high nervous torment just short of suicidal.

Yet when she spoke I turned, melted into the chair, all edges gone, utterly seduced by her tone, hardly despising myself at all for it. For sitting on the bed, her cigarette streaming, she spoke kindly of him. Kindly. Admitting liking.

My heart thawed. Almost, my body wept. I said, 'Oh, Helen!...I must take off this polish,' and found cotton wool and polish-remover in the top drawer.

'I suppose coming from me this is a funny question, but has he any religion?'

I wiped my thumb-nail. 'Anglican. Very high, he said. (Naturally.) They do have confession and he talks of throwing himself on the mercy of the Church but—he isn't capable of doing any good to himself. Or anyone else. He hasn't the will. And he's too ashamed...'

'Can't, you persuade him to go?'

'Persuade him? I'd have to take him. And while he's with Olive only a fairly large loan makes it safe for him to

273

meet me except for the nights he has permission to come here. Remember what happened to the appointment you made for him? It would be the same again. He wouldn't go alone and couldn't defy Olive. According to her I invent these appointments as pretexts to be alone with him.'

'He's so completely dominated?'

I looked at my half-cleaned nails. 'Right now he's like someone on a trapeze—he won't jump till he's certain I'm going to catch him.'

Helen looked at me steadily. 'And do you intend to catch him?'

'I put no pressure on him to decide. But I wouldn't let him fall. He's waiting to be assured of that. Somehow I don't do it. I don't know why.'

'I'm convinced that people do what they want and nothing else. You don't want to.'

I stared at her. 'Oh, no. It isn't so simple. People can be afraid. And I don't *want* to have to dominate and bully him.'

Wandering across the room Helen stubbed out her cigarette in the glass ashtray on the window-sill. She said, 'You've every reason to be afraid. I'm more than relieved to hear it.'

How easily she spoke! How glibly! Amazement flickered. I gazed at the small bottle in my hand. 'But I despise caution—especially cautious emotion.'

She bounded back onto the bed, wrapping her gown round her legs. 'But this time the cost could be too high, as I think you realize. Clem, you have a lively mind. You care about what happens in the world. You meant to travel.

You've studied hard to equip yourself to do useful work that you like.'

All this news about me! So brightly delivered! I was dying, in a sense, I was dying, and brightly, logically, she discussed me with myself.

But temperately, for I was curious to understand, I reminded her, 'You've got Quentin.' What did she think the world was to me, that it wasn't to her?

'I know. But I sacrificed nothing.'

I left it. Yet I could not be silent. I could not stem the enormous urge to self-betrayal. 'Sometimes I wish a minor plague—a triple death—would solve it all. Do you remember that murder last week?'

'Lewis wondered why the husband hadn't walked out instead of killing his wife?' Helen felt in her pocket for her cigarette-case. She was really quite happy. How should she understand what I said?

'Yes, that one. Lewis thought it was incomprehensible.'

'Well, wasn't it?'

'No. Not for someone at the end of his tether. There is a sort of unbalanced logic about it, I can see that now. A crisis comes—after what sort of strain?—and we say, quite smug, since we aren't involved, "That man should go away from his wife." But his mind is shackled by her very existence. Simply never to see her again doesn't seem, at that moment, sufficient relief. While she breathes, the problem—whatever it might be—the great insoluble problem of his life will torment him. So he kills her.'

'And is hung.'

'That wasn't news to you?'

'I don't think I've thought about it much. I suppose I just don't think the subject's very amusing. In this situation of yours—to me, the possibility of a disaster has been by far the most unnerving thing.

'This is something I think you don't know. One morning some months ago I had a call from Olive. We hadn't met, but she and Christian were friends of yours, she said, and then she started to cry. They remembered that I was a doctor and wanted me to have a look at a gash on his head that wasn't healing properly. Anyway, after more tears and frantic appeals I agreed to see him on my way to work that morning.

'His head needed attention, certainly, but they hadn't dared to call the local doctor in case he asked questions. Olive admitted what had happened. I saw the poker she hit him with and, you know, she could very easily have killed him.

'Now I don't know why it seemed best not to tell you. But as you hadn't mentioned it to me...And to tell the truth I was too disturbed. I felt I might say too much and drive you to—'

'Well,' I said vaguely, still examining my nails. 'The things that happen! He didn't tell me either.'

'I should say I'm sorry.'

I shrugged. 'Doesn't matter— And you thought Olive was dangerous?'

'I remember her expression, that's all. She's threatened you, hasn't she?'

'Oh...I suppose so. But you say to yourself, "I have an enemy who would like to kill me!" It doesn't make much sense.'

276

'No,' Helen said without expression. 'No, it doesn't.' She stood up, automatically fixing the cord of her gown, and added, 'But just be careful.'

Something precariously suspended in me settled blissfully to earth. I am, he is, we are, here and living in the present. He stood inside the door and it was like the violent relief of being abandoned by a violent toothache.

This was an island in the air, not a small bed-sitting-room in London—a warm, bright place, subject to hurricanes now and then, true, but still...

Shortly he was saying, 'So I should grow up and stop searching for a substitute family in one person? Is that right?'

'Well, it might be a good idea.'

'I'm thirty: it's now or never, I suppose. You don't want me to be your family if we live together?'

'I do not!'

'And you refuse to be mine?'

'Exactly.'

'So what would we be—orphans and lovers? Since you would insist on "living in sin".'

'Just lovers.'

'What about babies? Would you ever want children, Clem? What do you think about that?'

'Nothing. No.'

Nonplussed, he made a comic face. 'You wouldn't? Why not? I thought every woman did? Why? Or do you mean just mine?'

'No, no. Any. The world's over-populated. I hate crowds.'

'Be serious,' he pleaded.

'I am. There are plenty of people. I've got a social conscience. Children now are self-indulgence.'

He looked at me—a baffled youthful look, uncertain, afraid of being teased. 'What are you talking about? Talk in English. If it comes to that—talk in French—but talk sense, will you, girl? I want to understand.'

I lit the gas-ring, grimaced at having to explain. 'It's just—some people tie up the loose ends they've inherited, organize themselves and finish off the line. Then, when they're dead, it's neat and proper and the best conclusion for them.'

Christian listened holding his head with his hands. He looked up. '*Why?* Are you just afraid of the responsibility? I wouldn't want that—though with you…But then, I'm different. I admit I'm too weak to take it. But I've never thought of you as weak.'

I tried to explain. 'It's nothing to do with weakness or strength. It's to do with inevitability.'

'You'd be sweet. You'd be nice. You're a loving girl.'

'I'm a loving girl. I'm too old to have children. Yes, getting on for twenty-six, but I always was. Too old. I wouldn't have happy children.'

He pressed his chin into his neck, smiling and frowning comically to make me laugh. 'Hey, hey! Let me smell your breath. Have I turned you into an alcoholic? No. She's sober, only slightly bats. And her so young and gentle.

'Look! The idea is—together—we'd be happy. Understand? I don't think I'd want children but if there were any, why shouldn't they be, too?'

278

'I might be jealous.'

Very shocked and sad, he said, 'That's a dreadful thing to say, darling. But I know you don't mean it. If you had a son he would respect you, and you could never disappoint him. *I* never would.' The idea moved him deeply. His face was transfigured.

I held one of his hands quite hard. 'I know that, darling.'

In a moment I said, 'But if you make things right with yourself, and I make things right with myself—'

'What'll happen?'

'We'll have done our duty.'

'Ah, but that's selfish,' he said reproachfully, sentimentally. Then he laughed a bit, wagging his head from side to side. 'But true. You know, it's funny. You're a mystery to me. Your whole life is. For instance—have you ever known another actor? Have you got a middle name? Have you seen the Taj Mahal?'

'Yes to everything.'

'Really? Is that true?' He was delighted to be proved right. 'Well there you are! And I'm for you.'

'Hullo, darling. This is Christian. Now it's all right. Don't panic. I *am* coming tonight.' He gave me a résumé of the events of the day since he'd called in the morning. And I listened like a scientist, I listened like a lover.

After a while he said abruptly, 'By the way, I've got the money for you. Carruthers gave it to me yesterday.'

Yesterday? I said, 'Oh? Good.'

For days I'd been receiving frantic assurances that he would repay me by the end of the week. 'You must believe me. I know I've treated you badly, Clem, but I could never be dishonest with you.'

I believed him, for he meant what he said. Or rather, I knew he believed what he said.

But another day he sneered, 'Do you think I'm thinking of robbing you?'

I ignored that though I realized that at the moment this was his exact intention. I guessed it would pass. He would overcome that particular devil on his shoulder, that whispering in his ear.

But this method of self-defence—the contemptuous accusation of mistrust—was one of his tricks that was thoroughly familiar to me now. Caught at a safe with a blow-lamp, Christian would have said with indescribable disdain, 'What do you think I'm trying to do—blow open the safe?'

And that cold self-possession and that disdainful smile would very successfully have burgled the conviction of his discoverer.

Now he said, 'Yes, I've got it. Old Carruthers had trouble getting rid of some—I don't know—rubber or something at the right price—I don't know what.'

Idly I doodled on an open notebook.

Christian gave a short uneasy laugh. 'I don't mean to be unkind, darling. I'm not *blaming* you, but I wish like hell you hadn't given me that money when I asked for it. It's all gone and there's practically nothing to show for it. Most of your fifty—Carruthers's fifty, I should say—went in two days. Drinks for the kids in the house here. The room was afloat.' He gave a peculiar sobbing laugh. 'I actually burned some. Did you know that? Put a match to some notes! Christ, what a bloody maniac!'

I said nothing but through him I felt the nightmare pressure of Things, Them...He did feel this whatever the purpose of his words, whatever cunning hope had prompted them. It was simply that he had to use even his most genuine feelings.

At length he said sullenly, 'So I've got the money and I'll come round in an hour.'

I could feel the twist of reluctance in his shoulders and see the frowning smile as he added, 'But the thing is—I don't want to give it to you.'

'Oh, you don't! That's too bad!' I said good-humouredly. 'Because it's mine. And I certainly want it back.'

'You really do?' he said, laughing too, in the same uneasy way.

'Quite definitely. I need it.' And we were all the while smiling strangely at each other through the telephone, gambling, contesting, both laughing softly and elevated with shock.

Need, I had said, deflecting the argument. 'Lewis and Helen would help you,' he coaxed in a charming uneasy voice. 'You wouldn't be stuck. If they're your friends they should help you.'

The fantastic effrontery of this speech laid me low, but still I smiled, determined, saying, 'But I don't need their help. I don't intend to be stuck. I want you to return that money to me as you promised.'

'Well,' he half laughed. 'If you really insist, I haven't much choice. I'll be round in an hour.'

281

We both spoke with peculiar dreamy elation, but I was solid with resolution as I jangled the receiver back on the stand, and swung my legs from the divan.

I *would* hang on. He *must* keep his promise. I wouldn't let him wriggle out of this. My heart pounded as I whirled about the room, brushing hair and teeth. Oh, I didn't *want* to be cheated. He mustn't...

The hour was up. In front of the mirror I was pulling a face, gritting my teeth and showing determination when the one-two ringing of the telephone started.

If it's—

'Hullo?'

'This is Olive, Clem.' Meek and triumphant. 'Chris can't face you tonight. He'll come at the end of the week. His nerves are bad. It's the money. He needs it, you see. He's sort of hysterical. When he does come—make it easy for him, will you?...'

A tug-o'-war.

He sat on the divan in his old raincoat, staring at the floor, being confused and depressed and ashamed. I let him.

A hand came out to touch me.

'Oh, all right!' He stuck the rejected hand back in his pocket. There was another silence. Outside it was raining.

'You make me feel like a criminal...I suppose it is stealing—in a way. But I'll pay you back later. You won't lose anything. Don't worry!'

I resisted this and other tactics with cast-iron inflexibility, and he argued uneasily back, with quizzical lop-sided grins, with frozen grimaces, with abrupt alternations

282

between scorn for me and self-castigation for himself. But always the little treasure, the little prize, he held high in one hand out of reach.

Stony, I sat, making it hard for him. It was all I could do now for either of us. The surface of my mind did seethe and surge with disappointment, indignation and wounded pride. And I was remotely frightened of the future this would create. But I knew by the demoniac glint behind the blue eyes that he was literally taken over, possessed. I knew that fearful threats or violence might part him from his trophy—but nothing I had at my disposal.

Off the rails...Not a phrase I'd ever used, but I knew now that it was coined to describe just this look in other strange eyes. I had the impression of being in the company of two separate men who conversed together in glaring gay asides that I was supposed not to notice.

'You told Lewis and Helen and Bertrand, I'm sure? And probably dear Lucy Turner and a few of the cleaners?' He prayed I had not.

'Lewis and Helen—yes. You like to be understood, so it's only right that they should have a clear picture. Let's be honest about it, as you're so fond of saying.'

'Ha! You would!...What'd they say?' He threw off a whole gallery of agitated and disapproving friends, then gave a very cynical grown-up smile, one corner of his mouth tucked in, a rakish Regency sort of smile.

It melted, thawed, collapsed, fell in ruins of childish woe and incredulity. '*Not* to send for the police?' He laughed and surveyed the ceiling, his mouth wide with wonder and fright. 'You aren't thinking of doing that? You're—too fond

283

of me—aren't you? In spite of everything? Just as—in spite of everything, and the way this looks—I'm too fond of you for my good or yours.'

I also had a cynical smile at my disposal.

'How do you feel now that I've done this?' he asked, leaning forward with genuine curiosity. I said, 'Surprised. Disappointed' and he turned away, disappointed himself, drawling, 'Now don't give me that childish stuff, Clem, as if I'd taken your ice-cream.'

But he *was* ashamed, and bitten by his nerves, and sat frowning fist to mouth in silence—yet restlessly, with awful mental agitation. He was mauled by guilt, was almost physically tormented by something invisible to me, crawling over him...

Yet for all that our words were often sharp, the temperature of the room was mild and acrimony out of place. The facts existed complete, I felt, and without threats or violence, what action was left open to me was as rigid and complete as what was past.

Looking at me in soft astonishment to explain it to him, Christian said, 'I never dreamed I'd do a thing like this to you. I didn't plan it. I always meant to give it back. But—these things just happen sometimes...'

Memory after memory filtered through my mind: Christian recounting with distaste and wonder the numerous swindles in his past seeming to stem from him, which had actually happened to him. The good old passive voice!

Still, I had to remember if he truly thought that, then it was so indeed. One day when there was time I would follow this philosophy further...

But I lit the gas-ring and moved about the room collecting cups and making coffee while we discussed the surprising event objectively, neither emotional nor deliberately distant.

'You wouldn't threaten to cut off my lessons because of this, I know.' Laying confidence on me so carefully. 'And I don't *think* you would disclose my—misdeeds—to Rollo, for instance, or Mrs Carruthers, or anywhere where it would do me harm?' Weighing my expression he said slowly, 'Yes, one can always—count—on your discretion.'

I smiled and had a picture of him sitting with Olive seriously calculating, 'One can *allow* for Clem's discretion...'

And beneath the reasonable debate about his strange behaviour to me, silent messages flew fast and plain.

'You wouldn't like me to accuse you of blackmail,' his eyes said. 'And if you did take reprisals—by stopping lessons—or telling Rollo or anyone important—that is what it would be. No, you must always set me a good example. And how disillusioned I'd be if you of all people threatened!'

An apprehension of the branching complications intoxicated me. Clearly, I couldn't win. If I acted, it was moral blackmail; if I acquiesced he would take that inference which most flattered—that my will was weakened by a deathless passion.

Let him! I thought. I wanted that. He knew nothing of me. I defied him.

Tiredly at the door he said good-bye. It was quite late. He had actually agreed to give the money back. I hardly thought he would, but it was something even to have made the intention light up for a second. His raincoat rasped as

285

he put it on; watching him I fingered the little white knob of the electricity switch.

'I suppose you haven't got someone planted in the cupboard?' he looked up from the raincoat business very cagily. 'Hearing all this? Or a tape-recorder?'

'In the cupboard?'

'Yes. You know. Listening to me. Evidence.' And he smiled an atrocious foxy smile as if to say: 'I wouldn't be surprised. It would be the clever thing to do.'

'No,' I protested, widening my eyes. 'No, of course not,' I said earnestly, reassuring him, beginning to understand. Then I repeated it with smiling indignation. But the more I admitted the knowledge of his suspicions to my understanding the more my mind sank and shifted, readjusting yet again to the tortuous ways of his.

286

CHAPTER THIRTEEN

It was very quiet. An ornate bronze clock on the wall ticked slowly. Dr Craig sat at his desk writing on a beige card. A soft leather armchair supported me. And someone was taking care of me.

A shrewd, well-tailored, laconic man, the doctor. What was he writing? What had I gabbled? For instance, when he asked, 'How are you sleeping?' I said I slept from five in the morning till nine while the eye of my mind stayed on duty. True enough. But wasn't it neurotic to say so? Oh, God only knew what I'd said! A lot of nonsense probably.

Smoothly and fast his pen went over the orange card, mesmerizing me.

'Now, Miss James.' He shifted his chair out at an angle from the desk and crossed his legs.

'You're not sick!' Christian said that night.

'I didn't say I was.'

'Then why did you go to see the doctor?'

'Headaches,' I said innocuously.

'*I'm* the one who's ill.' He looked worried at the sound of his words. 'I've lost too much weight. I don't like my face to get too haggard. For my height I should be about—' he went off into statistics.

When he'd worked all that out, he said, 'By the way, where's your wireless? Sold?' He smiled grimly, raising his brows. 'The programmes are rotten anyway. I hardly ever listen. Well, it was worth a bit. That'll pay your rent for a few weeks.'

He watched and waited. Can I make her angry? Can I make her rave? His lips parted with eager boyish curiosity. No, sweetheart, I thought, my heart warming to him. I did cherish him. He was so awful.

'A little work, a little work,' I said. 'You can read if you like.' And I turned to look at the books stacked on the chest behind my chair.

'Villon? Yes, I insist on Villon. I'm contrary. I want to know why you so cleverly edged me away from him before.' Already standing, hand on the volume, he held my eye.

'Did I?…All right.'

So he stretched out on the divan, and juggled with the lamp on the table till the circle of light fell on the page, then he began and I closed my eyes.

> *En l'an de mon trentiesme aage,*
> *Que toutes mes hontes j'eus beues,*
> *Ne du tout fol, ne du tout sage,*
> *Non obstant maintes peines eues,*

Lesquelles j'ay toutes receues
Soubz la main Thibault d'Aussigny...
S'evesque il est, seignant les rues,
Qu'il soit le mien je le regny.

For an hour or more he read, and reading, used his voice to such effect, with such humility and grace, that my senses moved with joy. The complementary beauty of sound and meaning purged me instantly of premonition, tangled feeling. A lightness of the spirit, of joyful gravity, enveloped me.

And he was subdued by what he had at his command, and used himself with abnegation.

Afterwards in our clothes we lay side by side, gently, in horizontal voices, talking about Villon, falling silent, and finally, not having moved, almost slept.

But at last he roused me, turning to say, 'Am I to come to you, darling? Could you just let me go? If you would, you can't feel very deeply about me. Would I drive us crazy with guilt over Olive? You know what I'm like. And how could you respect me now—after what I've done?' he persisted. 'You must despise me, Clem. I know I can be really very nice—I *am* really nice—but the other half is pretty rotten, isn't it?'

I faltered under the barrage of talk. Was his aim to wring a disclaimer from me about the money? Was I to say, 'It was nothing. I'm glad you did it'?

Out in the corridor Helen was going to and from the kitchen. Christian pricked his ears and rose on one elbow. 'Listen! Does she know about us? Does everyone?'

289

I looked up at him with stony friendliness. 'I've no idea.'

'I bet they do...Don't they wonder?' he asked discontentedly, unwilling to think himself of so little importance. He smoothed the collar of my blouse.

Not everyone exists to think about you! I felt like saying. But would he believe me? Weakened by that much egotism (as I was by its converse when I saw him deflated out of all proportion by a word or look that touched his quick) I was silent, simply catching his hand and biting his forefinger gently. His eyes leapt and laughed in mine, he was distracted, but inevitably he returned to the future.

'Olive *knows* but won't admit it. She's been looking at single rooms in case you and I go off to Paris together. But I don't think she needs to worry, do you? I don't think you'd leave your safe little world to go anywhere, would you?'

Wryly I remembered Dublin. I would have gone *then*. I might even now...

He said, 'We're wasting time, we're wasting time,' and drew his arm from under my shoulders and stood up. I followed him. He drew the curtains and I undressed with an automatic blankness that might or might not have been feigned. I could no longer judge the authenticity of my actions or feelings.

Yet, after all, he was no enemy. After all, when he had gone I could—in thinking of a parting that would never be, to test myself—feel weak, annihilated, with impetuous grief.

Oh, I was alive, no doubt! And weak, fragile and ill I could feel with his departure from my arms and this small room.

Ten past twelve.

Was he with Olive now? With *her*?

Oh, no! Not jealousy, too! A few exhausted tears drained from the sullen swamp of despair in my chest. Really, it's amusing, I thought. In a moment you will tell yourself that your distaste for his whole dreary bag of tricks is a sham, dreamed up to deceive yourself so that you can think: is that all he is? So that you won't break to pieces when he goes.

I picked up a book and began to read. My love, it said. My love...

The long ingenuous twilit evenings passed, and now in late October milky mists puffed along the streets above the lamp-posts. From my window I could see a car being towed by a yellow truck, and on the footpath opposite two boys in leather jackets were looking at a motor-bike, squatting on their haunches to tinker with the engine.

'May I come in?' It was Helen with a brown paper shopping-bag which she dumped on the table. 'Some food. How are you?'

'Oh, thanks. Thank you. Fine.' I was a bit apologetic for it was inconsiderate to let things slide like this. Why should Helen, who was busy at work all day, have to shop for me? If I found it too much of an effort, why shouldn't she? I couldn't at all feel that I would do the same for her.

'Been working?' She pulled off her string gloves and looked round the room.

'Of course. Ready to post.' I flapped the weekly foolscap envelope at her. 'I thought I heard Lewis and Bertrand a moment ago?'

291

'Men!' She lifted her eyes. 'They think they're being kind collecting me for a drink instead of meeting me somewhere. They're in my room checking some of Bertrand's facts, I gather. Right in the middle of my room! I can't move.'

During his summer vacation, Bertrand had completed a prodigious research project and was tonight to address a student organization on some such subject as 'Advertising, Television and Youth'. Helen and Lewis were pledged to go with him.

'Hope you enjoy it,' I said unconvincingly, beginning to unpack the bag. Oranges, apples and bananas, she had brought, and eggs, bread, butter, cheese and steak. I looked at it all spread out on the table: the round bright oranges with their sickly fragrance, the weighty cheese…And I felt somehow abused to be made to own so much, cruelly hedged in by the problems of disposal. But one or other of my two disguises—the polite, the petulant—which Helen imagined were me, saved me from her understanding.

Lewis came in as I started to wash some gloves. I looked in the direction of his tie and turned again to the basin.

He lit the fire, and asked me about my work, and outlined the theme of Bertrand's lecture, his manner seeming somewhat forcedly enthusiastic. I let my gloved hands float about in the warm water. The mirror above had little white flecks of toothpaste spattered on it, not rubbed off this morning.

'We thought of coming back about ten from the club,' Lewis was saying, 'and if you're free, going on to Bertrand's. He's got some new records and a piece of equipment for his gramophone that revolutionizes listening, he assures us. Why don't you come?'

Ten o'clock. If I had seen Christian in the meantime it would be loathsome to be set upon by their three alien personalities: on the other hand, it was lonely, lonely, to be left without him, with years of darkness between me and morning.

'All right. If Christian's gone.' I hadn't meant to sound as ungracious as that, but Lewis smiled with pleasure.

Rollo sat astride the upright chair by the basin, resting his arms on the back; beside him on the chest of drawers was a white china cup full of brandy. In the far corner by the bed the lamp glowed without much relieving the density of the dusk.

On the edge of the armchair I was facing the divan where Christian lay, and looking twisted across my shoulder at Rollo.

Now he stopped speaking and lifted the cup and drank. I stared glassily at his hand, the long arm in the black sweater.

'He'll sleep for half an hour more at least.'

His dispassionate glance indicated yet again that this evening was nothing unusual. The slow crumbling-up of one friend was much like that of another. Of no shattering importance, he seemed to say, to someone in his position.

I found his calm paralysing, insupportable. His detachment seemed not human.

Christian had arrived with Rollo's assistance at seven o'clock after five telephone calls spread over the afternoon to herald his approach.

He was very drunk. Violently drunk. 'Come to celebrate. Date's set for Paris. You're coming with me. I've left
Olive. Don't argue.' He barged into the room and hulked
unsteadily about, clumsy and hoarse, seeming enormous
and curiously sombre, as if the blacking out of something luminous in his nature had caused a visible light to
snap off.

In a minute he fell against the wall in the corner and
slid to the floor and went instantly to sleep. Then Rollo
stepped forward to lift out the two brandy bottles from his
clasped arms. But he woke at once with a sort of guttural
roar and rolled against the wall, hugging his bottles. And
from the corner, not knowing who his enemies were, he
glared out at us.

We seemed to tower over him. By some simple transference his sense of defending himself against Titans, of our
power and magnification in his eyes, did make us seem
to dilate. He looked fantastically small and breakable, so
expecting to be broken...I couldn't bear it.

Rollo was talking now, very quietly, leaning over him,
making him cower back, saying that he wasn't trying to
steal his bottles, only to open them for him, so that he could
have a drink. Because, as Christian knew, he wasn't in a
condition to do it himself.

I looked at him in wild despair. Was he mad? What did
he *mean*—so that he could have a drink? Couldn't he see
that Christian was half-crazed with the stuff?

Rollo caught my look. 'We couldn't stop him now.
Don't worry. We'll water it. He won't notice. Then he'll
go to sleep.'

Shortly, sullen and mistrustful, Christian clambered up off the floor and after another half-hearted struggle to dash one against the side of the basin, allowed Rollo to wrest the bottles away from him.

'Come on,' Rollo said, 'you aren't launching anything.'

And he gave a short reluctant laugh and allowed himself to be wooed over to the divan, still frowning theatrically and unsure of his identity.

Rollo tore the foil from the neck of the bottle and turned the cork-screw. On the divan, his face flushed, his expression disordered, Christian was mumbling something, complaining, starting to haul off his sweater and yank off his shoes and socks, flinging them about.

Swinging his lowered head, he tried craftily to get Rollo's business with the brandy into focus. He was very suspicious. Up he got and lumbered across to the basin where Rollo stood easing out the cork, and seemed to try to climb over his shoulders to see what was happening. He was dreadfully suspicious.

Now he wove about, glass in hand, arms extended, brandy slopping, 'I might've been—I might've been—'

He wandered about, immensely noisy, incredibly never falling. With two or three words he'd begin, then halt abruptly as if he'd been tapped on the shoulder and reminded of something important that, nevertheless, he couldn't quite remember.

The rapid bated changes of mood, expression and tone, the enormous confusion of voices and emotion gave the nightmarish effect of twelve stricken men arguing out some mysterious and tragic event in their common past.

295

He was relatively unaware of the presence of anyone in the room. If now and then he noticed me it was not with recognition.

Noisily, anguished, he pleaded with those other people. But they were cruel and meant to hurt him, and he crumpled piteously. Or else they were stupid suddenly, and he was very cunning and crowed and smiled.

It was likely that someone would complain about the noise soon. Downstairs, upstairs, across the hall. No one was deaf.

But there were periods of silence during which he sat head down, gliding in and out of consciousness. Then he woke coughing, and groaned and shuddered. He went to hang over the basin in silence for a few seconds, and this was somehow a trick, designed to mislead those unseen persecutors.

When he lifted his glass and turned again, he realized that he was not alone and hesitated, childishly at a loss to know what to do. Then with a secret smile he poured his glass of brandy over the carpet and waited.

No one reacted.

At this failure to communicate he screwed up a vaguely disgruntled expression and trotted back to the bed where he fell face down, and promptly slept.

Was it a trick? No one moved. Was it the real thing? Sleep? So tightly strung that natural functions—breathing, blood flowing—were almost painful: then seconds had passed, and I dared to breathe out and Rollo did, and we looked at one another blankly eloquent, relaxing.

First of all we arranged the arms and legs and body on the bed in some sort of order. I paused to look at the large fair head on the pillow, saw the shoulders slowly rise and fall as his breath came and went.

Rollo prepared another glass of watered brandy against a certain demand, and I collected the scattered clothes from the floor. Then what was left in the first bottle, and all of the second one I poured down the sink.

Mean, low, despicable it felt, sneaking about like solemn puritans doing things for his good while he was helpless.

You had to be cruel to be kind, they said. To children, perhaps. To sad-eyed pups that overeat. But adults? To adults?

To this adult, it seemed. Scruples and fine feelings were self-indulgent, hindrances in the way of his survival.

When we sat down again in the increasing darkness, now that it was dark outside, Rollo began to talk. And because the light was dim and it was no known hour, like survivors of a shipwreck adrift in an open boat, we spoke without misunderstanding, not knowing facts about each other, but aware of all that mattered.

When he spoke about Christian, it was to recall piteous anecdotes that Christian would have suffered to know I heard—exposing more of his vulnerability than was right to be known. I turned the talk away, saying, 'I wanted to help him.'

'He isn't easy to help. He never has been. For some people, you know, Clemency, it's too late.'

Too late, he said.

My heart emptied at the finality of his tone.

Too late?

297

Like an oracle, with a weird impassive authority, he had said it.

Almost beyond bitterness, incredulity or sorrow, but as if I'd heard him sentence Christian to death, I stared at his face, waiting for a denial.

He only said, 'If Paris comes off—do you intend to go with him?'

A pause. '*If?* I thought it was settled. Didn't he say...'

'Ah, yes. To sound me. But at the moment it's all—poised, ready to be confirmed by my father. I have to approach him now.'

Abruptly he lifted a hand and nodded.

There was a movement on the bed. Christian stirred. It was quite late now, entirely black outside; no light at all came through the drawn curtains. I could just see the humped bulk of his body against the pale wall.

Slowly he dragged himself up, strangely grunting with effort, bed creaking, clothes rustling, and again the noises of great exertion.

He paused suddenly. The commotion stopped. Even the sound of breathing. Twisting up from the bed, supported on his arms, he hung—listening.

The room was black. He was afraid of it. He was listening to the dark. Trying to think.

If only the light was on! But sudden light might unhinge him.

We waited in the dark.

A blood-curdling stream of gibberish came from the bed. A thin scream of gibberish. Weirdly it ripped through the silence, gibbering shouts and warrior exclamations.

298

Nothing intelligible, no single word. Yet up and down went the tone of the noises, small animal noises, a travesty of speech.

Lower I felt myself sink, empty and chill. I stared through the dark.

Hoarse cries and gurgles of incoherent sound reverberated from the walls, against my ears, against my heart.

Abruptly it was silent again, the noise on the bed. As if it was waiting for, listening to, a reply.

No one moved.

'My sister! Stella! Stella!' he shouted, jumping round on the bed, starting up entranced, one arm raised to touch, or ward off, an apparition.

His eyes were fixed on something in the air above and behind me. And the projection of his vision came from him with such overpowering force that the room did feel inhabited by spirits and strange lights.

Across the carpet he went unevenly, arm upraised in supplication, babbling softly, babbling.

By Rollo's chair, standing between us, he halted. But again he addressed what he could see with cries and whimpers, more noisily pleading, pausing now and then for irregular periods to listen acutely.

Gradually, very slowly, Rollo began to talk to him. Matter-of-factly and softly he started to answer those rushing scalp-pricking noises with words and sentences. He was recalling him to himself, calming him as though he were a high-strung animal.

I attended to the crazy dialogue in frozen horror, as if I were blind and deaf. What was happening? What were they saying? What was it?

I knew nothing, yet through him I somehow knew too much. An endless phantasmagoria we were in. Mad dreams under ether. Like temporary insanity.

'Talk to him,' said Rollo.

Had I a voice? Say what? My mind was glacial.

Christian was reaching into the air, face transfigured, sound pouring from his mouth.

Was there no one to help him, save him, stop him?

Occasionally I could make out a word, a phrase, now.

Still Rollo spoke to him in disconnected soothing sentences, and I found I could speak, and did.

'I'm not afraid to die,' he whispered, leaning down, soft-faced, 'just please tell me when it's to be. *Please*.'

He was on his knees, head bowed, talking to Stella, and yes, it was all right now, I said. Yes, she did forgive him and want him to be safe. Nothing was wrong. He would see. Yes, he did have to struggle with his own nature but he was good. And we did all care very much about him. Would all help.

Rollo got up and turned on the white centre light and more and more Christian seemed to recover. Minutely the atmosphere untensed, claws of the mind retracted. A lifetime we'd hung on, a lifetime we'd talked.

Recognizing us now, he declared monotonously, at length, that Rollo must go away: he wanted to be alone with Clem.

'If it wasn't that I'm expected somewhere—long overdue,' Rollo said. 'He's still pretty bad. He's going to be intractable. Do you think you can cope?'

'Now,' said Christian, as soon as we were alone, 'we're going to bed. I've left Olive.' And he lunged at me with a great show of strength and certainly was stronger than ten ordinary men. He was going to be as malleable as a sledge-hammer, I could tell.

I had a very small stock of tricks in my repertoire, however I tried one now, complaining a little reproachfully that I disliked the taste of brandy.

Slowly horror registered. His politeness was at stake! He flinched away, almost blushing his apologies, and went to rummage in the cupboard for his toothbrush.

'I'm terribly sorry, darling,' he kept turning to say.

I stood trying to think while he was engaged at the basin. If I could persuade him to drink gallons of coffee…If he would sleep again…If he would shout less…If no one complained or called the police…I knew if I showed any signs of resistance he'd be violent as I had only heard he could be. This was a very temporary truce.

'Clem!' It was Bertrand's voice. Christian had just hauled off his white T-shirt and was washing his face with the ineptitude of a four-year-old.

'Clem! Bertrand here!'

Christian looked round at me, instantly diverted. On went the shirt and he emerged, somewhat pettishly bothered by his hair, which he was incapable of fixing, and whispering to me, 'Where are your manners, darling? Don't keep a guest waiting at your door.'

He shouted, 'Please wait a moment, Bertrand.'

It all had to happen. There was no way out. I called, 'Two minutes, Bertrand,' and getting my comb from the chest, fixed his rumpled hair. Restlessly, but at the same time with a sort of grateful passivity, Christian submitted to this, and to having his face wiped clean and dried. He felt warm to be near, and alive.

In his best grey suit, Bertrand stood at the door, an air of considerable embarrassment overlaying a look of being well pleased with himself. He looked tanned and extremely fit. He protested, 'Why didn't you just say, "Go to hell!"? I feel like—'

But he saw how Christian was.

Helen and Lewis were coming upstairs. The door was open. 'Who's that? Who's that?' Christian cried, somehow emotionally. 'Please come in! It's good to see you Lewis. And you, Helen, my dear. Please sit down. Bertrand, would you move that chair? No, please don't go!'

They weren't to go because he had to tell them all he loved me. Yes, he'd been drinking but would they please not belittle him or what he felt on that account. He worshipped the ground I walked on. He would never make me unhappy. He knew and agreed with all they might think about him, he knew what he was, but would they please not belittle him *now*, or what he was saying, because of it. This was his last chance.

Loudly he spoke and with a naked private sincerity, his voice racked and from a depth I'd heard sounded perhaps once, if ever, in my life before.

Like a Greek chorus Helen and Lewis and Bertrand watched and listened. They had an air of outdoors, of being other creatures from another world. Yet for all their difference and long-held hostility, they were moved, not sceptical; they had no scorn.

302

I should take two steps and touch his arm. I should speak and claim him. I should...

It was arranged that Christian should go home with Bertrand to his flat. Helen and Lewis seemed to speak to me, saying reassuring things about 'in the morning' and 'after you've slept'.

At the bus stop Jan bounded up to us, all her fair curls jumping. 'Haven't seen you for years! Do you know there's only a big hole where Miss Evans's used to be? They've pulled it all down. You've lost weight!'

'You know Helen Reid, don't you?'

Jan had on a dark blue suit and carried a paper bag with a dress-shop label. 'Shopping. Don't know how I'm going to pay for it!' Leaning back on her high heels she laughed very gaily showing a lot of sound white teeth. 'What've you been doing? Just working? There's a good thing on at the Academy—Italian—would you like to go one night?'

'Can I ring you later this week? Here's our bus. Nice to see you again, Jan. I'll ring in two or three days and fix something.'

We went upstairs to the very front through the cigarette smoke, swaying.

When we met, rather than walk, rather than sit still, I had said, 'Let's catch a bus somewhere,' so here we were. Helen got tickets to the terminus, wherever it was. I sat slumped, staring out at the road ahead.

Saturday crowds paraded busily up and down Knightsbridge. The flower-stalls were dazzling in the lovely autumn light. At Hyde Park Corner the traffic was thick, choking

303

the roads, but the buildings and the park seemed to glitter with sunny solid prosperity and assurance.

Wrapped in my overcoat, looking straight ahead, I felt tears start again to trickle down my face, slide coolly to my neck.

'Are you sure you want to stay here? Perhaps we should go home.'

'No!…I don't want to be inside a house. I'm not upset.'

I had gone to Bertrand's flat at nine o'clock, and Olive arrived shortly afterwards. Christian had bathed and was in bed wearing a pair of Bertrand's pyjamas. Though he must have been quite ill he looked fantastically healthy and vital. Beside him even Bertrand had the air of a displaced person.

Till this morning Olive hadn't known where he was, so last night she had had a taste of—where is he? What's happening now? Is he with her?

The socialization of suffering. I *liked* equality.

'Can't you tell me what happened?' Helen said, and added humbly, 'I promise not to—say anything.'

As if it mattered! It was just a question of finding breath.

'Well—I went in. I'd decided, as I told you, that I must take care of him. It seemed the only thing. In the beginning I'd hoped it would be possible to—cure him, I suppose—make him—what he ought to be—could have been. But last night when Rollo said—did I tell you, Helen? He said *it was too late.*'

Again that little poisonous gush of anguish as words and meaning stabbed to the quick. Real blood might have gushed from my mouth and not surprised. I waited a moment.

'Well—for the first time I faced the idea that all anyone might be able to do would be to look after him. After my high hopes it seemed—sad—but I thought I would do it. That I could still, even at that, be better for him than Olive. For I do respect him in some way I don't understand.'

Looking down at her gloved hands, Helen listened, and dusty sunshine through the dirty windows lighted her face.

'Did you change your mind then?'

'No, not exactly…When I got there Bertrand was making breakfast. I went in to see Christian and he—sat up in bed in an excited sort of way as if he'd been planning and waiting. He looked quite luminous—I know it sounds funny, but he did. Very happy.

'I was rather stunned, I suppose. It seems a fairly permanent state with me lately. I took his hand and his eyes glittered at me—all sorts of questions. Just stood by the bed like that feeling—enormous relief to be with him. A weird sort of peace, because till that moment I'd felt ghastly. But standing there, and looking, it felt as if both of us were smiling faintly through and through, smiling into one another…

'Bertrand came in eventually and Olive arrived being quietly tragic. She was very smart in all her new clothes, and she'd put on a martyred expression. We were very polite to one another. She sat up straight in a straight chair and folded her hands and legs away neatly, so ladylike.

'Well—Bertrand said should he go, but everyone said no. And Christian started to talk. He said if I asked him to leave at once, he would, without thinking twice about Olive. They were through. Olive said she'd known that for a long time and in a way it was a relief. She just wanted to know where she stood so that she could make a life for herself.'

A life for herself! I had felt a twinge of jealousy, envy.

'It was odd. Christian and I were both somehow extremely animated and fluent, smiling this heart-to-heart smile as if we were enjoying ourselves. As if it was a party. But *not* enjoying...I was on the carpet by the bed. Bertrand and Olive just sat, rather astonished by our liveliness...'

I remembered Christian propped up on one elbow, his brilliant elation. As if we were alone, he mused and reminisced. There was a cloudy look of wonder about his eyes. Now and then we smiled at each other warmly, sweetly, with familiarity and forgiveness—I from the floor, he down from the bed.

'Olive said, "She's got no more money, you know. She won't be able to keep you. How are you going to live?" He was very biting. And she was easily cowed. I felt—rather low—shameless. It wasn't unpleasant.

'Because she was undivided in her mind Olive seemed—more serious than either of us. She wasn't. But she's seriously obsessed. Anyway, Christian talked about our life together in the future. I listened with the others and said nothing. I couldn't make myself speak.

'So then gradually it changed. He'd invited me to say, "Come away!" and I hadn't said it. If *he* had said it, I'd have had no decision to make. And I wouldn't have hesitated. It was what I'd intended. To be with him. But I couldn't say it myself.

'So he began to worry then if Olive would have him back. And he said that though he'd been prepared to come away with me at once, wherever I chose, now he felt he had obligations to Olive.

'So I put on my coat and cried in a slow theatrical way. I owed him tears. And he was very gentle. Olive must have been relieved. When she asked what we intended to do, neither of us spoke—not a word. I felt physically a bit wrecked but nothing really...So I came away...'

'Are you seeing him again?'

'Oh, yes! Tomorrow. Till Rollo confirms the Paris job. He was so agitated about not stopping anything till then. And really, after all...'

It was ironic—his having been willing to come with me now, when he had murdered feeling, made me too weak to be of use to him, to withstand or turn the tide of his personality.

Funny. He had given me a long and complicated trial. And I had passed. And then I'd broken up.

'Poor Clem!' The movement of Helen's body as she turned caused a wave of perfume to advance over me, into my lungs. I had been given a bottle of the same perfume for my last birthday, knew it much too well. 'Poor Clem! You've been pulled in all directions. I don't feel I've helped. Neither has Lewis. But then he isn't disinterested.'

Sympathy was not what I wanted! I despised it and all soft things.

Vaguely I said, 'I feel very ineffectual. Not much staying power. Reach the outside limits of a situation like this very quickly...'

Helen was making excuses I didn't hear above the flat jumbled perturbation of my spirit.

A sense of the irrelevance of talk, and something else—like a suppressed memory of tragedy—flared in me, lit my mind.

'Where are we? Where do you think this is?' I peered out of the dirty window. Then was pushed back against the seat by a thought that made me say, 'One thing surprises me to realize: I know I could have stood the strain of feeling for Christian, loving him, if I'd been supported by—I don't know—a family—religious belief. On my own account I knew all about—endurance tests—passive resistance. I never needed help. In that sense I've been tough all my life. And for Christian—so that he wouldn't be hurt any more—I tried to suffer, and did. But I cared more than I had about myself, so I couldn't—take it, I suppose. Not for a lifetime. Not without faith. Which is not to say I have the inclination to dump any burdens anywhere. Just—I didn't realize I had limitations. In my head I did. But I hadn't touched them.'

The bus braked suddenly and everyone lurched. It moved again and the passengers vibrated, swayed and stared out of the windows. Leaving it, we would all smell of cigarettes.

Lucy Turner came in just as he was going. With her shoulders braced and her motherly shape swathed in bronze wool, Lucy looked at us with large alert eyes, affecting benign interest.

Christian and I stared at her, the broken conversation dangling, jangling in our ears.

308

'Off already, Mr Roland? This is a short visit tonight!'

Of course she had seen him come in.

'I have an engagement,' he said curtly, then turning to me, 'Good night, Clem. I'll ring you. Good night, Mrs Turner.'

Hypnotized, Lucy slid out of the way to let him pass.

Slam! The quickness of the exit deceives the eye!

Lucy and I let out soft sighs of bewilderment to see him gone, and gazed uncertainly at each other for a second.

'Well, I'm sorry to have disturbed you, but I just heard half an hour ago that a friend's coming from Cambridge tomorrow for the Motor Show. So I want to clear up the meters and accounts tonight.'

Rattling her shillings, and eyeing herself surreptitiously in the glass above the chest, Lucy admired the freesias in the pottery vase. A figure in a dream, she was, trying in the ennervating fashion of dream-figures to hold my attention. Finally she disappeared.

He had exploded into the room, his hair damp with rain, light raincoat flapping, then swiftly off and tossed aside, catching my arms. Fair, flushed, his teeth sparkling, and brow uncomplicated as a jar of cream—I had the feeling of being held in the arms of a charming but precocious adolescent, the head-boy, the hero of the school.

Amazement moved in me during these silent seconds to feel his enormous eagerness for this meeting. As if something was *starting*...We had all but renounced each other!

'Faint heart!' he mocked, smiling into my eyes. 'Faint heart!'

Abashed, I looked away. Faint heart. But we smiled together and my heart, not faint at all, went out to him. While inside me someone groaned, 'Oh, not again! I'm tired! It can't start again...'

His hands were on my shoulders. 'Come here, darling. Clem. I've been watching the clock, been waiting...'

I could have fallen on him.

I swayed, and moved away decisively, reminded by my brain that we had chosen, said: not all that again.

'Oh, yes!' Understanding, he sat down on the edge of the bed, hands on knees, repulsed and growing venomously angry. 'That promise to Olive! Good little teacher and pupil act we're supposed to play, huh? You'll get a halo one day for sure!'

We stared fixedly.

Lucy Turner knocked and announced herself as he pulled on his coat again...Now he was gone. And here I was alone, instead of with him. Alone with four pink walls and two nickel taps and a pile of books and a vase of freesias and two windows and a telephone and a floor and a ceiling. And there was a soupy night outside, and a face made-up with care, and silence, and no laughter, and my spirit craving for him, turning on me with hatred, and nothing to remember, and words unsaid, and time wasted...

And Lord, how I regretted it!

One thing: if I chose not to be with him, it wasn't in order to be shackled by politeness or obligation to anyone else. Alone I would be—not touched, looked at, entreated, needed.

Everyone assumed it was all over. Soon Christian would go to Paris, and I would settle down to a nice routine, unchanged except for a natural attitude of repentance.

Meanwhile, for the first two weeks of November, he came regularly to see me.

'Going round the world to forget me, darling?' he teased gently. 'How do I forget you? I don't want to. I'll keep expecting you—the way I do here if I haven't seen you for two days—when someone knocks at the door or the phone rings. It's never you, but I always expect it will be...I'd never be surprised to see you...'

I knew that feeling too.

With him now I was happy as ever, but calm, knowing it would end. Well, *saying* it would...But really, was it in the nature of things that we could ever not be together? Everyone mistook him for a messenger from fate, but he was mine and it was no illusion.

'Christ,' he whispered. 'Oh, Christ, what'll we do? We can't say good-bye...'

After a time like that we were nervous and frosty and I was piously lectured on Olive's rights. If we meant to part we were not safe together. But did we?

'Don't worry. I'll break from Olive. It's the psychological moment—when I leave the country. Timing's everything.'

Well, perhaps. We would see. Nothing was final, after all. If you could just find some marvellous elixir to restore you...But, really, all you had to do was eat a bit more, and sleep a bit more, and breathe a bit of air. With all that, if you were with him, too, you could feel so different, and strong...

Almost before I woke from that thickly-woven aching sleep, I was at the basin being violently sick. Icy face and scalp and fingers...Now the water was running. I clutched the edge of the cold white basin and spat and rinsed my mouth with a mixture of surprised resentment and self-pity. And again, as the steam from the hot-water tap rose to my face, another shattering head-splitting wave of nausea. Black and starry and cold.

It was this bad flu everyone was catching.

Oh, don't faint!

The world reeled and catapulted into dark ether. Vast icy spinning spaces...Then it shrank, contracted with fantastic speed till it fitted once more inside my pounding skull. Head down I opened my eyes and saw the carpet and on my left the wooden knobs of the drawer handles. Oh, nice! *Won't* faint. Get Helen.

In the corridor at her door I banged twice and lurched back inside to the basin. What fun! I thought, but the thought went under in a wave of blinding pain as I got back into bed. As if the protective bone had been removed and among the tender contents of my head a seed of nitro-glycerine had been planted, it started on an endless series of explosions...

Then Helen was here in her dressing-gown. A noise came from her mouth and made me sick. My eyes closed and would not open. For it was noisy with voices, this vast blinding aching country I was lost in—tiny tiny chattering voices, tiny voices buzzing, saying words I couldn't hear.

But Helen was here again. And the racking blaze of all the suns was shut out by the curtains. Temperature was taken. Nasty flu. Bad flu.

In my conscious moments I was learning its habits. If you spoke it made you vomit. And also if you heard a voice...

Coming to again I gathered from a careful movement of my eyes across the shaded room that Helen had dressed. She was sitting in the armchair in the dark.

'Rotten,' I complained to let her know I was around. But a phlegmy croak was all that came out. Helen felt my head and pulse and indicated that she'd asked Dr Craig to call in.

'Rotten flu,' I tried again. She nodded sympathetically and I was at the basin, and sick, and drifting back into the rowdy house of semi-delirium where I lived.

Taken over, commandeered, yet conscious of unconsciousness, I was obscurely, profoundly, terrified of what was happening and what I might be made to do.

'*Don't go away...*'

Once I heard Dr Craig and Helen talking in a corner together. Did they know each other then? They were both doctors, of course, but it was hard to remember.

Over me he stood, reaching to the ceiling, frowning in the distance, with grey hair above the frown and a silver instrument in his hands.

'Flu,' I told him.

He said, 'Your temperature's below normal.'

Dully I tried to understand. 'How?' I asked at last. When you had this awful new flu you deserved at least the compensation of a high temperature.

But he was saying, 'I warned her that something like this might happen...She wouldn't tell me...' Then I

313

heard, '—not flu, of course. Minor catastrophe...danger signals...'

For timeless days it lasted—the sick explosive universe in my head, the cold white basin, the tiny tiny voices, the wide-awake sleeping, and the fear...

Always there was someone with me. I could not be alone.

But it seemed to be receding one day. Surely I was coming back? Helen had gone to the kitchen to make herself some lunch, and the phone rang beside me. Was that my arm? Could I command it? Could I so far project myself back into that fabulous ordinary world where arms lifted receivers and people spoke, expecting brisk replies? I lifted it to my ear.

And Christian's voice burst into the room—vital and forceful as ever, seeming to pursue me, to beat me down, even through this black instrument.

His voice and words and personality flooded relentless and impervious into my head, talking, talking. Cold and rich and bright.

He was trying to fix a date for our next meeting, I dimly realized.

My voice shrieked of its own accord, 'I'm sick! You're not to come! We're never to meet again! I don't want to see you! I don't want to see you!'

He was puzzled and joked and said he would certainly come on Friday night at seven.

After that wild weak outburst I was silent. His voice in my head made nausea reach a climax. Helen was taking the receiver away and I was sweating coldly at the basin, throbbing and racked. What fun! I tried to think.

314

The doctor came and went. People gave me things to swallow. I lay flat and seldom spoke—invaded, and very frightened.

Before this hallucinatory voyage, in picture my mind presented itself as something contained in my head in a saucer-shaped vessel: the mind and vessel had been one, cemented together like adamant, almost dully incapable of movement.

Now the impossible happened: the saucer tilted. Balance was threatened, giving a hair-raising demonstration of its slippery potentialities...

And I noticed...It was funny. I bathed every day more than once. I *would* do it over all Helen's protests, though it was all white and slippery and chattery alone in the bathroom and so much water, glass-green water, somehow seductive and dangerous. But the door was unlocked and ajar, even.

It was funny, because the room was beautifully clean and cool and there were flowers. But there was a funny smell.

My arms were bony. I had no flesh. I smelled like someone dying. Through scented skin, and fresh linen and laundered nighties, I smelled like death, and decomposing matter.

But on Friday morning I was well—light-headed, weak and unused to my body, but definitely well. No thunderous pain, no little voices, no electric silence.

Christian would come. I would see him. I would say good-bye.

All day I leaned against the pillows in the shaded room and waited.

315

It was seven exactly when he came. Outside, behind the drawn curtains it was foggy, but in here the gas-fire hissed and the lamp was on: the light was soft and the air faintly scented. This small pink cube was our only background. A hard one.

'*You* don't look sick,' he said with a sort of rallying artificial scorn. 'Up and dressed!'

'I'm not.'

We seemed to circle one another at a distance yet I, in a way, only for politeness' sake, for I felt calmly, kindly, detached.

I was on the edge of the divan and he sat in the black chair facing the fire, trying to act. In front of me it wasn't easy any more. His face and voice could simulate a remote formality, affect an interest in the movie camera given him by Mrs Carruthers, in yesterday's spectacular success of an actor who had once understudied him. He could simulate this and much more when he looked at the fire. His politeness and the care with which he selected his words was courtly—when he looked in the fire. Distinguished, like a consul visiting in a foreign prison, he could seem.

My poor love. How significant was the very fact that he did look down, not trying to transfix me with his eyes. How significant the unspontaneous lifting of hand to hair, the jagged rhythm of his voice.

With the indulgence, the courtesy, I'd have shown a stranger, I answered his unlikely remarks, leaving him to decide the duration of the piece.

But it was ludicrous to sit like this. It was impossible. His voice died away in mid-sentence. And he looked across at me.

He said, 'So I've come to say good-bye?...You're giving me up?'

I looked at my hands, limp on a green woollen lap.

'When you said—not to come again I—didn't know what to do. I felt—adrift. I almost went berserk. You didn't mean it?...How could we not even say good-bye?...Can you believe this is the last time we'll meet? I'm so used to depending on you. Always here. Or on the phone. No Clem any more.'

He wrinkled his forehead and seemed really to feel something. I watched him with a considerate sort of interest, as if I didn't know him very well. I looked at the flickering mobility of his features, the subtle changing lines of his face, feeling pleasantly absent and not at all unhappy.

'Give me your hand.'

317

I obeyed him easily, stretching out my arm. But there was my hand in his hard one, in his warm dry one; there was his reminding mine that they were old acquaintances, smoothing it, holding it against his face. And something wasn't quite so right as it had been...

Across the hall a wireless was turned on. Sweet music, soft music, came into the room, impinging on our senses and distracting. Now for the first time we smiled at one another, but unwillingly, in persecution, like old and tired and bitter people.

With a grimace, a small groan, he came from his chair to sit on the floor and lean against the divan. He studied one of my hands for a long time, saying muffled into it, 'I've left it late, haven't I, to be "tortured by remorse"?'

'So have I.'

I took my hand away, forestalling questions, asking, 'What time are you meeting Rollo tomorrow?'

Tomorrow, that glittering toy! He rose to it.

'In the morning. We're supposed to meet in our coffee-bar off Charing Cross Road, you know, the one we...And I get my embarkation orders for Paris. *Or else.*'

I was leaning forward and turned a little to watch him as he spoke. He was biting his soft lower lip, half-smiling. 'If Rollo tries to tell me there's been any slip-up, I've got my plans all laid. All neatly laid.'

His odd expression made me frown. 'What do you mean?'

'Rollo's involved in a certain—something—that wouldn't please his father.'

'*And...*' I looked incredulously into his face.

Almost smugly, gazing at the wall ahead, he smiled.

Seconds passed.

I said, 'Look at me!...You aren't going to do that to Rollo. Whatever he tells you tomorrow, you'll say nothing to his father. He's wished you well, Christian. He befriended you when no one else did. And even if he hadn't! I won't let you do that. For your own sake more than for his, promise me! Promise you'll say nothing!'

Christian was looking up, his youthful face alight. 'Oh, I love you when you're angry like that! I promise, darling. There's nothing I can swear on—is there?—that you'd believe, but I promise with all my heart. Clem, you could do anything with me. Anything.'

We kissed suddenly with loving impulsive enthusiasm, I leaning down to the upturned face, he holding my head, rising to his knees. But the release, the increase, the strange overturning, would not abate. And in our very mouths we discovered a profound dismay that was alarming, and made us draw apart. We were parting!

'What are we going to do, Clem?'

The dampness of his mouth was against my neck.

'Say good-bye,' I said very brightly. But the shape of his head was so familiar to my fingers.

And shortly my contented resignation was entirely murdered by the great simple fondness of the flesh, and the uncomplicated closeness. But for that we wanted to be kind to one another, we were mildly sarcastic, and if we could not speak sardonically spoke not at all.

Then abruptly, after a long silence, we turned together in the too small bed, and limbs and sheets were tangled

319

obstinately. We made an effort to undo the knots. It was a little bit funny.

Carefully, listening to one another, we began to laugh. We laughed. We roared. We lay side by side laughing till the bed seemed ready to founder. Tears oozed from my eyes. Oh, it was funny!

Oh. My eyes were crying…

And my heart turned inside out, and grief spilled through me, so that my body bitterly protested. Irrepressible wave on wave of long dammed-up despair rent my heart, annihilating me with dreadful tears.

I could hear him talking. He was holding me. To breathe I had to pull away.

'Oh, Christ! What have I done!' Beside me he was shrivelling with remorse and fear.

Choking, I sat up. And he found handkerchiefs and a towel for me, hovering, saying, 'Blow your nose and you'll feel better…Feel my shoulder, sweetheart. Feel my back. You're drowning me.' He was trying desperately, with desperate tenderness, to make me smile and I did in a way to reassure him, though I had no choice but to sob as hard as ever.

'What can I *do*? Can't I get you something? Oh, Clem…' Kneeling by the bed, half-frantic, he cried, 'Oh, Clem, I never really knew…'

Ah me. I never knew you cared. As she lay dying he learned the truth at last.

'Don't worry,' I said thickly. 'I was only kidding.'

'Oh, *Clem*.' He held me. 'How could I know…How could I believe someone like you really meant…And look what I've done…'

320

He always made me want to smile. One of the things I liked about him...Why had I cried? Not for so simple a reason as he supposed. Not for a reason I would soon know. But I said, 'See. I've stopped now. And never mind. We've been nice to each other...'

'That's not good enough!' He threw himself across the end of the bed, face down, and for a long time made no sound.

I lay flat, exhausted.

But it was time for him to go. It was really very late. Olive would be out with her hatchet.

'I can't leave you alone like this. Can't I get Helen or someone?'

'No.'

Then slowly he said, and against his will I could see he couldn't choose but think how romantic it would be, 'You wouldn't do anything—foolish—would you?'

She died of love for me.

Gently I shook my head and he turned away from me to comb his hair and inspect his face before returning to Olive. 'And you're not to say good-bye tonight. Goodbye! I refuse. It *isn't* good-bye. I'll meet you for dinner before I go away. You'll come to Paris to me. We can't be apart. *Don't* worry. So I'll deceive Olive. So it's the way I was made.'

Very nervously he approached me. Scenes really did upset him. He was so frightened, so confused. I looked steadily up, with just the strength to look up, but not to say as I felt someone should, 'No, no. There, there. It's all right...'

He bit his bottom lip, seeming to think, blue eyes agitated and not still.

'Tomorrow I'll see what our stars say in the paper! They'll tell us what to do!' And at this inspiration his expression turned with relief, subtly, to one of bright self-absorption. 'I believe in the stars, you know.'

'Do you?...Well, anyway...'

And again the dazzling eyes batted off in panic. 'No! Not "Well, anyway..." We'll meet for dinner next Friday at seven. I'll think of some lie to get out of the house.'

He sat on the bed and lifted me up to face him. He seemed barely conscious with nervousness. The dreadful inner confusion of his mind conveyed itself, perhaps for the last time, to mine. I said, 'Please don't worry, darling. Please take care of yourself. And try...'

Almost inimically, insultingly, we kissed, dry lip to lip. And we were silent then. And I did seem to feel my heart break—a very small quick and unimportant pang.

'I love you—very tenderly,' he said, and added swiftly, 'Don't say good-bye!'

He was at the door. He was at the door and really going. All my concentration in my eyes. Like seeing the sun set at midday.

In a jaunty unmusical voice he said, 'I suppose I should say thanks for all the work on the French. Thanks!'

'Don't mention it.'

'Friday,' he breathed, smiling weirdly. 'See you, darling. What do you think I'm going to do now—go out and get drunk?'

So that was what he was going to do.

The door closed.

His valedictory glances at the room and all its furniture, at my clothes on the chair, at the few books and ornaments, at the tube of toothpaste even, that we'd shared (for there was nothing too insignificant to interest him), and his glances at me, seemed to have drawn off the essence of us all, leaving us petrified.

And now the reasons for those tears were like a presence in the room, implacable, forcing me to know what I would not: that my tears were for a lost simplicity, for a failure I would lack the innocence to repeat. I cried because I wanted not to understand and would be made to, though it was difficult for me, and not fair.

Weak and meek and gently leaning I should be—not strong, not *now*. Another day I would be ready; another day I was willing to admit I would have no choice. But even now there was none. I was alive, and the way was ahead, and unsupported I would have to stand and walk. I was too tired, too old, to have to grow up any further. Was there no end to it? Why pick on me? The world was full of infantile adults. I knew a thousand not enrolled for kindergarten yet.

Long ago I had learned a fiery alphabet and thought my understanding quite complete. I knew! That there could be more pain to know, and other revelations, I hadn't dreamed. No single doorway out to understanding, but part of a circle of flame had I touched then? At one point only? Still encircled by the waiting patient beckoning unknown? So it seemed...

323

And rather than for any of that, those tears tonight had fallen for a feeling—simple, true and unadulterated—that was much maltreated and now lay crucified.

But he was very dangerous, and meant to be, to anyone less than heroic. And so that something else might miss destruction at his hands, I'd disengaged my clinging fingers and turned away, aware that I abandoned something phoenix-like along with all that was lethal. So here was the punishment for ignorance and folly—in the knowledge that I abandoned what I loved, and helpless grace.

If I had known at the beginning...If I had *now* the strength that by this weakening he bestowed on my future...If I could drink swiftly at some magic fountain...

Oh, and not only love and virtue I had left—a fine and hard and comforting ideal seemed fallible and seemed to fall. In not resisting actively, by any means, the twisted streak of suffering and sickness in him, I had been wrong perhaps. My honour, my integrity, so finely cherished, throve at his expense. There was a time and place for everything—including moral gestures. To have hoped thus to aid his soul's sickness seemed now to have the pitiful futility of signalling with flags to someone blind.

Of course circumstances hadn't helped...But I wasn't sure. I wasn't sure of anything any more. Except that I'd been naïve and arrogant and optimistic.

That survival was in no way easy I had always understood. But that anything in life, that any action, that to have virtue, or to lack it, that *love*, demanded this exertion of the soul, I simply hadn't known.

Perhaps if we had found the strength to go down before

324

each other, to be cut back, razed, we might have risen yet from the holocaust with something hardly gained and durable, instead of *this*...

But it wasn't likely. I wasn't sure. And now, anyway, it was too late.

Text Classics

textclassics.com.au